AS ALEC LED HER THROUGH THE STEPS

of the waltz, his fingers began to absently trace patterns across her back, generating waves of heat which spread through the thin fabric of her gown to the flesh beneath it. Kate stared hard into the center of his chest, trying desperately to ignore these sensations and focus on her purpose here tonight. But an undeniable excitement was bubbling through her veins as his lean body moved against hers with the rhythm of the dance.

"If you're done playing coquette to all our suspects, we need to talk," he began.

Kate paid his sarcasm no heed, for she sensed that tonight his words did not pose half so much danger to her as his body.

"Well?" she prompted him, the word honed razor-sharp. "What have you got to say?"

She noticed that he seemed as anxious as she to avoid making eye contact. "Not here," he said, pulling in a long, unsteady breath. "Not now. It's impossible for me to concentrate on business . . . while I'm counting the steps. We'll have to meet somewhere."

Kate knew that he was lying. All along his movements had been smooth and practiced. He was obviously an accomplished dancer; he hadn't a need to count steps. Kate closed her eyes to shut out the world and imagined, for the moment, that she and Alec were no more than polite strangers—just a man and woman enjoying the dance. Only then could she admit to herself what she'd been denying all along. Like it or not, there was more between the two of them than business.

DANA RANSOM'S RED-HOT HEARTFIRES!

CATHERINE WYATT
ROSE IN THE SHADOWS

ZEBRA BOOKS
KENSINGTON PUBLISHING CORP.

To the memory of Kate Warne,
who never let the fact
that she was a woman
interfere with what she had to achieve.

ZEBRA BOOKS

are published by

Kensington Publishing Corp.
475 Park Avenue South
New York, NY 10016

First printing: July, 1992

Printed in the United States of America

ACKNOWLEDGEMENTS

An extensive amount of research went into the preparation of this book, and I would like to offer thanks to all those who contributed with their aid and experience.

This story could not have been told at all were it not for the wealth of information contained in Allan Pinkerton's own series of adventure stories, especially those that chronicle Kate Warne's cases: *The Expressman and the Detectives, The Detective and the Somnambulist,* and *The Murderer and the Fortuneteller.* Also extremely helpful was Pinkerton's *Spy of the Rebellion,* which dealt with the war years, and as well his *History and Evidence of the Passage of Abraham Lincoln from Harrisburg, Pa. to Washington, D.C. on the 22nd and 23rd of February, 1861.*

I would like to offer my gratitude to the Chemung County Historical Society and to the staff of the Chicago Historical Society for their help in laying the groundwork, and to the staff of the Carol Stream Library, Carol Stream, Illinois, who never tire of aiding me in my obscure quests.

As always, I am grateful to my husband and daughters for putting up with my obsessions, and in this particular case, for giving up a day of their vacation to go headstone-hunting at Graceland Cemetery.

And finally, special thanks must go to Adele Leone, for her expertise and all the years of encouragement and advice, and to Marie Kuta, my sounding board from the very first, with the hope that I may someday repay the favor.

Chapter 1

Erin, New York
1853

Tonight, as always, the dining room of Harper's Inn was choked with hungry millhands. They sat, elbow-to-elbow, on rough wooden benches flanking the two long rows of trestle tables that spanned the room with scarcely space enough to walk between them.

Kate Warne backed through the swinging kitchen door, her muscles taut and aching as she balanced a platter piled high with biscuits in one hand and the heavy, enamel coffeepot in the other. She was met at once by the pungent odor of pine tar, sawdust, tobacco, and unwashed bodies—an unpleasant blend but all too familiar. And if she had any thoughts of her own as she went about her work, they were lost amid the din of gruff conversations and deep-throated laughter.

Kate had no more than set down the platter at the

head of the table before it was swept along the row, and thick, callused hands quickly laid claim to Mrs. Harper's hot biscuits. As she reached to pour the coffee, she wedged herself between the burly diners and felt a stray hand groping for her thigh through her skirts.

Instinctively, she moved to retaliate—perhaps hot coffee spilled in the lap of the guilty party. . . . Thinking better of it, she bit down hard on her tongue and kept to her business. She'd already lost one job on account of her failure to "treat the customers with the proper respect"; she couldn't afford to lose another.

Looking across the room, she locked eyes with Sarah, the Harpers' eighteen-year-old daughter, who was engaged in serving the men at the other table. As if reading her thoughts, the fair-haired girl sent her a thin smile, and Kate felt her spirits lift a bit. At least Sarah understood.

Kate was relieved when the coffeepot had finally been drained dry. She carried it back to the kitchen, then stepped outside and leaned heavily against the porch rail, swiping away the stray wisps of glossy, chestnut hair that had escaped her braid. There'd be a few minutes of peace, at least, before she was called back in to clear the tables.

The sky overhead was flecked with bright stars, and a crescent moon hung suspended high above the treetops. The breeze that swept through the valley was cool and scented with pine. It was a perfect night for walking, but Kate's time was not her own. Still, she ventured down as far as the pump at the bottom of the yard, where she filled the water pail, dipped in the ladle, and took a long drink. Then pulling a handkerchief from her apron pocket, she soaked it in the cool water, wrung it out and began to wipe away the sheen of perspiration from her brow and the back of her neck.

Her ears were ringing yet from the noisy dining room, and so she did not hear the man who drew up behind her until he spoke. "Well now, if it ain't the young widow come out for a breath of air."

Startled, Kate turned to see that the voice belonged to Sam Burns, a brawny fellow with greasy, black hair and all the manners of a jackass, who was— unfortunately for Kate—one of the Harpers' regular customers.

"Good evening, Mr. Burns," she replied coolly and started back toward the inn.

But Burns did not intend that she should leave him so soon and caught her arm roughly before she'd taken more than a few steps. "You're wastin' your time waitin' tables, Katie girl," he said, leering at her now as he backed her up against the wide trunk of a spreading oak tree. "A pretty thing like you has got a lot more to offer a man."

Kate swallowed hard, but could not fight the revulsion that welled in her as his hand slipped down her back, pressing her nearer to him. "Let me go," she warned. Blue eyes flashed, and her voice rose dangerously as she writhed against him.

"No need pretendin' to be shy with me," he told her. "You was a married woman. You know what's what."

Kate had reached the limits of her patience. For over a year now, she'd sweated over the kitchen stove,

9

scrubbed dirty dishes until her hands were raw, and waited on tables, all the while forced to ignore the crude advances and vulgar suggestions of all-important customers like Sam Burns; but this—this was too much to bear.

Giving vent to her pent-up anger, she raised her free hand and raked her nails across his face. The action stunned Burns momentarily, allowing Kate to break free. The sleeve of her sprigged cotton dress ripped as she did so, but she paid it no mind, only hurried back to the safety of the porch, where she clung to the rail, reassured by the sound of Mrs. Harper just inside, bustling about the kitchen.

Burns followed a few steps behind, scowling as he swiped the blood from his cheek. "I was just bein' friendly, that's all," he growled. "Reckon you think you're too good for the likes of me, Miss High-and-Mighty, but your pa was a millhand, same as the rest of us."

"My pa never treated a woman like a brood mare," Kate retorted, angrily blinking back tears as she rubbed the bruise his fingers had made on her arm. "You've all the subtlety of a steam locomotive, Sam Burns."

"Not like that husband of yours. Now, he was a smooth fellow, wasn't he? Well, Henry Warne might have charmed you with his big talk; but he's dead now, and what've you got? Nothin', that's what, Katie girl. A few more years waitin' on tables and you'll be beggin' for a man like me."

With that, he turned on his heel and left her. Kate lingered there on the porch, trying to deny his words. She didn't want any man just now, and even if she lived to be a hundred, she'd certainly never settle for a man like Burns. But she couldn't make a life waiting tables. What was she going to do?

When she'd composed herself, Kate stepped back into the kitchen, crossing her arms over her breast as if to ward off the evening's chill. Mrs. Harper was bent over the stove yet, and Sarah had just come in from the dining room, carrying a tray piled high with empty plates. As soon as Sarah noticed Kate's torn sleeve, though, and the pallor in her face, she set down the tray and went at once to her side. "What's happened?" she asked.

"I went out for some air and ran into Sam Burns in the yard," Kate explained, trying to sound light-hearted. "He got a little too friendly for my liking, that's all."

Sarah's eyes went wide. "Oh, Kate. He's a devil. Are you all right? Did he hurt you?"

"You needn't worry. I'm fine. He got the worst of it."

At this, Mrs. Harper looked up and swiped a weary hand across her brow. "You oughtn't to discourage him," she advised Kate, wagging a finger at her. "It's been more than a year now since your husband died. A man like Sam Burns is just what you need. He's a hard worker with a good steady job. You could do worse, Kate Warne."

It was late that night when Kate and Sarah finished their chores at last, climbed the stairs to the tiny, attic bedroom that they shared, and undressed for bed. Kate sat cross-legged on her narrow cot, and by the

11

light of a candle set on the bedside table, she began mending the torn sleeve of her dress, her needle flashing in and out of the worn fabric as she stitched.

Sarah, meanwhile, knelt on the floor before Kate's open trunk, admiring the marquetry work box from which Kate had taken her supplies. "What a pretty sewing kit," she remarked, as she lifted it from the trunk and ran her hand across the polished wood finish with its floral design.

"It belonged to my mother," Kate explained. "Pa saved up for a whole year so he could buy it for her one Christmas. She could stitch as fine as any of those dressmakers who have their own shops in the cities. Pa was always proud of her needlework."

Kate hardly ever spoke of her past. Sarah had always been curious, though, and seizing the opportunity, she encouraged her to continue. "I'll bet she taught you all she knew."

Without looking up from her work, Kate shook her head, and a wave of dark hair swept across her shoulder. "She died before I could learn very much, I'm afraid."

"I suppose I'm too young to remember much about your family," Sarah replied. "I do remember your husband, Henry, though. I saw him once or twice at the depot in town, fixin' to board the train. He sure had a way about him. Young as we were, all us girls envied you."

"He was a guard for the express company," Kate replied wistfully, as if she hadn't even heard the girl's final remark. "He spent a lot of time riding the trains."

Sarah seemed to sense that if the conversation

continued in this vein, it would wrest open Kate's scarcely healed wounds, and so she left off talking.

Instead, she gingerly put the sewing box back into its place in the trunk, then turned her attentions to what appeared to be a stack of papers tucked along one side. She drew them out. A closer look revealed them to be periodicals: several tattered copies of *Graham's* and the *Dollar Magazine*. "Why ever are you saving these old things?" she wondered aloud.

At the sight of the yellowed pages, a smile curved on Kate's full lips. Setting aside her mending, she reached for them. "They were a gift," she said as she clutched them to her breast. "I had to leave school after Mama died. Pa needed me to take care of the house; but I was only ten years old, and there was so much more I wanted to learn. The schoolmaster told me that if I kept up with my reading, though, I could learn almost anything, all on my own. He gave me these."

But it was clear by Sarah's furrowed brow that she was still not certain of the value of a few old periodicals. "They're full of all kinds of stories, Sarah," Kate continued, her words charged with enthusiasm, "stories that make you think. My favorites are by a man named Poe.

"This one here is *The Gold Bug*," she went on to explain and handed Sarah one of the folded pages. "It's about a pirate's buried treasure—and then there's *The Purloined Letter* and *Murders in the Rue Morgue*."

"Murders?" Sarah exclaimed, her voice trailing off in a nervous squeak. She let the paper slip through her fingers, loathe to touch it now. It floated down to the floor. "Why would anyone want to read about such things?"

"To follow in the footsteps of the detective and find out how the crime is solved, of course."

Kate unfolded her legs and left her place on the cot to retrieve the page. She regarded her friend with an irritated air. "Everyone ought to want to see justice done. It isn't fair that the guilty should go unpunished."

Sarah spoke without thinking. "You're not talking about any story, are you? You're talking about the men who killed Henry."

Kate's face paled as memories rolled in like cold, black clouds and gathered close around her, shutting out the light. She had tried to forget, but now her mind was recreating it all too vividly before her.

On the night the express car had been robbed, the doctor and two railroad men had come knocking at her door. It was late. She'd been asleep, and so she'd scarcely comprehended when they gave her the news. But they'd brought Henry's body with them, laid out in a wagon and hastily covered with a rough wool blanket. He'd looked so peaceful and still that when she saw him, Kate had thought he might only be sleeping—until she noticed that his waistcoat and shirtfront were soaked with blood. The doctor had told her he'd died instantly.

"I only wish that there was a man like Poe's detective to help me," Kate said absently. "I've pleaded with the sheriff and the railroad officials, but they say there's nothing more they can do. The express company won't pursue the matter any further. They've only lost four thousand dollars, but

I've lost my husband and my whole future."

And although she did not say so, Kate had lost something else as well. At the age of twenty-three, she'd lost her belief that there was some measure of justice in the world.

"It's been more than a year now," Sarah said soothingly. "You have to let it go, Kate. None of this will bring your husband back."

"I know."

Tossing her pages carelessly into the open trunk now, Kate crossed the room, propped her elbows on the sill and stared vacantly out of the open window. Sarah followed in her footsteps and laid a gentle hand on her shoulder.

"I'm sorry, Kate. I didn't mean to start you thinking about it again."

But it was too late for that. "Henry was always a dreamer," Kate said and breathed a tremulous sigh. "I think that's what I loved most about him. I tagged along at his heels from the time we were both children, listening to his fantastic tales, wanting to believe. . . . I lived for years on those dreams of his. I don't think I ever doubted that someday he'd make them come true."

There was a bitter edge to Kate's words, and when she heard it, she tossed back her head and stared up at the sky. "Just listen to me. It sounds as if I'm blaming him for dying."

Sarah stood by, wringing her hands. She did not know what to do for her friend. "It must be hard to lose someone that you loved so much," she said, unable to think of anything else.

Kate did not reply, but only got to her feet and

paced the length of the room restlessly. "I have to leave, Sarah," she announced. "I have to get away from here as soon as I can."

"Oh, Kate, you can't mean it. You were born here. All your kin are buried in the churchyard in town. You're just upset because we've been talkin' about Henry, that's all."

"No," Kate said firmly as she turned to face her friend. "No, it was something that Sam Burns said tonight that convinced me."

"Why, he's naught but a drunken halfwit! How could you put any stock in what he has to say?"

"'A few more years waitin' tables and you'll be beggin' for a man like me.' That's what he told me, and he's right. There's nothing here for me anymore, no future at all except maybe as the wife of a millhand, content with just scraping out a living. You heard what your mother said; she believes it, too. Well, I don't intend to marry, not ever again. I want something more of my life."

"But where will you go?"

Kate was deciding her future even as she spoke. "My mother had a cousin who lived in Chicago. Maybe I'll write to her and tell her I'm coming out. Things are different out west, you know—new people settling in every day, with all sorts of new ideas. Maybe there's a place for me in Chicago."

Chapter 2

Chicago, Illinois
1855

It was a brisk afternoon, and the biting wind which blew in off the lake wreaked havoc among the pedestrians, tugging roughly at the ladies' skirts and tossing off the hat of any gentleman not quick enough to clamp a hand upon his.

Lifting her skirts, Kate plodded impassively across the muddy width of Lake Street toward the establishment of J. G. Hewitt, the dealer in "ladies' furnishing goods" with whom she was employed. She was oblivious to any discomforts wrought by the weather, for her thoughts were full of the letter that she'd just picked up from the post office and now clutched in her hand.

She could see by the handwriting on the envelope that it was from her old friend, Sarah Harper. Actually she was Sarah Barnwell now; she'd married a carpenter from Elmira last fall. While she walked,

Kate tried to imagine what sort of news from home her friend would relate this time. She wouldn't read the letter just yet, though. She'd save it until this evening after supper, when she was alone in her room. Kate tried to deny that it was loneliness that caused her to place such importance on this fragile link with her past, but in spite of her efforts to deny it, she *had* been lonely since she'd come to Chicago.

Having crossed Lake Street, Kate began to traverse the unusual system of boardwalks which fronted the commercial buildings—climbing up a dozen stairs to the level of one building, then promptly decending half a dozen more to the level of the next.

The city of Chicago had a population of more than eighty thousand now, and there were more fine buildings and factories going up every day. But the city had been built on a swampy marshland, and for most of the months of the year, the streets were thick with mud. In order to alleviate this situation, the powers-that-be were now in the process of raising the grade of the city streets some six to ten feet, making basements out of the first floors of most of the buildings. In anticipation of the changes to come, some businesses had already moved their storefronts up to the new level, hence the need for the elaborate system of walkways.

The last building on this particular block was made of red brick, with the words "J. G. HEWITT, LADIES GOODS" printed in neat gold letters upon its large-paned window.

Kate wiped her muddied boots on the mat before pushing open the door. A bell jangled overhead as she entered. She heard voices from the back room as

18

soon as she set her package down on the counter; apparently they had not heard the bell.

"We shall have to cut back, my dear. No more bolts of French lace; they're far too expensive."

"But Jonathan—how are we to compete with the fashionable shops if we cannot offer our customers the very best?"

"After we've paid the rent, and Kate's salary, and the cost of these frivolous items in our stock, we're scarcely making a profit at all. If things continue as they have, we'll be out of business within the year."

Kate felt uneasiness rising in her. She'd been afraid of this for some time now. She couldn't bear to listen to any more. Turning back to the door, she opened and closed it again, more firmly this time.

As the bell sounded once more, Marcella Hewitt bustled out of the back room. In her claret-colored foulard, Kate's middle-aged cousin resembled a plump sofa pillow, stuffed rather too full of eiderdown. Approaching the counter, she patted down her silver curls and prepared to face her customer. There was no customer waiting, only Kate, but when Marcella saw her, a welcoming smile lit up her round, pink face nonetheless.

"Good afternoon, dear," she said cheerily. "You're back early."

"I wasn't very hungry, so I ran a few errands," Kate replied.

She did not meet her cousin's eyes as she drew off her bonnet, gloves and mantle and smoothed back the stray wisps of chestnut-colored hair. But Marcella regarded her like a disapproving mama. "You oughtn't to neglect your meals, Kate. You're welcome to the remains of our dinner if you like. There's some bread and a few slices of ham still in the basket on the table in back.''

Kate summoned a smile, and remembering the turn her thoughts had taken earlier, she told herself that she really had no right to feel lonely. The Hewitts had been very good to her. Marcella treated her more like a daughter than a distant relation, and while it was true that the older woman oftentimes fussed over her like a mother hen, she had proven herself a good friend.

Two years ago, when Kate had first written to her cousin and mentioned that she was coming to Chicago, Marcella had replied almost at once with an offer of room and board and a job as a clerk in her husband's store. Although Kate had insisted upon finding her own lodgings, the offer of employment had proven a godsend. To her dismay, Kate soon learned that—even in such a modern city as Chicago—a respectable woman without husband or father to support her had very few options to her. Why had she ever imagined that things would be different here?

The sales clerk's position that Marcella offered was a marked improvement over her previous situations, though. It provided her with income enough to lead a modest life, and through her exposure to the customers who frequented Hewitt's establishment, Kate discovered that she had a talent for dealing with people. It was easy enough, once she'd observed their habits.

Mrs. Patterson, for example, always came shopping after a battle with her husband and spent in a measure that was proportionally equivalent to the vehemence of the argument. In the wake of a small spat, she chose some trifle for herself—a lace collar, silk stockings or a pair of gloves—but a major altercation meant an extended perusal of bolts of the most expensive fabrics that Hewitt's had to offer, and Kate could count on a large sale.

Miss Clara Morrow was another such case. Her countenance was as easily read as a newspaper headline, and she had the uncanny ability to adapt her temperament to fit each of the two rival suitors who were vying for her hand. After a few weeks of study, Kate was able to ascertain at a glance which of these two gentlemen Miss Morrow had entertained the previous evening and, thereby, what purchases she was likely to make.

Kate had learned quite a bit since she'd come to work for her cousin. And so, with a comfortable position and Marcella for company, she had no right at all to feel as she did—lonely and restive. Still, there was something about the placid sameness of her life that left her ever more unsettled as the days passed.

And try as she might, she could not deny the conversation she'd just overheard between Marcella and Jonathan. Kate had suspected early on that her cousin had fabricated the clerk's job for her out of familial obligation. Kate worked hard enough for her wages, and her presence allowed Marcella the freedom to take a day off here and there; but when Marcella and Jonathan were both in the shop, there really wasn't the need for another clerk.

Kate knew that she was living off their charity, and increasingly she found that she could not bear the thought. There was no other decision to make. She would have to find employment elsewhere . . . and soon.

She hurried into the back room to hang up her things, and Marcella followed her. "I thought perhaps you might be having lunch with friends today," she said.

"I browsed for a while in Mr. Turner's bookshop, and then I picked up a letter at the post office," Kate told her.

Marcella's face mirrored a kindly concern. "I hope you don't mind my saying, dear, but you have been spending entirely too much time in your own company. You spend all of your free hours in that tiny room of yours, in that lonely boardinghouse. No one would say that you've not mourned long enough for your dear husband, God rest his soul. But you're still young; I daresay he'd not have wanted you to shut yourself up like you have."

"I'm not shutting myself up, Marcella, truly I'm not," Kate said in her own defense. "There are at least half a dozen people boarding at Mrs. Crawford's, more than enough to provide me with polite companionship. We dine together every evening, and afterward Mrs. Crawford's daughter, Annabelle, plays the piano and everyone visits in the parlor."

Kate did not bother to mention that she seldom joined the boarders for these after-dinner conversations, but Marcella's dark eyes narrowed as if she had her own doubts. Kate knew very well what sort of company her well-meaning cousin would like her to keep: the company of prosperous young gentlemen who were suitable for marrying. An advantageous

22

match was exactly what Kate ought to be aiming for. After all, what else was there for a respectable young woman?

But Marcella would not have understood Kate's feelings about marriage. The truth of it was that she'd determined never to put herself in a position where she might be hurt as she had been. Never again would she open her heart; never again would she allow herself to depend upon a man.

Kate hurried to put away her cloak and bonnet before Marcella could raise further objections. As she returned to her place at the counter, the bell on the door jangled again, and a woman entered, her broad face flushed beneath the brim of an outrageous bonnet, which was decorated with clusters of ribbons, red silk roses and curling ostrich plumes. Her dark brows were knit together in a deep scowl.

"Good afternoon, Mrs. Patterson," Kate called out, as a knowing smile formed upon her lips. "We've just received a shipment of the most exquisite French laces. I'm sure you'll want to see them all."

". . . As the strong man exults in his physical ability, delighting in such exercises as call his muscles into action, so glories the analyst in that moral activity which disentangles . . . His results, brought about by the very soul and essence of method, have, in truth, the whole air of intuition. . . ."

As Kate read again the passage prefacing *The Murders in the Rue Morgue*, which embodied Edgar Allan Poe's philosophy behind the creation of his detective, C. Auguste Dupin, a thrill ran through her. She understood so well. There was nothing magical in the way Dupin solved the cases in which he'd taken an interest. An analytical mind was the key to the unravelling of mysteries, as was a fundamental comprehension of human nature. Kate liked to think that she possessed both of these attributes. Perhaps she ought to try her hand at writing one of these mystery stories herself.

A sharp rapping on her door drew her abruptly from her reverie. Dragging herself out of the comfortable recesses of the armchair, she curled her fingers over the last page she'd read to mark her place and refolded the magazine, resting it in the crook of her arm as she went to stand before the door.

But for the soft glow of the reading lamp on the table beside her chair, the room was dark. Outside her window, the twilight had given way to a black, moonless night, and Kate wondered at the hour. After supper, she'd come up to read Sarah's letter; but rather than easing her loneliness, the reminder of home had left her strangely saddened, and so she'd turned to Poe instead. It could not be very late, she deduced, for she could still hear the dubiously musical caterwauling of Miss Annabelle Crawford as she entertained the guests in the parlor below.

As to exactly who might be seeking her company tonight, Kate had nary a clue. She rarely had visitors, and she had made precious few acquaintances among those who resided at Mrs. Crawford's.

"Who's there?" she called at last, when her deductive powers had failed her.

"It's me," an all-too-familiar voice replied

through the closed door. "Come along and let me in, Kate dear. I want to speak with you."

Expelling a deep sigh, Kate set aside her magazine at last and grudgingly opened the door. Marcella Hewitt swept in like a whirlwind. "I see you decided to forego the muscial program downstairs this evening. I ought to have guessed I'd find you holed up here, alone with your books."

Without allowing Kate a chance to reply, she marched across the room, wrinkling her nose as she surveyed the meager accommodations, and planted herself in front of the wardrobe. "I wish you'd come and live with us, Kate. We have a spare room, and you know we'd love to have you."

"I couldn't ask any more of you, Marcella. You've done too much for me already."

"Do you have an evening dress, dear? Of course, you must. Well, come along then; there isn't much time. Jonathan is waiting below in the carriage. The curtain goes up promptly at eight o'clock, and you'll need to hurry and change."

After a protracted moment of silence, Kate found her tongue; it took longer than that, however, to gather her thoughts. "But I don't understand. What's all this about?"

"Oh, haven't I said? I'm sorry, dear, but I have been in such a rush. Jonathan and I have tickets for the theater this evening. We'd invited my neighbor Mrs. Cummings to accompany us, but the poor dear isn't feeling well. I told Jonathan that it was a shame to let the ticket go to waste, and he suggested that perhaps you might like to go. I know you'll enjoy the performance. It's a delightfully naughty little melodrama called *The Life of an Actress.*"

Again Kate sighed heavily. "You are too good to me, Marcella."

Of course Marcella would have her way. As Kate had learned early on, Marcella always had her way. And Kate realized, too, that her cousin had carefully arranged this entire affair—even going so far as to invent the story of the invitation to her neighbor and the woman's sudden illness. She suspected that Marcella's plans had been prompted by the talk she'd had with her husband this afternoon; she was worried about Kate's future. As for herself, Kate knew what she had to do. Somehow she would have to find another position so that her cousin needn't feel responsible for her any longer.

For now, though, Kate allowed herself to be bundled into the blue silk which had once served as her wedding dress. Although it was plain and several years out of fashion, it was the closest she had to a suitable evening dress among the few that she owned.

Once Kate was dressed and standing before the glass, Marcella draped a lace shawl across her shoulders, attempting to buoy her spirits by assuring her that the dress was still perfect. "The color is especially flattering," Marcella exclaimed. "Why, it matches exactly the blue of your eyes!"

Kate was not deceived. She knew, even as her well-meaning cousin endeavored to arrange her unruly brown locks into a softer, more appealing style, that there was a purpose behind all this primping, and ere long she was to discover that purpose.

Chapter 3

Rice's Theatre had been a popular entertainment spot in the city for some years, and that claim was borne out on this night. Carriages clogged the street in front of the building, and the trio had to wade through the crowd milling about the doors to enter.

Before they'd even found their seats, Kate, who had been held fast by Marcella's firm grip since they alighted from the carriage, was introduced to more than half a dozen young men whom her cousin no doubt considered to be eligible bachelors.

When at last Kate managed to catch Jonathan Hewitt's eye, he only shrugged his shoulders helplessly. He could be a shrewd and inflexible man when it came to his business, but in dealing with his wife, he was softhearted and malleable as clay.

Kate could not blame Marcella. She was only trying to work matters out to the benefit of all. No doubt she'd decided that if Kate were to marry, she'd be comfortably situated and would no longer need the job at their store. And so Kate endured her cousin's machinations graciously, and despite the unabashed matchmaking which prefaced the evening, she had to admit that once the performance began, she did enjoy herself.

On the whole, Kate considered herself a dispassionate creature, but even she found this play poignant. It was the story of a young orphan girl who, in choosing the life of an actress, gave up all hope of a respectable life.

How unfair it was, Kate whispered to Marcella behind her fan, that the girl should be branded as something less than virtuous simply because she wanted more than the role of wife and mother that was expected of her sex. Marcella met her cousin's comments with an astonished air, then promptly changed the subject. It was the manner in which she dealt with all of Kate's peculiarities—she simply ignored them.

By the time the curtain came down for the intermission, Kate had worked up quite an empathy for the character, but she was certain that the poor girl was destined for an unhappy end. The audience, bound by convention, would have it no other way.

For a fleeting moment, Kate considered what a life on the stage might be like and found herself feeling less and less sorry for the "poor girl." Although she might give up her respectability, an actress gained freedom in the bargain: the freedom to travel, to play at different roles and live out fascinating lives, even if those lives were confined within the boundaries of a play. Contemplating her own uncertain future, Kate could envision nothing nearly so satisfying. Envy pricked at her like a sharp needle, and she hastily pushed away the thoughts, frightened by the intensity of her emotions. Perhaps she was not so dispassionate after all.

In the midst of the socializing that took place during the intermission, Kate found herself once more at the mercy of Marcella's matchmaking schemes. No sooner had Mr. Hewitt escorted them out to the lobby than they were promptly engaged by two of the "eligible" gentlemen whom Kate had met earlier, although "desperate" might have been a more accurate description for these two. They'd been freshly bathed and shaved, and their clothing was of an elegant cut; but their manners were more telling, and Kate soon learned that they were prosperous farmers who'd come to the city to find themselves wives.

Kate had no delusions about her own charms. When compared to many of the young ladies present tonight, she could only be considered passably plain and shabbily dressed at that. Yet in vying for her attentions, this pair preened like peacocks, each extolling his own virtues in a display that Kate found vulgar—partly because she sensed neither of them was as much interested in her as in gaining the advantage upon his rival. It was only when Marcella was drawn away to chat with a friend that Kate was able to make good her escape.

Leaning over to Mr. Hewitt, who'd been left behind to stand guard over her, she whispered: "I'm feeling stifled by this crowd. I need a breath of air, I think."

"Would you like me to accompany you?"

"No, you needn't bother. I shan't be gone a minute."

"Well, go on, then," he urged in a conspirator's tone. "Marcella is likely to return soon with another prospective suitor."

Making her excuses to the gentlemen who were positioned nearby like a set of matched bookends, Kate slipped away quietly, all the while keeping a close eye on her cousin, who was still conversing with her friend in an animated fashion. Thus, Kate did not take notice of the gentleman standing near the open doors until they had collided.

She apologized at once as she bent down to retrieve her pocketbook and fan which had dropped from her hand with the impact. "Forgive me," she said. "I was only going out to get a breath of air. I suppose I ought to have been looking where I was going instead of where I'd been."

"On the contrary, it was entirely my fault." The voice was a rich baritone. "Are you certain you're all right? You seem a trifle pale."

The stranger had already moved to rescue her belongings, and returning them now, he offered a hand to help her rise. As she looked up, Kate found herself transfixed by a pair of eyes as green as bottle glass. She was aware of the press of his fingers, hard and cool against the worn fabric of her glove, but it was his smile that wholly disarmed her. It was a knowing smile, as if there were some secret the two of them shared. To her dismay, her cheeks warmed with a blush, and she began to stammer.

"I—yes, well, perhaps I am just a bit light-headed," she admitted, raising a gloved hand to her temple. "I'm not accustomed to crowds—"

"Then, you must allow me to escort you outside." He did not wait for permission. In one swift movement, he drew her up beside him and led her out of the opened doors. He chose a quiet place for them, just beyond the lights of the theater and the sheltered portico where many of other theatergoers had gathered. It was an ideal vantage point for observing the crowd; but Kate suspected that this was not her companion's intent, for he'd turned his attention full on her.

A trail of heat spread out in the wake of his wandering eyes . . . from her slender nape, where loosened tendrils of dark hair lay dampened against her skin, to the pulsating hollow of her throat and lower still to the swell of her breasts, accentuated by the tightly laced corset she wore beneath the blue silk bodice.

Kate inhaled sharply, and the breath caught at the back of her throat as feelings that had lain dormant for far too long were reawakened with a startling suddenness. This man had an overpowering, almost hypnotic presence, and she knew she ought to go back inside at once; but her limbs were oddly lethargic.

She raised her chin to welcome the sharp chill of the night air against her flushed cheeks, hoping the stimulant would restore her faculties. But it was a futile hope. Despite all her best intentions, she remained fixed in her spot, awaiting his next move.

In the meanwhile, she studied the man, hoping to prove to herself that there was nothing unusual

31

about him, nothing at all that should have caused such a reaction in her. She sought to turn a critical eye on him, but he was strikingly handsome in his evening clothes—a pale yellow rosebud tucked into his lapel.

He was tall, with the solid build of an athlete. When first she'd collided with him, Kate had had the sensation of having strode headlong into the trunk of a massive tree. His hair was sandy brown in color, highlighted with warm gold where the light struck it. His jaw was square-set, his features stern, but when a smile curved on his lips beneath his thick moustache, all her attempts at objectivity evaporated.

"Are you feeling better now, Miss . . . ?"

"Yes, thank you," Kate replied, still flustered. "But it's *Mrs.*, Mrs. Katherine Warne."

With this, he assumed a disappointed air. "A pity! I suppose, then, I must send you on your way at once before your husband arrives to thrash me for making improper advances to his wife."

His dramatic stance made Kate think for a moment that he must be an actor—but the twinkle in his eye told her that he was only teasing. If it was his intention to put her at ease with his manner, then he'd succeeded.

"Improper advances?" she echoed, pressing her lips tightly together now in order to stifle the unladylike grin that threatened to burst forth. "Oh, is that what you've got in mind?"

"What? Why, no . . . ahem . . . no, of course not. That is to say, I—"

Kate's laughter rang in the air. She scarcely ever

laughed lately, but now she simply couldn't help it. The paragon of manliness who only moments ago had made her tremble with no more than a pointed stare was now tugging at his moustache and stammering like a schoolboy. She decided that he was even more likeable when he was disconcerted.

"You needn't worry about any angry husband," she told him gently. "You see, I'm a widow."

For an instant, he looked away. "I'm sorry. And you so young. That is a pity."

"It's been more than three years now. Time enough to adjust, I suppose."

Again he was silent, but as Kate was learning, he was a man who made good use of silence. "Ah, well then. . . ."

The voice had deepened once more, and he was flashing that dangerous smile of his. "Please allow me to introduce myself," he said and caught her hand in his. "My name is Brown, Jeremiah Brown."

Kate drew her hand back promptly, noticing now that even as he spoke, Mr. Brown's gaze appeared to be focused over her right shoulder, as if he were still anticipating the arrival of an irate husband. Or perhaps, she admitted more realistically, it was only that her charms were not sufficient to hold such a man spellbound.

"Are you enjoying tonight's performance, Mrs. Warne?" he inquired.

She could not help the small sigh that escaped her as the conversation turned polite. It might have been either relief or regret, and a long minute passed before she was able to give thought to his question. "As a matter of fact, I am. It's far more enlightening than I would have imagined."

"Enlightening? I'll wager that's not the description most of tonight's audience would use."

Kate remembered then that indeed Marcella had called it a "naughty" little melodrama. "No doubt you're right," she conceded, "but I think the playwright had something more in mind than scandal when he chose his subject."

"Something more than scandal?"

"Yes," she replied, though hesitant to voice aloud her unusual opinions. "I'd like to believe that he meant his work to apprise his audience of the plight of women—and of their lack of choices in this world."

Mr. Brown cast his eyes downward, but she could see that his lips were twisted in amusement. "You sound like a bluestocking, Mrs. Warne," he remarked, "or one of Mrs. Bloomer's followers."

Kate thought she sensed a derisive ring in the comment. She should have expected no less, but still she was stung by his words. Perhaps she was only disappointed to discover that the charming Mr. Brown was not so different from other men, after all.

"I'm not particularly well-read," she retorted, "but I've learned some rather hard lessons myself recently."

"Please believe me, I meant no offense," Brown insisted anxiously. "It was only my clumsy attempt at conversation. I honestly prefer a woman who's not afraid to have ideas of her own. You do forgive me, don't you?"

It was that damnable smile of his that won her over in the end. One man ought not to be allowed to possess so much charm.

For a moment, it seemed as if Brown's attention had wandered again. His brow creased in frown. It must have been the theater crowd behind them that he was surveying so intently; and then without so much as the hint of a warning, his arm flashed out, and he captured Kate by the waist, dragging her to him. The air left her lungs in a painful rush, and before she knew what he was about, his lips were on hers. There was nothing tentative in the kiss. His hard mouth demanded response, robbing her of what little breath was left her.

Fear knotted her stomach as she felt her body betray her. Suddenly she was responding to him, pressing closer to the lean, muscled body, her lips softening under his. Shooting stars flashed in brilliant profusion before her eyes, and her head was reeling, but even so, she was aware of the heavy tread of footsteps upon the boardwalk as someone passed nearby.

Her legs felt like India rubber, and she clutched desperately at Brown's lapels to keep herself from collapsing in a heap at his feet. When he pulled back finally, she fought to regain her balance while she stared open-mouthed, trying to decide whether to shriek a belated protest or to strike him.

She opted for the latter and felt a strange satisfaction as her hand connected sharply with his jaw. Brown was not at all disturbed. There was a mischievous twinkle in his eye as he put a finger to his lips to silence the protest he anticipated from her. But before Kate even had time to gather her wits about her, Jeremiah Brown let go a hearty laugh, turned on his heel and trotted off, leaving only the taunting ring of his laughter behind as he disappeared into the night shadows.

Kate stood there for a long while, trembling. There was no way to make sense of any of this. What had caused Brown to embrace her so urgently? Anyone who'd spied them would have assumed that they were lovers. Why had he run off? Exactly what sort of game did he think he was playing with her? And who was he? In the course of their conversation, Kate had learned nothing at all about the mysterious Mr. Jeremiah Brown save his name.

But there was no good in dwelling on questions that would likely never be answered. All in all, Brown did not matter. Kate was less angry with him that she was with herself for succumbing to his advances. For all her talk about independence, she had behaved like a fool—a lonely, love-starved fool— but she'd learned yet another valuable lesson tonight about trusting men.

When at last she was able to unclench her balled fists, Kate realized that the yellow rosebud which had once graced Brown's lapel was now no more than a heap of petals, lying crushed and broken in her palm. She very nearly dashed them to the ground, but after a long moment's contemplation, she opened her handbag and dropped them inside.

Chapter 4

His lips settled on hers once more, but this time
Kate responded willingly, reaching upward to coil
her arms about his neck, threading her slender
fingers possessively through the thatch of sandy
brown hair. He tasted of whiskey and cheroot—a
heady blend that further fuelled the aching hunger
within her. Only when the need for breath was
imminent did she break free of him, tossing back her
head to inhale deeply.

A soft moan escaped her lips as he bent to
concentrate his efforts upon the exposed white arch
of her throat, the brush of his moustache grazing her
skin as his mouth ranged upward to the sensitive
nape of her neck. Kate loosed her fingers from his
hair, and they fluttered downward, following the
hard curve of his arms. She could feel the tension in
him, coiled like a spring. An uneven breath rattled in
his chest as he strove to maintain control, and then he
pressed a hot kiss against her temple and began to
whisper pretty words in her ear—as if she needed

coaxing. And all the while his heart was beating a deep, even rhythm against her breastbone, setting the pace for their actions, his hands generating sparks of heat where they explored.

Kate gazed fully into the depths of his bottle green eyes, wanting desperately to know his secrets. There were so many questions she ought to ask him, but now, at this moment, it was exceedingly difficult to remember exactly what they were. Nothing mattered but fulfillment. It had been too long, she told herself, far too long.

And then with startling suddenness, he slipped from her arms, and the image of him, which scant seconds before had been so vivid, so real, melted away like a shadow, leaving behind only the harsh, hurtful sound of his laughter. . . .

Kate jerked bolt upright in her bed, her breathing ragged and unsteady, her body damp with perspiration. Tearing fiercely at the bedclothes entangled with her limbs, she sprang up and reeled drunkenly on her heels. She quickly reached out for the bureau and hung on until the whirling in her brain slowed to a more tolerable pace.

When finally she was able to walk, she crossed to the washstand to splash ice cold water from the basin onto her face. Her cheeks pinched and stung, but she bathed them again regardless, until her breathing returned to its normal rate. The face staring back from the washstand mirror was eerily pale in the moonlight.

This was the third night this week that she'd had the dream; and it grew more and more vivid with each occurrence. Kate did not consider herself a fanciful person—indeed, far from it—and the level of passion created in this dream by her unconscious imagination both frightened and shamed her.

Urgently now, she padded back to the bureau, rummaged through the contents of the top drawer, and eventually drew out the beaded handbag she'd carried to the theater. She rushed to the window, where she threw up the sash and upended the drawstring bag, sending a shower of dried rose petals raining down onto the street below. Surely this would break the spell. She couldn't go on as she had been, so plagued by the intensity of a mere dream that she rose exhausted from her bed each morning, her restlessness increasing as the days went by.

She hoped to concentrate her attentions elsewhere, but there was no peace to be found in her work, either. Each morning since that fateful excursion to the theater, Marcella had met her with an expectant look when she entered the shop, as if she were certain that one of her "suitable" young gentlemen would call upon Kate with a marriage proposal.

After a full week of being met in this manner, Kate could no longer bear to meet her cousin's eyes, and so, as she came in the door, she mumbled a greeting and took herself off into the back room to sit for a moment and hide behind the pages of the morning newspaper which Mr. Hewitt had already discarded on the table outside his private office.

First of all, she checked the employment column but, not surprisingly, found no position for which she was suited. There was nothing of particular interest in the advertisements, nor in the column headed "For Sale or Rent," but when Kate spied the name of Pinkerton within the text of a news story, it caught her eye.

Allan Pinkerton was fast becoming a well-known figure in Chicago. At a time when there was no adequate system of state or federal law enforcement, and the city's police force was no more than a barely organized gang of night watchmen, Pinkerton's National Police Agency provided an efficient alternative.

Kate remembered having read several accounts of the exploits of Pinkerton and his detectives. Not long ago, they had arrested a railroad station manager for stealing goods from a freight car belonging to the Galena Railroad and apprehended a postal worker for mail theft as well. This second arrest was effected by sending a decoy package through the mails. The guilty man was arrested as he attempted to steal the decoy.

This morning's offering told the story of Mr. W. S. Buck, who ran a large lottery business in the city. Having heard the account of the unscrupulous postal worker, he suspected that the post office was responsible for the loss of several of *his* letters containing cash. Mr. Pinkerton was consulted, and following a thorough investigation, he announced that the guilty party in this instance was not the post office, but an employee of Mr. Buck's.

The Chicago newspapers regularly related accounts of Pinkerton's cases, and one after another they praised the talents of the man, admitting their frank amazement at his successes.

Kate was reminded of a line she'd read in *The Murders in the Rue Morgue: "His results, brought about the very soul and essence of method, have, in truth, the whole air of intuition."* Well, the detective Dupin may have been only an author's creation; but Allan Pinkerton fit this description precisely, and he was very real. If a man of Pinkerton's abilities had been available to investigate Henry's murder, the men responsible might not have escaped the punishment due them. Maybe there was still some hope for justice after all, she thought now as she sat staring at the newspaper. But the world would need a good many more men like Allan Pinkerton. If only there were something she could do—

And then all at once, it struck her. She was in need of employment. Why could she herself not work with Pinkerton? She had a quick mind and a skill in dealing with people, and while it was true that she had never heard of a woman as a detective, that did not mean she could not prove a useful commodity.

Without realizing, Kate had put down the newspaper and gotten to her feet. The more she considered the idea, the less outlandish it seemed. She was not so naive as to believe that the criminal element was comprised solely of men. There were women who were guilty of theft and murder, as well as women who consorted with male criminals and shared their confidences—but the segregation of polite society put these particular women out of the reach of even the most determined male detective. A woman, though, a woman who was also a detective, might move freely through these feminine circles and attach herself to such a female suspect without arousing suspicions.

Kate knew that she would have to leave the security

of her position behind the counter at Hewitt's at any rate. But now she knew with an uncanny certainty where her future lay, and that simple knowledge filled her with a peace she had not known in some time.

She found herself distracted by her thoughts for the remainder of the morning and decided that she would go and see Allan Pinkerton that very day, before she lost her nerve. She could only hope that if he should deign to speak with her, he would not think her wholly insane.

"Would it be all right if I took my dinner break a bit early today?" she asked Marcella when she could contain her excitement no longer.

"I imagine so. Is there something wrong?"

"No, nothing," Kate replied slowly and then proceeded to tell the white lie she'd been perfecting. "It's only . . . well, I saw this smart little bonnet in the window of one of the shops on State Street, and I'm afraid if I wait too long, it will be gone."

Marcella smiled in an understanding way. "Go ahead, dear," she said, which made Kate feel all the more guilty. But she'd have to accustom herself to embroidering fancier lies than this, she reminded herself, if she was ever to succeed as a detective.

The offices of Pinkerton's Northwest Police Agency were located on the second floor of a building on the northwest corner of Washington and Dearborn. As Kate neared her destination, she rehearsed the approach she planned to take, mentally revising her little speech as she went along. Even as she strode firmly onward, her body was quaking within like a windblown leaf, but by the time she'd climbed the stairs to the second-floor office, she'd taken a firm rein on her apprehensions and adopted her most businesslike air.

"I should like to see Mr. Pinkerton, please," she said, addressing the clerk whose desk was nearest the door.

The young man set down his pen and looked up from the ledgerbook in which he'd been writing. "May I give him your name, ma'am?"

"It's Mrs. Warne. He doesn't know me, but I should like to speak with him nonetheless . . . about a business matter."

"Yes, of course. If you'll just have a seat, Mrs. Warne, I'll see if Mr. Pinkerton is available."

Kate knew that by the way she had phrased her request, the clerk would assume that she had come to engage the agency's services. Let him think what he would, she told herself, at least she would have her audience.

Perched stiffly on the edge of the chair she'd been offered, Kate studied the room while she waited. Several desks took up the floor space. All showed signs of habitation, blotters stained with ink, folders and sheaves of papers stacked upon them, although only the clerk's desk had been occupied when she came in. There were no signs of any detectives, but then surely a busy detective would not have much cause to remain tied to his desk all day long.

There was a door at the far end of the room, behind which the clerk had disappeared only a short time ago. This was no doubt Mr. Pinkerton's private office. Before long, the young man emerged, informing her that Mr. Pinkerton would see her now, and proceeded to escort her between the row of desks toward that inner sanctum.

Kate's mind had been occupied with a number of trivial subjects while she waited, but now as the moment of confrontation neared, she gave a last wild, female thought to her appearance. Would one look convince him that she was too young to take seriously? Would he dismiss her and her unusual notions as no more than frivolous and female?

No, she assured herself as she drew a deep, cleansing breath, she was properly attired for conducting business—in her sober woolen mantle and a pearl gray faille dress that was attractive, but by no means frivolous. In actual fact, Kate did not have a frivolous item in her meager wardrobe.

There *was* a spray of blush roses trimming her bonnet, though, and a fall of lace that framed her face in a most appealing fashion—but then perhaps it might not hurt to make some use of her feminine attributes. Was it not that very usefulness that she was here to prove?

Her escort departed, closing the door behind him, and Kate found that she was facing Mr. Allan Pinkerton himself.

He rose at once, put out a hand to greet her and then pointed to a comfortable leather chair opposite his desk. "Make yourself comfortable, ma'am," he invited, a pleasant Scottish burr rounding his words.

Pinkerton was average in height, and Kate, being tall for a woman, could address him across the desk eye-to-eye. She knew from the newspaper accounts that he was still a young man, only thirty-six years old, and he had maintained the firm grip and muscular build of one who had once engaged in physical labor to make his living. His hair and full thick beard were dark in color, but his deep-set eyes were sharp and as gray as steel.

One could not look into eyes such as his and coolly relate a falsehood; his very demeanor demanded honesty. Kate found the strength of his presence comforting, and as she settled into the chair he had offered, she felt herself relax and exhaled, long and low.

"I am Mrs. Kate Warne," she began. "I am a widow, Mr. Pinkerton, who must provide for herself, and well, to be quite honest with you, I have come here today to inquire whether you will employ me as a detective."

To his credit, Mr. Pinkerton's face showed not one hint of shock or surprise. He seemed only to consider her words in silence for a short time before he replied. "You do realize, Mrs. Warne, that it is not the custom to employ women as detectives."

"I realize, sir, that it has never been tried before," she admitted, "but, in my opinion, it is high time that it was."

"Well, well . . ." The hint of a smile which played on his lips as he tugged on his beard gave her hope yet. "What is it exactly, Mrs. Warne, that you think you could accomplish that one of my gentleman detectives could not?"

"Why, I should think that would be obvious, sir," Kate replied. "I could go in and worm out secrets in many places where it would be impossible for your 'gentlemen' detectives to ever gain access."

Pinkerton leaned back in his chair, hooked his thumbs in the armholes of his satin waistcoat and gave her his full attention. "Go on, Mrs. Warne . . ."

And so she did. She explained to him all of her ideas on the subject, unlearned though they were, from her observations on the female presence within the criminal element to the ways in which he could make use of a female detective to tap these sources. When she was finished, she stopped to draw a long breath, nearly certain she had convinced him. Even though his expression betrayed nothing of his thoughts, he was not a man to deny logic.

"Of course, I must have time to consider the matter," he replied at last and rose to signal the conclusion of their interview. "If you will kindly call upon me tomorrow morning, Mrs. Warne, I will inform you then of my decision."

The remainder of the afternoon proved interminably long. Kate found herself having to invent spurious excuses to explain to Marcella why she'd returned without the "smart, little bonnet" she'd gone out to purchase and wondered if it would not be easier to tell her cousin the unvarnished truth. But she came to her senses directly. It would be hard enough confronting Marcella with the news if and when Pinkerton decided to hire her; there was no use anticipating trouble.

That evening Kate dined with Mrs. Crawford and the other boarders, and for the first time, she regretted the polite but cool relationship she had cultivated with them. She wished that Sarah was not so far away, for this evening she needed a friend in whom she could confide, a friend who would share her anticipation and apprehensions. Kate had never wanted anything more than she wanted this chance. Pinkerton simply had to hire her!

Chapter 5

By nine o'clock the following morning, Kate found herself seated once again before Mr. Pinkerton's desk in his private office waiting, with carefully concealed trepidation, to hear his decision.

"Mrs. Warne," he began, after he'd spent what seemed an eternity pacing and posturing before the window from which he was able to look down on the street below, "I've given a great amount of thought to your proposal. To be quite honest, I've found myself able to think of little else since our interview yesterday."

With this, he settled down into his chair and leaned across the desk top to address her. "You might be surprised to learn that I agree with your observations. I like to think that we live in a progressive age, and I am not the sort of man who would allow mere convention to stand in the way of the successful resolution of any case put in my hands. If you are willing to go ahead with this scheme, then I shall be equally willing to give you the chance to prove yourself."

Kate had to struggle mightily to maintain a calm outward appearance. A chance to prove herself? She could hardly ask for more than that. She wanted to leap out of her chair, dance a little jig on the carpet and give Mr. Allan Pinkerton a hearty kiss. She managed to restrain her exuberance for a time, but the calm was once again threatened when Pinkerton took her out into the office to meet his staff.

Surely he had given them some warning of his plans, for a pair of gentlemen, who'd been nowhere about when she first entered the office, came out of hiding now. They replied politely when introduced and did not seem at all surprised to learn that there was to be a woman in their ranks. The clerk, whom Kate had already encountered, was introduced to her as Joseph Hamilton, though Pinkerton referred to him familiarly as "young Joe."

There were but two detectives besides Pinkerton himself. The first of these gentlemen had a sober demeanor. George Bangs was his name, and he was slim, with thinning dark hair. His suit was well-tailored, his manners impeccable. Kate thought that he bore more of a resemblance to a bank clerk or a lawyer than a detective, and perhaps therein lay his success as the latter.

The second gentleman had seated himself casually on a nearby desk top and was pretending to examine a newspaper he'd found lying there. But his seeming indifference did not fool Kate at all; he was as disconcerted as she, even if he was the consummate actor.

When Pinkerton introduced them, the gentleman came forward to shake her hand. There was not the slightest hint in Jeremiah Brown's expression to indicate that they had encountered one another before . . . that night at the theater. But then Brown was not his real name. Mr. Pinkerton had called him Alexander Dalton.

Realizing now that the mysterious man from the theater was one of Pinkerton's operatives, Kate found herself strangely pleased—and more than a little ashamed of herself because of it. The events of that night became clear to her now, and she understood why he'd seemed distracted, why he'd taken such liberties and then abandoned her. She might not so easily forgive him for the amorous advances he'd made, but Kate's pride was salved at least as she saw the truth of the matter. Nothing she'd done had prompted his behavior; he'd been working on a case.

"Just what are you up to, Mrs. Warne?"

When Pinkerton dismissed Kate, Alexander Dalton had brazenly followed her out of the office. Now, as she made her way down Dearborn Street, he endeavored to keep pace with her while she did her best to ignore him.

"How did you find me?" he persisted.

Kate could not deny that she was enjoying his uneasiness. It seemed ample restitution for all that he'd put her through. "You flatter yourself, Mr. Brown—or should I say Mr. Dalton—if you believe that I came searching for you," she responded at last.

51

"I came to Allan Pinkerton for a job. That you happened to be there was purely coincidence."

Dalton still regarded her suspiciously. "I don't believe in coincidence."

"Nor do I," she said with an equal dose of venom in her words. "Let's call it fate then, shall we?"

Dalton was silent. With hands thrust deeply into his coat pockets, he walked on at her side, all the while staring at the planked walk from beneath the broad brim of his slouch hat, as if contemplating his next words carefully.

"Surely you cannot be serious about becoming a detective."

"I can assure you, Mr. Dalton, that I am," she shot back, still without breaking stride.

Kate was disappointed by the change in him. He was not at all the same gentleman she'd encountered at the theater. Jeremiah Brown had been gregarious, lighthearted, charming—but she was beginning to see that it had all been pretense.

Alexander Dalton was stoical and secretive. There was no doubt that he disapproved of the idea of working with her, though he had apparently not shared this opinion with Pinkerton. What Kate couldn't understand was why he'd bothered to come after her. Did he believe her to be a threat to him somehow? Or did he think he could change her mind?

Anger welled up in her as she realized the truth. He thought her incapable—without any proof and wholly because she was a woman. Slackening her pace, Kate began to formulate a plan. If she was ever

52

to be taken seriously, she would need to prove herself . . . and maybe just teach Alexander Dalton a lesson as well.

As they approached the street corner, Kate reached to slip her arm through his so that he might escort her through the maze of wagon ruts that scarred the muddy street. Flashing him a brilliant smile, she leaned near enough to him that her breast brushed lightly against his arm as they walked.

"Tell me about yourself, Mr. Dalton," she began, her voice as smooth as warm molasses. "How long have you worked for Allan Pinkerton?"

He was wary still, but Kate was determined. After a drawn-out moment of silence, she blithely stepped onto an uneven patch of ground and was thrown off balance. As she'd anticipated, Dalton's grip on her arm tightened. He swung around and, catching her by the waist, drew her instinctively against him.

Kate's head was bowed, her eyes hidden by the veil of her bonnet, else he'd have seen the glimmer of triumph there. She remained in his arms a trifle longer than was necessary, very much aware of the effect she was having on him. Her hands were pressed upon the rigid muscle of his chest, and she could feel him responding to her, almost against his will.

Pulling a tremulous breath, Kate broke free. She thanked him before she took his arm once more and resumed their walk as though nothing of consequence had transpired.

They traversed the muddy street more or less unscathed, and Dalton helped her to regain her footing on the sidewalk. At last he replied to the question she'd posed. "I've worked for Pinkerton for nearly a year."

He didn't even sound like the same man, Kate realized. There was a faint trace of an accent threading through his words. Jeremiah Brown hadn't spoken with an accent. She was honestly surprised when she noticed it. "You're British, aren't you? Why, I'd never have guessed until now. I must admit you're very good at what you do, Mr. Dalton."

When at last he met her eyes, his expression was slightly less grim, and one corner of his mouth twitched perceptibly. Well, Kate thought to herself, it was almost a smile.

"I was born in Weymouth," Dalton admitted, "but my family emigrated to the States when I was a boy."

"Weymouth?" Kate echoed, endeavoring to draw him out. "That's on the Channel coast, isn't it? I've always wondered what it would be like to live by the sea. I suppose you must have been weaned on tales of smugglers and shipwrecks and pirates."

Dalton nodded, seeming to lose himself for a time in his memories. "When I was a child, my grandfather would tell me stories of how—on moonless nights—the local boys would cross to France and fill their holds with satins and silks and rum. They'd hide their booty in the chalk pits; then when it was safe, they'd send it on to London."

Kate had to admit that her interest was piqued. "Your grandfather was a smuggler?"

"No," he replied, amusement flickering across his face. "No, he was a customs officer, assigned to coastal duty. I've always admired him for sticking to his principles no matter what, although I can't say that his neighbors felt the same."

"No doubt his belief was that justice must be had, no matter what the personal cost," Kate remarked thoughtfully. "Perhaps he's the reason that you decided to go to work for Pinkerton."

"Perhaps he is at that," he replied.

As her eyes met Dalton's, Kate was suddenly overwhelmed by remembrances of the disconcertingly vivid dream that had plagued her lately, the dream in which this man was making love to her. She struggled to blot out the vision, but a thrill surged through her nonetheless.

"Have you any family, Mr. Dalton?" she inquired, trying to mask her uneasiness. "A wife? Children, perhaps?"

Dalton shook his head. "I'm afraid my work takes up all my time."

When at last he smiled in earnest, the sharp planes of his face softened, and his eyes filled with a warm light. Kate flushed behind her veil. She couldn't go on with this game any longer. She'd set out to teach him a lesson, to beguile him with her charms, but instead had fallen victim to her own foolish imaginings. Clearly she wasn't half so adept at subterfuge as she'd thought. Still, she was determined that Dalton should not know it.

"There now, do you see? I can gather information as well as anyone," she said, revealing her true motives at last. "In only a short time I've learned all about you."

Dalton released her arm at once, and Kate felt a

chill cut the air between them, a chill so sharp that she almost regretted having spoken. "No more than I wanted you to know," was his brusque reply. "The real skill, Mrs. Warne, comes in drawing out a man's secrets."

"Such as why you are so set against my becoming a detective?"

"There's no secret in that," he replied. "It is far too dangerous an occupation for a woman."

Kate was angry and irritated by his uncompromising tone, but met him with a self-satisfied smile as a thought came to her. "Ah, but you, Mr. Dalton, more than anyone, ought to understand how useful I can be. That fellow you were shadowing at the theater the other night never once suspected you. And why is that, do you suppose? Because you had the good sense to use *me* as a blind, that's why."

Kate had managed to keep her voice steady as she spoke of their "encounter," but she could do nothing to stem the blush that flooded her cheeks.

"And how can you be sure that business was all that I had in mind that night?" Dalton inquired, his green eyes perusing her shamelessly.

The action and his remark were meant solely to unnerve her, and she knew it. But Kate was not about to let this self-righteous detective get the best of her. "You may rest assured, Mr. Dalton, that in the future, business is all there will be between us."

Dalton pushed back the brim of his hat with one finger. His narrowed eyes glittered fiercely; clearly he was unaccustomed to challenge, particularly from a woman. "Take care, then, Mrs. Warne," he cautioned, his words sounding with an ominous ring. "If you go ahead with this plan of yours, you may well be risking your reputation in the bargain.

"It's no secret that Pinkerton's exploits make colorful tales for the local journalists. If they should learn about you, you're likely to become a curiosity, the 'fragile rose of womanhood' whom Pinkerton has allowed to be defiled by contact with the foulest criminals," he went on, waxing poetic. "Believe me, your life will never be the same."

But Dalton could not know that a change in her life was exactly what she was intending. Kate only smiled at his admonition, thinking it odd that he should take such an interest in her welfare.

"Then, we must make certain that this 'rose' remains in the shadows," she told him. "And isn't that precisely where a good detective belongs?"

Dalton pressed his mouth into a long hard line, swallowing a retort that would have made quite plain his ideas on just where he thought a hard-headed, shortsighted, manipulating female of her like belonged.

How could he have imagined, when he'd stolen a kiss from her that night at the theater, that she'd show up in his life again? If truth be known, he'd never done such a thing before. He'd always considered that sort of game unprofessional and dangerous. But somehow he'd gotten so caught up in the role he was playing that he'd acted without thinking, taking advantage of the presence of a stranger—a fascinating, feminine stranger—to conceal himself from the suspect he'd been trailing for two weeks.

More than once since then, he'd tried to convince himself that the kiss had been a spur-of-the-moment decision, a clever way of protecting his cover when it seemed his true identity might be exposed, but that wasn't so. He'd been thinking about kissing her from the moment they'd collided in the theater lobby and he'd looked down into those liquid sapphire eyes of hers.

Even now Alec's thoughts betrayed him as he met the glittering challenge in those same eyes, half-hidden by the veil of her bonnet. He was unsettled by the look on her face, flush from the heat of battle, and the rapid rise and fall of her breast.

There was no denying it; this particular woman had a queer effect on his sensibilities. And since it seemed he would be unable to dissuade her from this damned fool idea of hers to play at detective, the best thing for him to do would be to keep as much distance between himself and Mrs. Kate Warne as was humanly possible.

Without warning, Alec bid her a brusque "good morning," turned sharply on his boot heel and changed direction, without once looking back.

Far too restless to return to the office, and needing to be alone to sort through the jumble of his thoughts, Alec headed for home. He crossed the street, skillfully dodging the oncoming traffic, then rounded the corner, pushed through the door there into the narrow hallway, and hurried up the stairs.

For more than a year now, home had been a rented room above a tailor's shop on Randolph Street. As he shut the door behind him, Alec leaned heavily against it, hoping the familiar surroundings would ease some of the disquiet he was feeling. But try as he might, he found himself unable to stop thinking of "her." Regarding his room as if for the first time, he wondered what she would think of the man who lived here if she were to see this place.

The accommodations were undeniably Spartan. The meager space was filled with a single iron bedstead, chest of drawers and washstand, along with one battered chair and a narrow table that functioned as a desk. Upon the table lay the leather-bound notebook in which he wrote faithfully each night, making scrupulously detailed notes about each case on which he was employed.

"Empty room—empty life" a mutinous voice in his head echoed. But, of course, that was pure nonsense. Didn't he live an unfettered existence most men would envy? Didn't his work for Pinkerton allow him to travel the country meeting the most fascinating people? And wasn't he serving the most worthwhile cause of all—justice?

This room was exactly as he preferred it, he decided, orderly and organized, not cluttered with useless bric-a-brac that might distract his thoughts from his work. And yet, if he were to be honest with himself, he'd have to admit that to him its most attractive feature was the long, double-paned window that faced east and provided a view of Lake Michigan.

Alec had been pacing while he thought, but now he found himself drawn to that window, and he leaned heavily on the sill as he studied the view. Though the village of Weymouth on England's Channel coast was a lifetime ago and a world away, whenever Alec gazed out of this window at the gulls cutting wide arcs across an iron gray sky or a froth of whitecaps on the lake blown up by the wind, he swore he could catch a whiff of his mother's cinnamon bread baking or the pungent aroma of his father's favorite pipe tobacco, all-too-vivid reminders of the snug stone cottage they'd shared by the sea.

Three generations of Dalton men had lived in that cottage, three generations and all of them in service to the Crown: Alec's great-grandfather, who'd fought the French in Canada; his grandfather, the high-principled customs officer; and his own father, who'd been wounded at Waterloo.

Alec had felt himself destined to be the fourth. As a lad, he'd proudly tied Great-grandpa's saber to his waist and played at soldier. For years, he held tight to the dreams of the glorious military career he was sure he'd have—until the day that his father came to him with the news that they were moving to America.

An army pension wasn't enough for them to live on, he'd explained. Times were hard, and the English government didn't seem to have a care for the common man. Life would be better for them in America.

Alec had been thirteen at the time, nearly a man but not hardened enough for the blow. He had set his roots deep. For him, there'd always been a comfortable sense of permanence about the stone cottage. Sadly, it was a feeling that Alec would never know again—not once they'd settled into a crowded New York tenement flat, nor even after they'd moved west to Chicago, looking for a better life. And after his parents were gone, there'd been only a succession of cold, bare rooms and a single-minded devotion to his work.

Over the years, Alexander Dalton had learned well the wisdom in not attaching himself too closely to any place or any person, and regardless of what had happened today, it was a lesson that he would not easily forget.

Chapter 6

A good detective, as Kate soon learned, was often expected to get by on wits alone. Within a week's time, Allan Pinkerton had assigned her a case, but beyond a brief explanation of the situation and the role she was expected to play, she received little instruction. This, she surmised, was to be the test of her abilities.

After a great deal of thought, she decided to put off facing Marcella with the news of her new position. Instead she posted her a brief note explaining that she was going back home to Erin to nurse a sick friend and would be away for several weeks. It was a cowardly way to handle the matter, she knew, but there was so much at stake for her in this that she couldn't seem to summon the extra nerve that would have been required for that particular confrontation. Later, she decided, after she had proven to Pinkerton—and to herself as well—that she was worthy of her new profession, she would have the confidence to face Marcella with the truth.

Kate had to admit that Pinkerton had chosen her first case well; the affair was a delicate matter, just the sort to require a woman's touch. The proprietor of the Lakeview Hotel had enlisted the agency's services in order to apprehend the thief who had been stealing from the rooms of his guests' over the past few months. Already close to ten thousand dollars in cash and jewelry had been stolen.

This particular thief was a discriminating sort. He knew precisely which rooms belonged to guests who possessed expensive pieces of jewelry and which rooms were likely to contain large amounts of cash. Because of this, it was supposed that someone with daily access to the hotel was responsible. The servants, of course, had come under immediate suspicion; but one-by-one they had been replaced, and still the robberies continued.

Kate's part in all of this was to play the role of a wealthy widow, and Pinkerton's directive to her was succinct: "There is a small circle of guests who reside permanently at the hotel. Make a place for yourself in that group and learn everything that you can about them, without arousing their suspicions, for I suspect that one of them is our thief."

And thus it was that on a sunny afternoon in late spring, Kate arrived at the front desk of the Lakeview Hotel to inquire about a room. She introduced herself to the desk clerk as Mrs. Mary Barley, a widow from Buffalo, New York, who was visiting the city on holiday.

"How long do you plan to stay with us, Mrs.

Barley?" the clerk inquired, peering curiously at her over the rim of his spectacles as she signed the register.

Kate put down the pen, but did not reply. In fact, she had scarcely heard the question. Her gaze had wandered from the sweeping fronds of the potted plant in the corner to the archway beyond which lay a spacious parlor. Twin sofas of carved rosewood upholstered in crimson velvet, marble-topped tables and a grand piano, which stood before the tall windows that lined the front of the room, spoke of the hotel's elegance.

As she endeavored to maintain her composure, Kate was thankful for the veil draped over her bonnet, which hid her widened eyes. She reminded herself that Mary Barley would not be impressed by these accommodations; she was a wealthy woman accustomed to the finer things. But Kate Warne had never in her life beheld such luxury.

"What's that?" she asked, remembering now that the young man had asked her a question. "How long? A week, I should think, perhaps longer."

"Very good, ma'am."

"If someone would be kind enough to show me to my room," she requested then, drawing off her gloves and lifting her head imperiously. "It's been a long trip, and I should like to rest awhile before supper."

Kate's suite was just as impressive as the hotel's public rooms. Its floral-patterned carpet was so thick that her feet sank down with each step, making crossing the room a precarious task. A marble-topped dressing table with gilt-edged mirror graced one corner, and there were French doors which opened out onto a balcony providing the promised "lake view."

When her trunk was brought up, a maid came in to inquire if she required help in unpacking, but Kate politely dismissed her. This was a pleasure she wanted all to herself. She did not consider herself vain or frivolous, but she *was* a female and no less than human. Nearly everything within the trunk was newly bought, and Kate had never possessed such beautiful things. Just for a moment at least, she wanted to admire them.

Kate had learned that Allan Pinkerton was not an extravagant man, but he was a resourceful one. He knew that she could hardly pass herself off as a wealthy widow with her own meager wardrobe. And so he had convinced a jeweler, who was indebted to him for some past favor, to lend the agency several tasteful and expensive pieces of jewelry for Kate to flaunt.

As to her clothing, he promptly wrote out a draught for a sum to cover the cost of a suitable wardrobe. At first, Kate balked at this, but Pinkerton explained that expenses such as these would be charged to the hotel as part of the agency's fee.

"They'll be more than willing to pay for a few fripperies if we catch this thief for them," he'd told her.

"And if we don't?" Kate had inquired.

At this, the Scotsman had chuckled grimly. "Well then, you may rest assured, Mrs. Warne, that I shall take it out of your pay, a week at a time in small amounts."

She suspected that he was very much in earnest, but

took heart in the fact that he had sufficient confidence in her to believe she'd be with the agency long enough to repay such a debt.

Kate did not rest at all before supper, but spent the time in unpacking and perusing her new clothes. Like a child playing at dress-up, she held each of the garments in front of her and posed at the mirror before she hung them in the wardrobe.

There were two dresses suitable for evening wear, so intending to make a striking first impression, Kate chose the more elegant, a pale yellow brocaded satin. To complete the effect, there were matching yellow roses to twine in her hair and combs set with seed pearls.

Pinkerton's jeweler friend had provided a double-strand pearl necklace with matching bracelets. The pearls seemed to impart a warmth of their own as they lay against her skin, and even Kate—whose only piece of jewelry until now had been a plain gold wedding band—could guess by their size and luminous quality that they were fine specimens indeed.

It was early yet when Kate finished dressing, and so she decided to have a thorough look at her surroundings. The outside hall, she noted, was most always deserted. The lock on her door was a flimsy affair, and the tracery of heavy vines and trelliswork along the side of the building where her balcony was located made a perfect natural ladder. Anyone who wished could easily gain entry to the room when it was empty, search her belongings for valuables, then slip out unseen. It struck Kate that this was a daunting task she had taken up. However was she to identify the thief?

Poe's detective, Dupin, had once boasted that most men "wear windows in their bosoms," making their intentions easily read, but Kate did not think it would be half so simple as that. One had to know what to look for, after all.

When it was nearly time for supper, she left the quiet of her room and headed downstairs to meet her suspects. She had scarcely reached the lobby when an attractive young lady came forward and put out a dainty, gloved hand. "I'm Elizabeth Danby, and you must be Mrs. Barley."

"Yes, but how—? Oh, it must have been the desk clerk," Kate surmised finally.

Miss Danby nodded, and her golden curls bobbed rhythmically. "He told us to expect you. Those of us who reside at the Lakeview ordinarily meet in the parlor before supper. You're welcome to join us, if you like. I'd be glad to introduce everyone."

Kate smiled at her newfound friend. She couldn't have arranged a more perfect entree. "Why, thank you, Miss Danby. That's very kind of you."

With that, the girl took her arm and led her into the sumptuous parlor which Kate had first noticed when she'd registered that afternoon. It looked all the more inviting now. The gas lamps, with their sparkling crystal pendants, were all lit, illuminating the room and the hotel guests who'd assembled there.

A quartet of young men in evening clothes clustered at the center of the room, their voices raised in heated debate. Miss Danby carefully avoided this group and squired Kate toward the sofas, where the more sedate Lakeview residents were gathered.

The lone gentleman among them ran a hand over

his balding pate and got to his feet, then aided the matronly woman beside him in rising.

"Mrs. Barley," her companion began, "these are my parents, Cyrus and Lucille Danby."

"We're pleased to meet you, Mrs. Barley," Mr. Danby said, speaking for the both of them.

"And this is Mrs. Soames," the girl continued, indicating the elderly lady still perched upon the sofa.

Mrs. Soames was frail in appearance, swathed from chin to toes in black taffeta. The skin drawn over her bones was as creased and yellowed as old parchment, but she had sharp brown eyes and a voice as strong and clear as one half her age. "Where did you say you were from, Mrs. Barley?" she inquired.

"Buffalo, New York, ma'am."

"I visited there once with my husband . . . in '38, I believe it was. It was cold, frightfully cold. Can't blame you for wanting to leave such a place and travel about."

Kate might have argued that at this time of year Buffalo's climate was at least as pleasant as Chicago's, but she didn't think it worth the effort. Mrs. Soames' attention had already wandered elsewhere.

The younger gentlemen had given off arguing at last and now ambled over to join the rest of the group. The man in the lead had long sidewhiskers and thick, black hair which tumbled loosely over his brow, and he seemed to be trying to cultivate an air of genteel boredom.

"Ah, what's this?" he drawled. "A newcomer in our midst?"

As he reached to smooth his thin moustache, Kate

noticed that he wore rings set with gemstones on both of his hands and that the white satin waistcoat beneath his jacket was richly embroidered with gold thread.

"Gentlemen, may I introduce Mrs. Mary Barley from Buffalo," Miss Danby began. "Mrs. Barley, this is Mr. John Morton."

"And I'm Noah Gerard," the young gentleman behind him piped up as he came forward to take Kate's hand, "a fellow New Yorker. I'm from New York City myself."

Mr. Gerard had a friendly face, well sprinkled with freckles. There was a hint of mischief in his smile, and Kate could not miss the especial notice he took of Elizabeth Danby.

Finally Elizabeth turned to the pair of gangling, fair-haired lads who had yet to be introduced. The resemblance between them was so strong that they had to be twins. "These are the brothers Pratt, Richard and Samuel," she revealed. "I daresay you would have a time of it telling them apart, but that our silent Samuel scarcely ever speaks a word."

As if to dispute her claim, Samuel Pratt stepped forward. "Is your husband travelling with you, Mrs. Barley?" he inquired politely.

"I lost my husband three years ago last spring," Kate replied with a note of wistfulness in her voice that was not entirely feigned. "My family accuses me of brooding. They have decided that a change of scenery would do me good, and so here I am."

"Well then," Mr. Morton said, stepping forward, "we must do all that we can to make your stay here a

70

pleasant one."

Kate suspected that he would have taken her arm, but at that moment another young lady, who had been sitting unnoticed in the shadows, sprang up and sidled up beside him, slipping her arm through his.

"Oh, yes," Mr. Morton remarked, as though he'd quite forgotten her until now. "May I present my wife, Sylvia."

Kate could not imagine how anyone could forget a woman so striking as Sylvia Morton. She wore an expensive gown of crimson watered silk—with a low décolletage which accentuated her ample figure. The color was in vivid contrast to a complexion as pale and smooth as fine porcelain. She wore a ruby pendant at her throat, and her lustrous black hair was piled high upon her head and set with matching jewelled combs.

The woman seemed wholly unaware of her abundant charms, though, for she clung possessively to her husband's arm as if Kate might steal him away were she to release him.

It was a ridiculous notion. Surely anyone with eyes could see that Kate, in her borrowed finery, was no threat to the beautiful Mrs. Morton. But Kate developed an immediate sympathy for the woman and aimed to go out of her way to calm her fears.

"I'm so pleased to meet you," she said brightly as the members of the group began to drift away to the dining room, leaving her free to address herself to Mrs. Morton on a more personal level. "I cannot help but admire your lovely gown. I'm thinking of

71

having a few new things made myself, but I confess I don't know where to begin. Perhaps you might be so kind as to recommend a local seamstress."

It was after ten o'clock when Kate finally returned to her room. She'd spent the entire evening socializing with the Lakeview's residents and learning all that she could about them. Now it was time to sort out the facts.

Kicking off her shoes, Kate wriggled her toes in the luxurious nap of the carpet, then went to open the French doors. The night breeze was gentle tonight, the air full of the sweet scent of the blooming lilac hedges beneath her balcony.

Kate sat down at the dressing table, took up pen and stationery and began to compose her report to Pinkerton.

"Thursday, 24th May, 1855," she wrote at the top of the page. "Arrived at the Lakeview Hotel at 4:00 P.M., got a room and settled in. At 7:00 P.M. went down to supper and was introduced to the residents of the hotel . . ."

Kate went on to describe in full detail the facts she had gathered about each of them: Mr. Danby was a banker, and Mrs. Soames a widow, whose late husband had made his fortune in railroads. Young Mr. Gerard's father was an eminent lawyer who dabbled in politics in New York City, and the Pratt boys had come from Ohio and invested a portion of their considerable inheritance in the lumber trade.

Only the Mortons, whose appearance suggested a particularly extravagant lifestyle, did not make any

72

mention of their history. When Warne inquired of Miss Danby how Mr. Morton made his living, the girl had whispered behind her hand that no one knew for certain, but that one of the maids had told her that he was a gambler and apparently a highly successful one. Ah, here was a likely suspect, Kate deduced, pleased with herself. She'd been put off at once by Morton and his haughty manner.

She reread her report, then turned down the light, massaged her brow and ruminated for a while in the dark stillness upon all the information that she'd gathered.

Kate wasn't sure how long she'd been sitting there when she heard the buzz of hushed voices outside her window. Curiosity drew her out onto the balcony. The sounds were clearer here, the voices familiar. One of them was John Morton, and he was speaking with young Mr. Gerard.

"Are you coming?" Morton inquired.

"Perhaps I oughtn't. My father hasn't sent this month's allowance yet, and I—"

"Nonsense! That watch and chain you're wearing will cover any wager you care to make, and besides, if you don't go, you'll disappoint that charming little blonde who's so fond of you. I hear she's been turning away anyone else who asks for her."

There was a long hesitation and then a sigh. "Oh, all right, then."

Kate felt a wave of revulsion sweep over her. Her dislike for Morton was increasing by the moment. It was bad enough that he'd chosen a depraved life for himself, but to encourage a fine young man like Noah Gerard to engage in debauchery was inexcusable. She was so incensed that she had an urge to give up her hiding place and shout over the railing at him, but in the end, she bit her tongue and kept her place.

Then a more practical thought occurred to her. If she followed them tonight, she might discover the name of the establishment where Morton plied his trade, and then Pinkerton could investigate there to learn more of Morton's history and habits. Perhaps the evidence gathered might tie him to the hotel robberies. That would be the most effective form of revenge to deal to a man like Morton.

There was only the sound of retreating footsteps now, and so without further consideration, Kate slipped into her shoes and threw a dark woolen cloak over her evening dress. She came down by way of the back stairs and left the hotel through the rear door.

The two had headed down Randolph Street, and Kate set a rapid pace now to regain sight of them. She'd gone nearly two blocks before she saw them, walking shoulder-to-shoulder as they passed by the courthouse. Careful not to close the distance between them, she drew the hood of her cloak closer around her and trudged on.

Eventually, the pair turned on Wells Street and headed south. Kate knew well enough that this part of town was populated mainly by vagrants and street toughs. The ramshackle buildings there were a collection of cheap hotels, taverns, gambling houses and brothels. She shuddered with apprehension as she realized that there would be more activity here now than in the daylight hours. The darkness could hide a multitude of evils.

All at once, a drunk stumbled out of the shadows, passing close enough for Kate to breathe the foul, sour stench of him. With a gasp, she halted and pressed her back flat against the splintering clapboards of the nearest wall, wishing she could squeeze herself between the cracks and disappear. What a great fool she was! She, who had boasted that she could be a level-headed detective, had never even thought to bring a weapon with which to defend herself. Anything might have served the purpose—a letter opener, a parasol, even a hat pin—but here she was, empty-handed and trembling.

The urge to turn and run all the way back to the hotel was strong, but in the end she resisted. If she failed at this, she would prove them right—Alexander Dalton and all those who claimed that she had neither the strength nor the skills nor the brains for such work. But she would not fail.

Morton and Gerard had crossed the street now and disappeared into a building whose tasteful red brick facade made it appear an oasis in this desert of iniquity. There were even lace curtains ruffling gently as a breeze blew in the open windows. Kate lingered for a moment in the shadows, listening to the tuneless chiming of a piano and the shrieks of raucous laughter that betrayed the fact that this was no respectable house at all.

She'd accomplished what she'd come here to do, but she felt a slight regret at having to leave poor Gerard here in John Morton's clutches. Noah Gerard was probably very near to Kate's own age, young enough still to be expected to make mistakes. But what would his father, the respectable lawyer with an eye for politics, think if he knew that his son was spending his nights at the gaming tables and seeking comfort in the arms of a Wells Street courtesan?

In spite of the warmth of the spring evening, Kate felt a sobering chill. She turned away, intending to make her way as quickly as she could back to safety of the hotel, but she'd not gotten far before she was grabbed roughly from behind. In an instant, the arm closed like an iron band around her waist. There was no time to cry out; a well-muscled hand clamped across her mouth to prevent it as she was dragged backward into the alleyway.

Chapter 7

Kate writhed like a rattlesnake caught up in a gunnysack, and Alec Dalton had a devil of a time handling her. Focusing his efforts, he shoved her back against the brick wall on one side of the alley, using the weight of his own body pressed against hers to hold her there, his fingers anchored firmly over her mouth.

"Be still!" he ordered. "It's me. It's Dalton."

The hood of the cloak had fallen away from her face now, revealing her features to him. Kate Warne looked deceptively vulnerable in the moonlight, with those blue eyes wide and as dark as the night sky and stray wisps of soft brown hair curling across her pale brow.

The air was full of her scent—lavender and roses—and beneath the tangle of the cloak, the sleeve of her yellow gown had slipped, baring one smooth white shoulder. Dalton's eyes were drawn to the spot. He could scarcely keep his wits about him, and it made him all the more angry.

"What in God's name do you think you're doing skulking about in such a neighborhood at night?" he hissed against her ear.

His breathing was ragged, partly from exertion, but mostly, he knew, because of the feel of the supple body writhing beneath his. When he was certain she would not scream, he removed his hand from her mouth, but selfishly, he did not step back to release his hold on her.

"Doing?" Kate echoed, her voice rising dangerously. "I was doing my job! I needed to know where those two men were headed, so I—I followed them."

The catch in her voice made him suspect that she, too, had been affected by their struggle. There was no longer a need to keep her pinned, he told himself. He ought to free her at once, but the effect she had on him made him curious. He was acutely aware of her breath, warm against his cheek, and the rising and falling of her breast, which had slowed now to a regular rhythm. But this was a dangerous game he was playing; it made him weak.

Squeezing his eyes shut, he drew a deep breath, mustered all his strength and stepped backward, hoping he'd regain control. "*You* followed them?" he growled. "What in bloody hell made you think you had to do that?"

He was determined to use harsh words, threats, whatever it took to convince her that she didn't belong here, in this place, or indeed in this profession. "George and I are stationed outside the hotel to handle such things. What do you think I'm doing here now? You're not so naive as to think

Pinkerton is letting you handle this case all on your own, are you?"

"No," Kate replied, after some hesitancy, "no, of course not. But this is my only chance to prove myself, Mr. Dalton, and I shall do whatever I have to do—"

"I don't doubt that you will," he retorted sharply. "But Pinkerton is taking a gamble with you, you know. He's hoping that this little experiment will pay off handsomely, but as for me, I think—"

Dalton struggled to find words that would dissuade her. She was so young, and there were so many dangers. Hadn't she seen that tonight? She could as easily have been seized and dragged into this alleyway by some drunken lunatic. No woman ought to put herself in such a position. He allowed his gaze to linger upon the soft curve of her face. If anything had happened to her—

That one simple thought stunned him. Was that it? Were his opinions not so much a product of reason and rational thinking, but rather based on some as yet unexamined feelings for this particular woman? The realization robbed him of his self-righteousness and left him grim and silent.

"Well, Mr. Dalton?" Kate prompted. "What *do* you think?"

Women only distracted a man from his goals; that was what Alec Dalton thought. He had always kept them at arm's length, never allowed one to intrude upon his life. He'd had something to prove to himself, a career to build, and before long, his work and his life had become one in the same. It was hardly the sort of life any woman would want to share, but he'd been satisfied and certain of his future. And now along came Kate Warne.

Of course he was physically attracted to her. What red-blooded male wouldn't relish the thought of a vibrant young woman like her warming his bed? But there was nothing more to it than that. Oh, he supposed he would have to concede that she was not an ordinary female. She strayed where she did not belong. She was brash and opinionated. She had a fiery temper and a stubborn streak a mile wide. Together, the two of them couldn't seem to carry on a conversation for more than a few minutes without raising their voices, and yet. . . .

"I have my doubts," he told her when he finally found his tongue.

It was all he could say. He was no longer treading on firm ground, certain of his motivations, and so he had no choice but to resign himself to the inevitable.

"But if you intend to make a go of this, Mrs. Warne, never forget that we function as a team. Let George or Allan or me handle this sort of thing. From now on, you confine your activities to those places suitable for a respectable young woman."

There was a hint of annoyance in her expression, and Dalton suspected she might deal him a hot retort. But after a moment of silent contemplation, she accepted his advice without a word and blithely began to rearrange her cloak.

She may well have recognized the folly of her actions this evening, but she was no less determined to proceed with the case. Dalton shook his head solemnly. He'd learned a valuable lesson tonight, even if she had not.

* * *

There was no mention of the encounter with Alec Dalton in Kate's report to Pinkerton, and while she could not be certain, she strongly surmised that Dalton's own report would be silent on that point as well. Their highly charged encounter and their animosity for one another was irrelevent to the case at any rate.

In the course of the following week, Kate continued to gather evidence. From a garrulous chambermaid, she learned that the Danbys had been the latest victims of the hotel thief, only a month before. Miss Danby had lost several expensive pieces of jewelry as well as Cyrus Danby's gold pocket watch and chain. Even Elizabeth had not been spared. A cherished sapphire ring, which her parents had presented to her on her sixteenth birthday, had been taken from her dressing table and, oddly enough, a lavender silk evening dress.

Kate could not help but wonder why the Danbys chose to stay on, but as she thought on it, she realized that they, like most of the hotel's other permanent guests, considered the Lakeview their home—and a mere theft would not be enough to drive them from their home. Then, too, there was a camaraderie among those who met in the parlor each evening; one might say they comprised a family of sorts—with Mrs. Soames as their eccentric matriarch, the Danbys as benevolent parents, and the others, a host of young cousins. Then, of course, there was John Morton. Kate thought him perfect in the role of wicked uncle and the family's black sheep.

81

As a part of her daily routine, Kate would take a walk each morning after breakfast, and in this way she was able to pass her reports on to George Bangs, who regularly took up a post just across the street from the hotel. She had not encountered Alec Dalton at all since that night in the alleyway on Wells Street, though once or twice she thought she'd spied him keeping watch outside the hotel at night as she peered from her balcony windows.

After looking over the details of her latest report one last time, Kate folded it, carefully sealed it inside an envelope and prepared to go down for her walk. When she passed by the mirror, though, her eyes were captured by the reflection. The woman staring back at her through the veiling of gauze draped over the brim of her bonnet—with the exquisite gold and enamel brooch displayed prominently on the bodice of her bronze faille walking suit—looked so unfamiliar and yet so genuine, almost as if the elegant widow Mary Barley were becoming increasingly more the reality and Kate Warne only fading into illusion. It was a sobering thought.

The day was warm, with only a few cottony tufts of clouds dotting the sky, but Kate could not linger to enjoy the fine weather. After delivering her report, she walked around the block and hurried back to the hotel dining room, hoping to catch some of the regulars still at their breakfast.

The early-morning crowd had thinned, and the air was full of the sound of clanging silverware and clattering plates as a bevy of young girls in white aprons went about clearing the tables. Elizabeth Danby was there, though, and her mother as well, although Mrs. Danby had moved a few tables off where she was wholly immersed in conversation with a pair of lady friends.

But Elizabeth was not alone. Noah Gerard had taken up the place beside her, and as Kate observed the pair from her vantage point at the archway entrance to the room, Gerard made a bold move, reaching across the table to lay his hand upon Miss Danby's arm.

Kate had suspected for some time that Mr. Gerard was smitten with the girl, and for her part, she thought that friendship with a refined young lady like Miss Danby might be just the impetus the young man needed to break off his dealings with John Morton and his sordid Wells Street crowd. But it was more than clear now from Elizabeth's reaction that Noah Gerard's feelings were not reciprocated. Distaste was plain upon her fair features, and her eyes had gone as gray and icy as a winter's day.

For the merest instant as Gerard withdrew his hand, Kate discerned a look in his eye that struck her cold. She found herself moving in a rapid stride toward their table, although she had fully intended to hang back awhile longer to watch.

"Good morning!" she called out in her cheeriest voice.

Elizabeth seemed pleased—or was it relieved?—at the interruption. "Mrs. Barley, won't you join us?"

"Thank you. I think I will. Oh, but I see that they're clearing the tables. Is it too late for me to request a cup of coffee, do you think?" Kate wondered, directing the question at Mr. Gerard.

The young man rose and offered Kate his chair. "If

83

you will forgive me, ladies, I must be off. But I will see to it that someone brings you your coffee, Mrs. Barley."

A broad smile brightened his boyish face now; there was no hint of a darker side. Regarding him, Kate might almost have doubted what she'd seen with her own eyes. But she would not forget. For in that moment when she'd watched him from a distance, she'd been sure he'd meant to strike Miss Danby.

"He appears to be quite fond of you," Kate remarked after Gerard had left them.

The waiter arrived and poured both ladies a fresh cup of coffee before retreating silently. Elizabeth spooned sugar into her cup, then stirred absently, focusing her gaze on the curl of steam that rose up from the brew. "He's made that plain enough to everyone. Now he's after me to accompany him to the masquerade ball at the Tremont House next week."

"He seems a personable enough young man," Kate ventured. "You don't find him attractive?"

Miss Danby's moody silence was as good as an assent, yet still she would not meet Kate's eyes.

"I understand that he comes from one of the finest families in New York City," Kate continued, hoping to prompt a reply.

At last Miss Danby came to life, her eyes blazing. "That's what Mama keeps telling me, but it wouldn't matter to me if he were royalty, Mrs. Barley; I should still think him arrogant and self-centered."

Kate digested this information and sipped at her coffee, giving the girl ample time to collect her emotions before she replied. "Well then, of course, my dear, you were right not to encourage him."

A few awkward moments of silence ensued before the timely arrival of the Pratt brothers served to lighten the mood. The young gentlemen stood shoulder-to-shoulder, eerily alike in their appearance. Their smooth blond hair was lightly tousled, their tall, spare frames clad in sober black frock coats and trousers, although Richard was sporting a green-and-yellow-striped waistcoat, as if to proclaim his individuality.

"Good morning to you, ladies," he began, as usual speaking for them both. "We were wondering, Mrs. Barley, if you'd found an opportunity as yet to explore our fair city?"

"I'm afraid I've not been bold enough to venture more than a few blocks from the hotel," Kate told him.

"Well then, may we offer ourselves to you as guides? If you're agreeable, Samuel can see about arranging for a carriage, and we can be off at once."

"Why, thank you, gentlemen. That sounds wonderful," Kate replied, quickly smothering a lopsided smile with her fingertips as she contemplated the absurdity of being shown the sights of a city she'd called home for the past two years.

Miss Danby had been sitting, quiet and demure, all throughout this exchange, but Kate could not help but notice that her features had grown more animated when Samuel's name was mentioned. Gathering courage, the girl finally looked up, but just as her eyes met those of the young man in question, she flushed prettily and cast her glance downward once more.

Kate was irritated with herself for not having seen the signs sooner. She ought to have realized—on that first evening when Elizabeth had playfully introduced "silent" Samuel—where the girl's true affections lay. No wonder she hadn't the slightest interest in Noah Gerard. She had set her sights on Samuel Pratt.

"I wonder," Kate proposed, "if I might be so forward as to suggest that Miss Danby accompany us?"

After all, she said to herself, what harm could come of mixing her business with a little matchmaking?

Richard appeared genuinely surprised by the idea and paused to consider. A well-placed elbow jostled him, but when he turned his sights on his brother, Samuel was concentrating fully upon the shoe with which he was busily scuffing the carpet.

"We hadn't thought to include Miss Danby— seeing as how she's a native to our city," Richard explained. "But, of course, if she would not find such an outing tiresome, we would welcome her company."

And so it was that Kate found herself seated beside Richard Pratt, who held the reins of the spacious open carriage, leaving Elizabeth and Samuel to occupy the seat just behind. And in the end, the silent twin proved to be not so silent after all. For most of the drive, he kept the fair Miss Danby pleasantly entertained with his conversation, leaving his brother to point out the city sights to Kate.

They began the tour near the mouth of the Chicago River, where Richard directed Kate's attention to the McCormick Reaper Works. "McCormick employs several hundred hands," he explained. "This year alone it is estimated that his company will build more than two thousand grain reapers and grass mowers. Across the river there, you can see two of our largest grain elevators. Chicago has become a leader in the grain trade, and each winter these elevators are filled to bursting. Last year we shipped four million bushels more than new New York. The grain was so plentiful that the owners found it necessary to moor ships nearby to hold the over-flow."

He took them next down Michigan Avenue, past the Illinois Central Railroad terminal and the cavernous stone freight shed with its gaping half-moon arches. Beyond this there was the lake to admire, its calm waters a brilliant aquamarine today, and farther south along the boulevard were the imposing mansions where resided the city's most wealthy and influential citizens.

Kate asked a number of eager questions as they continued on. She was careful to listen politely to her companion's replies, convincing him that she was impressed with his knowledge about the city, though, in fact, none of it was new to her.

She was not able to forget that this was a role she was playing, however, and in the quiet moments, while Richard was concentrating on the traffic, Kate could not prevent her thoughts from straying to more personal concerns. She'd had no word from Pinker-ton yet, no way of knowing whether he found the information she'd been gathering useful or if he was pleased with her progress. He seemed willing to allow her the opportunity to prove her natural abilities. But now more than a week had passed uneventfully, and Kate was growing anxious. Would she be able to justify his trust?

Only one person had deigned to voice an opinion thus far on her capability for this job—and that opinion had been a doubtful one. Although she had not seen him face-to-face in days, Kate often sensed that Alec Dalton was somewhere nearby, keeping a keen eye on the suspects and coolly waiting for her to make some mistake.

But she sensed as well that Dalton was intentionally keeping his distance. He'd gotten too close that night on Wells Street; she was sure that she'd not imagined his labored breathing when he held her in his arms. Kate could not deny that she had been affected, too, and those memories filled her own dreams now on more nights than she cared to admit. Perhaps the truth was that Dalton was avoiding her because he had decided that he would not aid her cause, of which he so heartily disapproved. Yes, perhaps it was only that. Kate dared not explore any other reason.

The carriage was travelling westward now, rattling over the plank-covered streets which cut through blocks of balloon-frame buildings fronted by board sidewalks. They had reached the heart of the city, and her irrespressible guide pointed out the imposing edifice of the courthouse as they passed it by.

Ahead lay the south branch of the river, lined on either side by wharves and warehouses. Dozens of tall ships lay at anchor here, their masts and spars branching out against the pale blue sky like leafless trees.

When they crossed the river by way of one of the center-pier bridges, Richard took the time to explain its operation to Kate—how in response to a tugboat's whistle, the bridgetender would start the mechanism that would turn the bridge a full ninety degrees so that its ends swung out over the river, allowing the ship to pass by.

Next he told them all of the time an impatient tugboat captain, making free use of his steam whistle, had very nearly caused the stampede of a team of excitable horses caught midstream on the bridge. "If not for an admirable effort on the part of that teamster," he explained, "all of us waiting there on the bridge would have had an unwelcome bath in the river."

It occurred to Kate then that Richard Pratt reminded her of someone, though she couldn't put a finger on who it was. He had rather a flair for telling tales and was doing his best to show Kate a good time. Samuel was the one, though, who suggested that perhaps the ladies might enjoy a tour of the brothers' own establishment, Pratt Brothers Lumber and Supply Company.

The idea was well-received, and Richard obliged, directing the team at a rapid pace through the commercial streets until they reached a choice section of river frontage with a long, low warehouse building wholly surrounded by open ground that was piled high with lumber.

Kate surmised, from the bustling of men and

machinery on the property, that this was a thriving concern, and it soon became apparent to her that while Samuel Pratt might have been wholly unassuming in a social atmosphere, he was as well-spoken as his brother when it came to business affairs. And with gray eyes wide, Elizabeth Danby hung on his every word, like a devoted acolyte.

"Each day more lumber arrives by ship and train from the forests of northern Wisconsin and Michigan," he informed the ladies as he helped them alight from the carriage. "With all the construction going on in this city, we could easily make our fortune selling to contractors alone. But there's good money to be made as well in the handling of lumber. From our central location, we can ship throughout the country. You mark my words, ladies, before long Chicago will be the largest center for the distribution of lumber in the world."

Kate learned a good deal about lumber that day and about the Pratt brothers as well, enough to convince her that they could likely be eliminated from her list of possible suspects. With the profits they were realizing from this lumber venture, they would soon be able to build their own fine mansion on Michigan Avenue and gain entree into the more high-toned city circles, if they chose. Stealing bits of jewelry from hotel rooms would not be in their best interest; the Pratt brothers had far more lucrative prospects.

The outing might have ended harmlessly enough, had it not been for Kate's gloves. Having completed their tour of the lumberyard, the gentlemen proceeded to help the ladies back into the carriage, and when Kate moved to take Richard's hand, she accidentally dropped the gloves she had been holding. He attempted to retrieve them at once, but they'd had fallen into the mud beneath the carriage wheels and were now hopelessly ruined.

Kate tried to dismiss the loss as unimportant, but Richard had noticed that the gloves were new and insisted upon replacing them. She assured him repeatedly that it was not necessary, but before she knew what he was about, he had driven back across the river to a block of fashionable shops on Lake Street that Kate knew only too well.

She sat very still, her heart slowly sinking in her breast as the carriage drew up along the sidewalk and her companions discussed among themselves which shop to try. As a stranger in town, Kate could hardly be expected to offer a suggestion, nor to dissuade them from the choice they made. And as if guided by the perverse hand of fate, they decided upon the one called HEWITT'S.

Chapter 8

The bell over the door jangled briskly as the two smartly dressed young couples entered the shop. Marcella Hewitt met them at the counter with a gracious smile.

Kate's body had gone rigid with tension, and if she had not been held fast on Richard's arm, she might have turned and run. But it was too late for that. She had no choice but to face up to the precarious situation she found herself in, and precarious it was, indeed. If Marcella were to recognize her—to call her by her true name—Kate's position would be compromised, she would lose the trust of her companions, and all the work she'd done at the hotel would be for naught.

Her first thought was that she was getting no less than she deserved for lying to Marcella. But more rational instincts prevailed. Perhaps her cousin would not recognize her dressed as she was, in the latest fashion, her face obscured beneath the veil of her bonnet. Still choosing to be cautious, though,

Kate endeavored to keep herself hidden within the circle of her friends.

"Good afternoon," Marcella said, greeting them all. "May I help you?"

"Yes," Richard piped up, drawing attention at once to Kate. "The young lady here has lost a pair of gloves—fawn-colored kid gloves—and I should like to replace them for her. Have you got anything like that in your stock?"

"I think we can accommodate you, sir," Marcella replied and reached beneath the counter for the long wooden display box. "If the young lady would like to have a look at these—"

"This really isn't necessary, Richard," Kate whispered to him once more. But he was adamant.

She hesitated, then resignedly stepped nearer to the counter, deliberately tilting her head to one side as she pretended to examine the goods on the counter so that her face was shadowed by the brim of her bonnet. From behind, a hand touched her arm. It was Elizabeth's.

"Samuel has asked if I'll walk down to the post office with him," she explained in her soft voice. "We'll return directly, I promise. So you take your time in deciding."

Well, at least Kate had managed to do one thing right today. Elizabeth and Samuel were getting on famously. The girl leaned nearer to her then, her voice only a whisper. "I want to thank you, Mrs. Barley . . . Mary, for inviting me along today."

"Samuel seems particularly glad of your company," Kate observed, and the two conspirators cast a furtive glance at the gentleman, who was waiting by the door.

"I think Richard is rather taken with you as well," the girl replied, nudging Kate's arm playfully before she turned to follow her young man out.

The words caught Kate completely unaware. In her astonishment, she forgot all about Marcella. Considering now what Elizabeth had said, Kate looked back over her shoulder at Richard Pratt, who stood in bold silhouette against the sunlit store window. He was a pleasant young man with an engaging manner, and he *had* been doing his utmost to be entertaining all morning.

After she'd thought on it awhile, she realized that the girl could be right, that Richard might indeed have been trying to charm the young widow, Mary Barley. And all at once Kate felt ashamed. She'd been so concerned with her own purposes that she'd never even considered his.

It was only then that Kate began to grasp the full meaning of what this job of hers was all about. Richard Pratt had been trying to win the favor of a woman who did not even *exist*. Kate had not forgotten how she had felt when Dalton left her standing alone outside of Rice's Theatre. No matter what the motive, she was the one who was coldly playing with people's lives now, and the thought was a hard one for her to accept.

When Kate turned back to the counter, she made a hasty selection and handed the gloves to her cousin, wanting only to escape before anything else went wrong. But it was not to be. The widening of Marcella's eyes as the color drained away from her face made it quite clear that she had realized at last who the well-dressed young woman across the counter was.

However, the confrontation Kate feared did not take place after all. She could not imagine what Marcella must be thinking, but the older woman had apparently decided not to give her away, for she transacted the sale with an uncharacteristic silence.

Richard paid for the gloves, handed them to Kate, and taking her by the arm, led her from the shop. But Kate could not resist the urge to look back, and when she did, her cousin met her with a look that left her feeling utterly cold and empty inside.

It was late in the afternoon when Kate returned at last to the hotel. The Pratts had insisted upon treating the ladies to dinner at the Sherman House, and she could do no less than oblige, though with all that was on her mind, she'd found herself scarcely able to engage in light conversation.

Safely inside her room, Kate pressed her back against the door and breathed a long sigh of relief. The day's events had left her feeling drained, and she could only hope that a nap before supper might restore some of her vigor.

Untying the ribbons of her bonnet, she dragged it off and started into the room. A gasp caught in her throat as she spied a man's dark form sitting in the corner chair, and she drew up short, thinking for one alarming moment that she was about to meet the hotel thief face-to-face.

The man rose smoothly, though, and stepped out of the shadows, tugging thoughtfully on his dark beard.

"Mr. Pinkerton!" she exclaimed as relief washed over her. "I wasn't expecting—"

"Forgive me if I startled you, Mrs. Warne; but I need a word with you, and this seemed the most inconspicuous method. Do sit down," he bade, pointing out the chair he'd just vacated. He was chuckling to himself as if her disquiet amused him. "Poor girl, you look exhausted. So those Pratt boys did a thorough job of showing you the city, did they?"

Kate tossed her bonnet on top of the bureau and dropped obediently into the chair. She must have appeared startled to hear that he knew precisely where she'd been, for he took the time to explain.

"I spoke to George before I came up. He saw you go out. Now, I've been reading your reports . . ."

It was the impassive tone of his voice that made Kate uneasy. Had he found them inadequate? Had he decided that she hadn't the skills necessary to do the job? She studied her employer for a hint of what was on his mind. Pinkerton began to pace before the windows, as if sorting out his thoughts. His head was bowed, his brow furrowed, but there was no indication at all of his mood.

"Is anything wrong?" Kate prompted.

"No. No, on the contrary, you've done a fine job. We've been able to discover quite a bit using the information you've supplied to us. This John Morton, for example, is an interesting character."

Kate nodded thoughtfully. Discovering that she'd been clenching the fabric of her skirt in two tight fists she loosed her fingers now, endeavoring to relax as she listened to his words.

"A gambler who spends his money on living the

high life. He's run up bills all over town. A likely suspect, don't you think?"

"Yes, sir," Kate agreed, her enthusiasm building. "I'll admit that he's been my first choice all along, but something's happened that's gotten me to reconsider my theories. You see, I was watching Mr. Gerard, the young man from New York, this morning, and well, some of his actions lead me to believe that he's not all that he seems to be."

"You're quite right about that, Mrs. Warne. We've done some investigating at Flora Desmond's—that's the gambling house he's been frequenting with John Morton—and it seems that Mr. Gerard is quite the gambler himself. Papa provides him with an allowance, but nothing like what he's been spending."

After having observed him with Elizabeth Danby this morning, Kate was not at all surprised to hear that Noah Gerard was not the innocent young boy she'd first thought him to be.

"For several months now," Pinkerton went on, "he's been keeping a mistress there. The girl's name is Nell, and her friends tell us he's given her several pieces of jewelry. Under the circumstances, that isn't unusual, but I'd like to have a look at those pieces. Dalton and I both tried to talk to her, but she'd have none of us. She's a greedy little piece of work who knows a good thing when she sees it."

Kate wondered what she herself might be able to learn if she could talk to the girl, but of course she'd never have such an opportunity. As Alec Dalton had pointed out to her once before, she would have to remain above reproach and confine her activities to those places suitable for a respectable young woman if she wanted to prove the usefulness of a female detective.

"So," Pinkerton concluded, "I think you'll agree that Morton and Gerard are our most likely suspects. Now we have only to catch one of them at his dirty business."

"I've been showing off my jewelry at every opportunity," Kate assured him, "but thus far no one has made a move. How long do you suppose we shall have to wait?"

"Not long, I suspect," he replied, his mouth curving in a self-satisfied smile. "You see, I've a plan to draw out our thief. I trust you've heard about the masquerade ball next week at the Tremont House?"

"I believe it's been mentioned."

"And do you think you might wrangle an invitation from one of your new gentlemen friends?"

In fact, Richard Pratt had offered that very afternoon to take her, but Kate had not given him an answer. After what Elizabeth had pointed out to her, she did not feel comfortable leading him on. "I don't know if—"

"Make the arrangements," he said simply. The tone in Pinkerton's voice made it clear that he intended that nothing should stand in the way of his plans. "Both Morton and Gerard have already rented costumes for the affair," he told her, "and so I want you to be there—with the bait."

Pinkerton insisted upon handling the rental of Kate's costume, which arrived at the hotel two days before the ball. The "bait," as he'd called it, was delivered but a few hours before Kate was set to depart, by the hand of none other than Allan Pinkerton himself. And as soon as she set eyes upon it, Kate understood why.

This most-important part of the plan was a collar necklace, strung with chains of marquise diamonds which hung in varying lengths—like sparkling icicles. Kate had never seen anything to compare with it, and how Allan Pinkerton had managed the loan of such a magnificent piece of jewelry, even for one evening, she could not begin to guess.

Her costume was a personfication of winter, no doubt chosen because it would complement the necklace of diamond icicles. The white silk gown was scandalously low-cut and trimmed in deep green holly leaves and red ribbons, and a white velvet cape had been provided to complete the ensemble. Kate had at last given in and enlisted the service of one of the hotel maids to help her dress. The girl took great pains with her hair, arranging it into a mass of dark ringlets, which were piled high upon her head and set with pins whose dangling silver heads were wrought to resemble lacy snowflakes. When at last her sequinned mask was in place, Kate scarcely recognized herself.

After she'd taken stock of the woman in her dressing table mirror, she felt a rush of apprehension. She'd been plain for all of her life; there was a certain comfort in anonymity. Tonight, though, she was meant to be the center of attention, the one upon whom all eyes must be fixed—even if it was only because of the fabulous diamond necklace she wore. Such a woman must be vibrant, entrancing, and wholly in control. But would Kate be able to play this part that Pinkerton expected of her?

In spite of all her doubts, Kate could not suppress the childlike enthusiasm that infused her as she prepared to meet her companions in the hotel parlor. Whatever the outcome, tonight would be an adventure, an adventure such as she'd never experienced before.

If the reactions of her own little group were any indication of what the evening held in store, Kate decided that she might have a chance for success after all. As she swept down the stairs and posed in the archway framing the entrance to the parlor, all conversation ceased.

"Mrs. Barley," Richard greeted, voicing his pleasure as he advanced to take up her hands. "I shall be the envy of every gentleman in the ballroom tonight with you on my arm."

Even if he hadn't revealed himself by speaking, Kate still would have recognized him by his choice of costume. Richard Pratt was a dreamer, just the sort to crave the role of dashing cavalier, plumed hat and all. The purposeful look with which he continued to regard her distressed her, though.

Miss Danby was dressed as a fairy-tale shepherdess—in golden locks, pinafore, and petticoats, and carrying a tall crook. The girl looked positively radiant upon the arm of Samuel Pratt, who was for tonight an august Roman senator in toga and sandals. For once, Kate thought to herself, the two brothers looked nothing alike.

"Oh, Mary, you do look lovely," Elizabeth agreed. "And that necklace! Wherever did you come by such

101

a beautiful piece?"

Kate had rehearsed a response for just such a question, and she was thankful for the opportunity to be able to use it now. "It was a gift . . . an anniversary gift from my husband," she replied, her voice effectively quavering as she placed a trembling hand over the jewelled collar.

As she'd hoped, Richard nervously shifted his gaze across the room, freeing her at last. Perhaps if he thought that she'd not recovered from her husband's death, he would not expect so much.

The Tremont House was only a short carriage ride away. Once the couples arrived there, they found the expansive ballroom choked with a queer assortment of humanity: harlequins, knights, and pirates, queens in courtly robes and gypsy wenches. Kate could only stand there, clinging to Richard's arm. She had never seen such a colorful spectacle, and she was struck dumb behind her mask as she studied the costumed revellers.

Once she'd gotten over the initial amazement, she found herself having to juggle a polite conversation with her companions with an attempt to concentrate on the business of locating the two men who were to be the focus of her attentions tonight: Morton and Gerard.

It was difficult at first to pick them out, with everyone masked and wearing elaborate disguises, but Kate could not help but smile to herself when she finally spotted Morton. He'd given himself away by his very choice of costume: a devil in crimson cloak, with pitchfork and tail—a stark contrast to his all-suffering wife, who tonight wore the guise of an angel.

Noah Gerard appeared a short time later as an Elizabethan courtier in black velvet doublet and hose. There was a Grecian goddess on his arm, her costume no more than a length of filmy material artfully draped over her slim figure and bound at the waist with gold cord. The girl's carefully painted face did not seem at all familiar, and as Kate studied her, she wondered, with a rising exhilaration, if this could possibly be the canny Nell.

When Kate saw the girl separate from her partner and head off in the direction of the dressing room that was provided by the management for the convenience of the ladies, Kate excused herself from her companions and followed her inside.

After the brilliant blaze of light from the ballroom chandeliers, she had to blink her eyes to adjust to the dimness of the dressing room as she closed the door behind her. A line of gas jets along the far wall, where the mirrored dressing tables had been arranged, provided some light, but still the room was hung with hazy, blue shadows.

Kate spotted her quarry at once. She was seated before one of the mirrors, arranging her hair. Its color seemed, in this light, a most unnatural shade of blond. While she planned her strategy, Kate hid herself in amongst the ladies who were busy chatting and making final adjustments to their costumes. If this girl was indeed Gerard's mistress, then Fate had provided her with an opportunity that could pay off handsomely—if only she would tread carefully.

First, she removed her mask and set it aside, then discarded her white velvet cloak and borrowed one of soft, dark wool from among those hanging on the wall hooks. Carefully arranging the cloak's enveloping folds so that they hid her costume and the magnificent diamond necklace, Kate then raised the hood and glanced at her reflection in the nearby mirror. For the first time in her life, she was grateful for her ordinary features, for without the aid of the striking costume and Pinkerton's diamond necklace, Kate knew that hers was a face easily forgotten.

When the crowd in the dressing room had thinned somewhat, she made her move, casually approaching to take up the stool directly beside Gerard's friend. "Nell?" she inquired, effecting a voice with a tone that was much coarser than her own. "Is that you, Nell?"

When the girl turned to Kate, her powdered brow creased as though she was trying to place her, and Kate felt flush with success. Her suspicions were right; this was Gerard's mistress. "It's Mary, Mary Brown," she went on, bluffing boldly. "I worked for Miz Desmond a while back. Aw, but you probably don't remember me, do you?"

The girl cocked her head, as if the action would jog her memory. "Well, I . . ."

"Don't let it worry you none. It's hard to remember all those girls, and I been gone almost a year now."

"So how are you faring, Mary?" The question was phrased politely enough, although her narrowed eyes warned Kate that she had not entirely abandoned her caution.

"I got up in the world some," Kate told her. "Got me a real gentleman to take care of me now. An' I can tell you, I don't plan on ever goin' back to Wells Street. But what about you? You still in thick with that gambler fella? A gambler ain't the best invest-ment you could make, you know."

"He treats me real good," Nell said in Gerard's defense. "He brings me presents—flowers and chocolates—and he treats me like a lady. Why, he even bought me a fancy silk dress—lavender-colored, it was, and just drippin' with lace. Liked how I looked so much that he made me wear that dress just about every night."

Kate quietly took in the information. She had to fight the revulsion that welled in her as she recalled that just such a dress had been stolen from Elizabeth Danby's room. Could it be that Gerard was indulging some sick fantasy in making his mistress up to look like Elizabeth?

"And what does Miz Desmond say about your entertainin' only this one fella every night?" she asked next, hoping to keep Nell talking awhile longer yet.

A smile twisted on the girl's rouged lips. "Noah pays her well enough to leave us be. Besides, we'll be gettin' married soon."

Kate widened her eyes in exaggerated fashion to reflect Mary Brown's utter astonishment at the news. "Well now, don't that beat all?" she cried, all the while her mind calculating furiously. "An' I'd wager that such a fine important man as Noah Gerard probably bought you a diamond ring, too."

Nell hesitated for a moment, as if considering the risks, and then proudly waved her fingers—and the ring she was wearing—under Kate's nose. Kate took up the girl's hand to examine it more closely. The stone was a sapphire, flanked by two diamonds. Elizabeth Danby had lost a sapphire ring to the hotel thief.

"Well now, ain't that a fine piece!" Kate replied as

she pretended to admire it. "You're one lucky gal, there's no denyin' it. But I'd watch out for him, Nell, just the same. His friend, John Morton—you do remember Morton, don't you? Well, he told me that Gerard had his eye on a rich widow."

After a long pause, Nell smiled knowingly. Kate could see some cracks in the facade, though. "That? Oh, that's only business," the girl assured her.

"Just the same," Kate said, rising from her stool to end the interview, "I'd keep a close eye on him, were I you. A rich widow is a mighty temptin' prize . . . maybe too temptin' to pass by."

With those ominous words hanging on the air for Nell to consider, Kate made her escape, disappearing promptly into the shadows.

It was not difficult later on—after Kate had reassumed her original costume—to arrange a dance with Noah Gerard. She had only to wait for an opportunity to find him alone, and then guilelessly inquire as if she had not promised him the next dance. As she'd hoped, he did not hesitate to take advantage of the opportunity.

"It seems that I have been concentrating my efforts in entirely the wrong direction," he remarked as he led her out onto the floor.

"And how is that, Mr. Gerard?" Kate asked, brimming with innocence.

His dark eyes fixed on hers momentarily, but then slipped downward, following the arch of her throat. For a time, he seemed wholly mesmerized by the diamond collar that lay sparkling against her skin. Kate was well pleased with herself and reckoned that she had him just where she wanted him—until his gaze dropped lower still.

"I've been wasting my time on green apples," he said, his voice deepening, "when all the while here before me was the sweetest fruit of all and ripe for picking."

With this, his arm tightened across her back, and Kate fought back a frantic impulse to break free. But she could not. She had to see this through; she had to put on a convincing show in order for her plan to work. And so she swallowed hard, met his words with a beguiling smile, and accepted his advances.

The dance seemed to wear on endlessly. Gerard had whirled her about the room so many times that Kate felt dizzy from the exercise. Her persistence was rewarded finally, though, when she caught sight of Nell. The girl was standing alone by the windows and watched them closely, a look of wounded betrayal written plain upon her painted face.

When Gerard led Kate from the dance floor at long last, he asked her pointedly if he might meet her later. She had encouraged him—there was no doubt of that—and so the look of indignant surprise that she sent him as she refused his offer left him silent, but obviously enraged. If his greed were not sufficient motive to send him after the necklace, Kate reasoned, then perhaps revenge would spur him on.

Kate danced one dance with the devil, Mr. Morton, and then spent the ensuing hour keeping company with Richard, lest he begin to wonder at her absence. When the tall, mysterious Arab arrived to claim her, though, Kate had no chance to refuse.

"I believe this dance is mine," he announced as he snatched up her hand and led her away.

Kate could see a squared jaw, but a black silk mask effectively concealed the rest of his features. A hooded burnous made from a rich, striped fabric of crimson, gold and black enveloped his body to mid-calf, where wide-legged trousers had been tucked into the tops of his boots.

His fingers gripped hers tightly, almost as if he expected her to flee, and as he turned her into his arms, his hand splayed across her back, pressing her full against his hard-muscled chest. It was a purely possessive gesture—whether he was aware of it or not. And when Kate looked up into those familiar bottle green eyes, her heart skipped a beat. Dalton!

Chapter 9

As Alec Dalton led her through the steps of the waltz, his hard fingers began to absently trace patterns across her back, generating waves of heat which spread through the thin fabric of her gown to the flesh beneath it. Kate stared hard into the center of his chest, trying desperately to ignore these sensations and focus on her purpose here tonight. But an undeniable excitement was bubbling in her veins as his lean body moved against hers with the rhythm of the dance.

"If you're done playing coquette to all our suspects, we need to talk," he began.

Kate paid his sarcasm no heed, for she sensed that tonight his words did not pose half so much danger to her as his body. Beneath his mask, his jaw was firmly set. He seemed as cold and solemn as ever, except for the achingly sensual brush of his fingertips. Was this some cruel game he was playing? Was he out to prove she could be distracted from her purpose?

Kate willed herself to concentrate. "Well?" she prompted him, the word honed razor-sharp. "What have you got to say, Mr. Dalton?"

Only now did she notice that he seemed as anxious as she to avoid making eye contact. "Not here," he said, pulling in a long, unsteady breath. "Not now. It's impossible for me to concentrate on business . . . while I'm counting the steps. We'll have to meet somewhere."

Kate knew that he was lying. All along his movements had been smooth and practiced. Dalton was obviously an accomplished dancer; he hadn't a need to count steps. Could it be that he was just as much a victim of this strange ailment as Kate herself? She dare not even consider—

"Where shall we meet?"

"When the dance is over, lose yourself in the crowd," he directed, "and then slip into the alcove, behind those curtains. Over there, do you see?"

She told him that she did, and then neither of them spoke again. Kate closed her eyes to shut out the world and imagined, for the moment, that she and Alec Dalton were no more than polite strangers—just a man and woman enjoying the dance. Only then could she admit to herself what she'd been denying all along. Like it or not, there was more between the two of them than business.

Dalton paced the narrow confines of the curtained alcove, tore the mask from his face and tossed it aside impatiently. Kate Warne had only been doing her job tonight, he reminded himself. It was Pinkerton's idea to dangle her like a scrap of meat before the hungry wolves. Damn him! Nevertheless, Alec found himself unaccountably irritated with her for playing the part—and playing it far too well.

Alec had scarcely been able to contain his rage as he'd watched Noah Gerard, a miserable profligate better acquainted with Wells Street whores, lay his hands on Kate. It angered him almost as much to realize how close he himself had come to losing control. But he had handled difficult assignments in the past, and he swore to himself now that he would overcome his personal feelings—whatever they might be—and handle this one.

When Kate pushed back the heavy damask draperies and swept into the alcove, she found Dalton already waiting there. He'd cast aside his mask, and she could see that his handsome features were set in a deep scowl. In his dramatic costume, with eyes fixed on some invisible spot on the floor, feet planted firmly apart, and his arms folded across his broad chest, he bore more than a little resemblance to an implacable Arab sheikh.

Kate's heart fluttered inexplicably. It would be wise, she warned herself, to get down to business at once. "Gerard has his mistress here with him tonight," she informed him as she removed her own mask. "She's wearing a sapphire ring. I've had a good look at it, and I'd be willing to bet it's the same one that was stolen from Elizabeth Danby last month."

Dalton's brow lifted, but no more than a fraction of an inch. "That would appear to narrow our list of suspects," he admitted. "Just the same, we'll need hard proof. The girl hasn't been anxious to cooperate with us.

"Pinkerton wants you to make yourself scarce tomorrow," he went on to inform her. "Once you've had breakfast with your new friends, let them know that you've made plans for the day and then leave the hotel. You're to set the jewel case out on your dressing table; we don't want to make things too difficult for our thief."

As Kate silently digested her instructions, soft strains of music and odd bits of conversation from the ballroom filtered through the draperies, reaching her ears. And then all at once, she heard a voice she recognized. "I wonder where she could have gotten off to?"

"Anyone could get lost in this crowd, Mr. Pratt. But don't worry, we'll find her."

Kate stiffened instantly as she realized that these voices belonged to Elizabeth Danby and Richard Pratt. By the sound of it, her companions were outside—just beyond the draperies—and they'd come looking for her.

Drawing in her skirts, Kate edged closer into the corner of the alcove where Dalton was ensconced. He seemed to sense her alarm, for he stretched out one long arm, hooked her waist and pulled her deeper into the shadows.

The stillness in the tiny alcove was broken only by the ragged intake of their breathing. Entrapped within the circle of Alec Dalton's arms, Kate hastily put aside all thoughts of the danger without, for the danger before her was far greater.

As she savored the rugged feel of the body now

molded against hers and the warmth of his breath against her ear, desires she had all but forgotten sprang fiercely to life, and Kate could not help but wonder if this was only another of her vivid dreams. On their own, her hands slipped beneath his Arab cloak and ranged across the soft linen shirt beneath and the broad, muscled planes of his back.

Alec fought back a groan as his body responded to her touch. His eyes lingered over the soft white flesh nearly spilling out over the top of her tightly corsetted bodice, but his hands were strangely numb. He knew that if he touched her, he'd be lost.

They remained where they were, clinging to one another, long after the danger of discovery had passed. Deep within, Kate still harbored doubts about Dalton's intentions. When she found the courage at last to look into his eyes, though, she was relieved to see that his expression had softened. She opened her mouth to speak, but she'd no more than uttered his name before he gently put a finger to her lips, as if fearful of what she might say.

Curious now, Alec traced the soft outline of her mouth with his fingertip, and with that, the barrier was broken. He captured her face in his hands, and when his mouth closed hungrily over hers, it caught them both unaware.

Kate's head was reeling. She was no novice to lovemaking; she understood full well the urgency fuelling his kisses, and if she'd been half so strong as she claimed to be, she could have used this knowledge to best him at this game he must be playing with her. But Kate, too, was a captive of powerful needs, needs that had gone too long unfulfilled, and it

113

shamed her to admit that she wanted this man, regardless of his motives.

She may have been experienced in such matters, but never before had she felt so utterly powerless. The scent of tobacco and sandalwood wreathed the air between them; it was an intoxicating blend. Alec Dalton filled up her senses. His deft hands played over her body with the skill of a virtuoso playing upon a familiar instrument and striking each chord with perfection. He had control over her every breath, her every thought—

Despair welled in her as Kate realized that in seducing her, Dalton had proven his point. She hadn't the strength of which she'd boasted. He'd made her forget—if only for the moment—her role here tonight, her suspects, and the whole case she was supposed to be building. . . .

In the half-light, Alec saw the shimmering of unshed tears in Kate's sapphire eyes, and it brought him at once to his senses. Reluctantly he released her, and she stumbled back awkwardly out of his arms before regaining her balance.

Both of them realized that they'd made a mistake— but it was Alec who apologized.

"I'm sorry, Kate."

Kate passed a thoroughly sleepless night. Thus far the hotel thief had chosen to strike while no one was about. There was, of course, always the possibility that he might come after the necklace tonight, but it was not this thought that kept her wide-eyed and anxious. It was rather the fact that in this evening's encounter with Alec Dalton, she had allowed her emotions to rule over good common sense.

She reminded herself that there was nothing she wanted more than to be accepted into Pinkerton's circle of detectives, to have a part in seeing justice done. A few stolen moments of pleasure were not worth jeopardizing an entire future.

Doubtless Dalton had only been toying with her in order to prove his point. It was no less than she deserved, Kate admitted to herself, for she'd once used much the same methods on him. There was no use in denying the physical attraction between them; both of them had been perceptive enough to recognize it and use it to their own advantage. But Kate knew that if she was to remain in Pinkerton's employ, she must learn to fight these dangerous desires and somehow make her peace with Alec Dalton.

The next morning, in keeping with Pinkerton's instructions, Kate breakfasted with the hotel's regular guests and casually announced that she had an appointment which would keep her away for all of the morning. She left the hotel with no particular direction in mind, but she soon found herself heading west to Lake Street and toward a confrontation she'd been dreading, but which she could put off no longer.

When Kate entered the shop, Marcella stood alone behind the counter. The older woman glanced up, but as soon as she saw who had come in, she turned away at once, without a word, and immediately took herself off into the storeroom. Kate did not let the cold reception daunt her. Straightening her back, she marched behind the counter and followed her cousin.

"Marcella, it's not what you think," she began, when finally she'd cornered the woman among the storage shelves.

"And precisely what am I to think? Your note said that you had to leave town for a bit, but then only a few days later, you show up here on the arm of a rich young gentleman, who wishes to buy you something. I've tried to tell myself that he must be a close friend of yours, even though I've never met him, for no lady would think to accept such a personal gift from a stranger—"

"It was only a pair of gloves, Marcella, for heaven's sake. He felt responsible when mine were ruined."

"And what sort of relationship is this that would have you lie to your family? Where did you come by all of these fine, new clothes you're wearing? Did *he* buy them for you?" Marcella tried to form her argument further, but the words eluded her. She could only shake her head and sputter. "Nursing a sick friend, indeed!"

"I-I'm sorry that I didn't explain earlier. But I wouldn't have let it go on. I planned on telling you."

"Telling me what?"

As she met her cousin's eyes, Kate drew an uneasy breath and then forged ahead. "The truth is that I've taken a new job. I am now employed by Mr. Allan Pinkerton, as one of his detectives, and we are presently engaged in an effort to catch a hotel thief."

"You're what?" Marcella's eyes went wide, and she had gone dangerously pale. "Why, that's an absurd story! I don't know what you hope to gain by inventing such a tale, Kate—"

"It is the truth."

116

At last Marcella began to accept that Kate was serious. "You can't do this. It's not the proper sort of work for a woman. What do you know about being a . . . a detective?"

"Enough to convince Allan Pinkerton to hire me," Kate replied. "And what I don't know I shall learn along the way."

The older woman began to wring her hands as she paced between the rows of shelves. "I ought to have tried harder to find you a nice young man. That's what you need. You've spent too much time alone, Kate, and those books you've been reading have put all sorts of queer notions in your head."

"This isn't a queer notion," Kate insisted. "It will allow me to do something truly important with my life."

"Devoting your life to a good man and being a dutiful wife and mother is what God intended. It's the most important choice that a woman can make."

"I made that choice once, if you remember," Kate retorted, her patience finally eluding her, "but God had other plans. I . . . won't . . . be hurt like that again, Marcella."

With Kate's breathless revelation, Marcella seemed to soften. But while the mothering instinct was strong within her, the need for reason was stronger. "A respectable woman would not take a job which might expose her to the company of strange men, Kate—even if they might be gentlemen. How can you possibly consider a position which will have you consort with criminals?"

"There is nothing sordid in what I'm doing, Marcella, nothing of which I need feel ashamed,"

117

Kate insisted, "and I shall gladly ignore social conventions if justice is the end result."

Marcella was unaccustomed to encountering any challenge to her ideas. She looked flustered but then finally composed herself, arranging her expression into a stern mask.

"You and I are blood, Kate, and so it's my duty to try and make you understand. I owe it to your poor mama and papa, rest their souls. If you do this, you'll not only shame yourself and your family, but you'll ruin any chance you have for happiness in the future."

Kate listened to the pronouncement solemnly. An impasse had been reached. Perhaps they never would agree. It was something Kate would just have to accept. "I'm sorry," she said finally. "I've made my decision."

Marcella gave her one last hopeful look, and then, seeing that her cause was lost, she whirled on her heel and strode off into Jonathan's office, shutting the door firmly behind her.

For the first time since she'd come to Chicago, Kate felt entirely alone. Perhaps she'd known all along that it would eventually come to this. Marcella was generous and well-meaning, but though her expectations reflected dreams that were shared by most women, Kate could never conform to them. She had already been bitterly disappointed by such dreams, and now she had to find something else.

As Kate stepped out onto the sidewalk, it began to rain—cold, heavy drops that splattered where they struck. Pulling her mantle closer around her, she cast a baleful glance at the lowering mass of gray clouds which the wind had swept in off the lake. She'd planned to take a long walk this morning in order to pass the time, but it seemed that today even the weather gods were conspiring against her. A few minutes more of this downpour and the streets would be rivers of mud. Still, she had to keep away from the hotel for several hours yet, and so she trudged onward until she reached Turner's Bookshop, where she took refuge for a while.

Yet even as she tried to decide if she could afford to purchase Charlotte Brontë's latest novel or perhaps Mr. Hawthorne's *House of the Seven Gables*, Kate could not keep her mind from conjuring up thoughts of what might even now be transpiring in her room at the Lakeview Hotel.

This was perhaps the most difficult part of the work—she was learning—to have been such an integral player in the game all along, only to miss its culmination. Oh, Kate understood full well that it was necessary for her to be absent, but still there was a part of her that wished she could be there to watch as Noah Gerard was unmasked as the thief.

And she knew that he would be. All their weeks of hard work pointed to that conclusion. Unlike the mystery stories she was so fond of reading, there would be no surprise ending here. The entire case had progressed precisely according to Pinkerton's plan. In fact, the only questionable element in it had been Kate herself.

She hoped that her contributions had made her worthy of the trust that Allan Pinkerton had placed in her. It was only her good fortune that he had not been witness to her humiliation at the hands of Alec

Dalton. But Kate had learned a painful lesson in that regard, and it was a lesson she would not soon forget.

When she left the bookshop, Kate changed direction and headed down Clark Street. She could hardly go back to her lodgings at Mrs. Crawford's. Dressed as she was, in clothes much finer than Kate Warne could ever afford, she'd be bound to set off a spate of gossiping and unfriendly speculation. But surely no one would mind if she spent the remainder of the afternoon at Pinkerton's office.

As she passed by the Sherman House, Kate peered into the window glass at her own bedraggled reflection. The rain had spotted her skirts and wilted the silk roses that decorated her bonnet. But as she stared, Kate noticed something else as well, something that caused a violent shudder to run through her as she turned away and hurried past.

She should have been amused. Inside the hotel's dining room she saw Richard Pratt, who'd been her ardent suitor these past few days. Now, though, he was sitting beside another young lady and was endeavoring to charm her with his words. All along Kate had been so concerned about playing with his affections, and yet here he was blithely entertaining another woman. Kate *should* have been amused by this scene, but she was not, for in that brief instant as she regarded him, she'd realized something. She had thought once before that Richard Pratt reminded her of someone, and now finally she'd realized who that someone was. Oh, not so much in looks, perhaps, but in his bluff, easygoing manner and propensity for storytelling, he was the very image of Henry . . . her dead husband, Henry.

Henry Warne had had a penchant for spinning wonderful tales, too. But they'd been married for more than two years before Kate discovered that he'd not been content to share his dreams with her alone. He'd been away for more than a week on a special job for the railroad when she decided that as a surprise, she'd go down to Elmira and meet him at the depot. It was she who was surprised in the end, though, to find Henry there in the arms of a pretty young woman.

Kate knew from the first that she oughtn't to have married Henry. But she'd been so lost after her father died, and Henry was there to comfort her, filling up her empty life with his dreams and insisting that they belonged together. They'd known one another since they were children; Kate understood Henry Warne better than anyone else ever could. He was the dearest friend she had; but in the end she came to see that she could not love him, not the way one ought to love a husband, and Henry needed desperately to be loved. He needed someone for whom he could play the hero, someone to believe in his dreams, and Kate was fast outgrowing that role. If she'd been able to give him a child, things might have been different for them, but she'd failed him in that, too.

Although Kate accepted her share of the blame, she could not forgive his betrayal. Henry begged her to understand, swore that he would change, but she had been wounded. And then suddenly Henry was dead, and Kate never got the chance to forgive him. Perhaps that was why she'd fought so hard to see justice done on his behalf, in order to assuage some of her own guilt.

Kate walked the rest of the way to Pinkerton's

office consumed by her memories. By the time she'd climbed the stairs to the second floor, her eyes were brimming with hot tears. She hadn't been able to face the truth about her marriage in so long, and now that she had, she felt painfully numb, as if she'd lived those awful days all over again. It had been an unsettling afternoon, and Kate was chilled inside and out. She had burned all her bridges with Marcella. All she had left now was her job with Pinkerton; her whole future depended upon the success of this case.

Kate brushed away the traces of her tears, removed her rain-soaked mantle and bonnet and drew a deep, cleansing breath as she prepared to enter the office.

The staff was assembled within, seated at their desks; the clerk Mr. Hamilton, George Bangs and Alec Dalton. Kate turned away for a moment to hang her things on the coat rack, and when she turned back into the room, the conversation they'd been engaged in ceased at once. She felt very much the intruder, standing there with all eyes upon her. And then it occurred to her that this was odd, indeed. With Pinkerton's detectives all assembled here in the office, who was keeping an eye on the hotel?

As she stood there, confusion plain upon her face, Alec Dalton got to his feet. Offering her a genuinely warm smile, which she did not expect, he began to clap his hands together as though he were applauding a performance. Kate could not tell by his expression if this was some manner of taunt, but after a brief moment, the other gentlemen stood up as well and joined in. She felt the warmth as color flooded her cheeks.

The door to Pinkerton's office swung open in

response to the outburst, and the man himself stepped out. What was all this? she wondered. Had everyone forgotten about the case? Pinkerton came forward to take up her hand. "Congratulations to you, Mrs. Warne, on a job well done."

"Is it over, then?" she asked, still endeavoring to comprehend all that had transpired.

"Aye, that it is. I apprehended Mr. Gerard myself in the process of making off with the diamond necklace and delivered him into the hands of the police. You'll be pleased to know he's made a full confession. No doubt his father will make restitution for all that was stolen—that is, if we agree to keep the boy's name out of the papers."

"A full confession?" Kate repeated, amazed.

"He really had very little choice," Dalton chimed in. "His mistress came into our office this morning and offered to tell us all she knew."

"I can't imagine what made her change her mind," George Bangs remarked. "Until now, she seemed set on protecting him."

Kate's eyes went back to Dalton, who was sporting a mischievous grin. He, at least, had guessed that Kate had had some hand in the woman's change of heart.

"I'd like you to go back to the hotel," Pinkerton directed her. "Stay there for another few days, just to allay any suspicion regarding Mrs. Barley's connection to this matter. Once you've checked out of the hotel, come back to the office and we'll give you your next assignment."

The chill Kate had been feeling was gone now. Her next assignment. She liked the sound of that.

Chapter 10

1857

Kate copied the long row of figures into the ledger and checked her addition one last time. The agency had realized a healthy profit on this particular case, even with the added expense of sending two operatives to Philadelphia for six weeks.

Whenever she had an opportunity, Kate offered to assist in managing such business details, for she'd decided early on that it was important for her to understand all facets of the organization. Most of her time was occupied in detective work, though, for as Allan Pinkerton had discovered, that was where her true talent lay. In the two years since she'd come to work here, the agency's business had thrived, and Kate had been kept so busy that lately she'd begun to wonder if it wouldn't be wise for Pinkerton to consider hiring another woman to share the work load.

As she recalled her own fitful beginnings, Kate was

reminded again of the difficulties she'd faced. Even though she had managed thus far to remain more or less an invisible member of Pinkerton's team, her cousin Marcella had not forgiven her for deciding on this career. And in fact, it had taken some time for her to prove herself and overcome the prejudices held by some of the male members of the agency staff—and one in particular.

After the Lakeview case, she and Dalton seemed to reach a silent agreement to maintain the distance between them. This wasn't a difficult task; their separate duties within the expanding business kept them from seeing much of one another anyway. Dalton's time was occupied in overseeing the activities of Pinkerton's newly organized private police force, a portion of the agency charged with protecting business and property, while Kate was kept busy working on those cases that required a woman's touch. This arrangement was a fortuitous one, to Kate's way of thinking, for the emotions that Alec Dalton stirred within her were dangerous, uncontrollable, and on the whole, better left undisturbed.

When the door to Pinkerton's private office swung open, Kate looked up from her desk and turned in time to see her boss's dark head as he peered out.

"Kate," he called to her. "Would you join us, please?"

Obligingly, Kate set down her pen, checking to make certain that the ink had dried before she shut the ledger. She tried to recall who was closeted with him, but realized that she had been so engrossed with her figures in her quiet corner of the room that she hadn't been aware of any of the comings and goings elsewhere in the office.

She rose from her chair, arranged the folds in her gray wool skirt and crossed to the threshold of Pinkerton's office, where she hesitated for a moment to survey the scene. The three gentlemen rose almost simultaneously when she appeared. Pinkerton had gone back behind his desk and waved a hand now to indicate the young man who had occupied one of the chairs opposite him. "Kate, this is Elias Green, one of our new operatives."

Kate came forward to take his hand. "I'm pleased to meet you, Mr. Green."

"And I, you, Mrs. Warne," he replied, brimming with enthusiasm. "I've heard quite a bit about you."

A slow smile curved on Kate's lips. "Yes, I would imagine you have. But don't you believe a word of it."

Young Mr. Green had a round, boyish face generously sprinkled with freckles and an unusually vivid shade of red hair. There was a genuine sincerity in his manner and, too, some naivete—both engaging traits, but ones that Kate knew would be sacrificed if he worked for Allan Pinkerton for very long.

Pinkerton didn't bother to introduce the second gentleman, and Kate regarded Alec Dalton as if she'd only just now noticed him standing there. But, of course, it wasn't true. His was the first face her eyes had settled on as she'd surveyed the room, and in these last anxious seconds, she'd been trying to ascertain what this summons was all about and why it should concern Dalton.

127

"Hello, Kate," he said softly as he offered her his seat.

She accepted it without speaking or meeting his eyes, afraid even the slightest acknowledgement on her part would reflect her disquiet. Alec pulled up another chair for himself, and when all were seated, Pinkerton began. Kate had to will herself to concentrate on his words.

"You know that I've just returned from Mississippi. I was asked to make the journey there by the officers of the local bank in the small community of Atkinson, in order to investigate the murder of their paying-teller, George Gordon, and the theft of over one hundred and thirty thousand dollars."

"One hundred and thirty thousand dollars?" young Mr. Green echoed, his jaw dropping in astonishment.

A wry smile played about the corners of Allan Pinkerton's mouth, but he ignored the boy's outburst and continued solemnly. "Mr. Gordon was murdered in the evening, after normal business hours. The lock on the door had not been forced, however, and the money was taken from the open safe after Gordon had been bludgeoned to death with his own cancelling stamp."

"That tells us something," Kate observed as she began to focus her attention on the facts of the case. "The murderer would have to be someone Gordon trusted—a friend or a very good customer—else Gordon wouldn't have allowed him in the bank after hours."

Pinkerton leaned back in his chair, tenting his thick fingers. "And our murderer was no fool. He started a fire in the hearth to burn any evidence which might incriminate him," he said. "But I managed to find a twist of paper beneath the grate, which he probably used to start the blaze. Amazingly, the paper was partially unburnt—enough for me to recognize it as a promissory note. There was also a bloodstained scrap of paper with calculations pencilled on it found beneath the body.

"The signature on the note was that of an influential local gentleman named Matthew Drysdale," he went on to explain. "The figures that George Gordon penned on the scrap of paper, which later came to be stained with his own blood, correspond to the last three entries in Drysdale's account. And I've been told that Drysdale was a good friend of Gordon and one of the few men he allowed to do banking after regular hours."

"It would seem that this Drysdale is our man," Dalton concluded.

"Yes, so it would seem," Pinkerton agreed. "But— as you are well aware—in order to obtain a conviction, we shall need direct proof. I'm putting this case in your hands, Alec. I want you to get close to Matthew Drysdale and test the mettle of the man, so we'll know what we're up against."

Dalton nodded solemnly.

"The three of you will travel to Atkinson at once. Kate, you'll need to cultivate information from the ladies of the town and strike up a friendship with Drysdale's wife, then somehow get yourself invited into the house."

Kate's curiosity about the murder evaporated in an instant as she realized that she and Dalton were both

129

being assigned to this case. They would be working together. It was a possibility that she'd been dreading for some time.

"Kate?"

Although she had heard Pinkerton's instructions clearly enough, she was so distracted by her own troubling thoughts that she started in surprise as he called her name a second time.

"Is something wrong?" he asked her.

"No, nothing," she replied, rather too quickly. "I can certainly handle such a simple task as that."

"And now I expect that you're wondering, Mr. Green, as a newcomer, just why you've been chosen. Quite frankly, what recommends you for this particular case is a strong resemblance to the dead man, George Gordon."

This comment sparked everyone's interest, but it was Alec Dalton who gave voice to their question, turning a gimlet eye on his employer. "Just what is it you have in mind, Allan?"

"It's devious, yet simple, and with a man such as Drysdale, I think it just might work. Are all of you acquainted with Shakespeare's *Macbeth . . . ?*"

Atkinson was a tidy, well-ordered town nestled in the gently rolling hills of northern Mississippi. There was much in the feral beauty of surrounding countryside to appreciate, but Kate was far more pleased by the contrast of its mild climate with that of Chicago, presently suffering in the icy grip of a long Midwestern winter.

The City Hotel on Main Street, where Pinkerton

had instructed them to lodge, was the most comfortable establishment in town. Many of the county's best families came up from their plantations to reside there during the winter and spring months, and so once the detectives had situated themselves there, they found it an easy enough task to ingratiate themselves among Atkinson's elite.

Dalton was the first to arrive. He introduced himself to the hotel guests as Mr. John M. Andrews, a cotton broker from Baltimore who was considering settling in the area, if he could find the right property. Kate came nearly a week after, playing the role of Mrs. Katherine Potter, a widow from Jacksonville, Florida, who was in fragile health and had come for convalescence to the dryer climes of northern Mississippi. As yet, Kate had not run across young Mr. Green, but Dalton informed her that he, too, had already appeared on the scene and was quartered inconspicuously in another part of the town until his presence was required. And so they set about the business of putting Pinkerton's plan into action. . . .

In the valley, the scent of moss and damp earth hung heavy on the air. The last gleaming rays of sunlight faded now beyond the treetops, and the evening mists began to rise, carpeting the hard-packed dirt road in cottony layers and blurring the sharp edges of the rocks that cluttered the hillside. It provided an eerie effect, this combination of place and time of day, precisely what Alec had hoped for.

He spurred his horse onward. Beside him rode the object of his investigation, Matthew Drysdale. Alec had to admit that he was perplexed by the man;

Drysdale had not proven at all what he expected him to be. He hardly seemed a villain, this middle-aged man with a slight paunch and thinning auburn hair, his soft features lost in a pale, broad face whose only remarkable feature was a drooping moustache.

Just ahead, beyond the bend in the road, the waters of Rocky Creek meandered through a pasture of tall grasses, shimmering in the waning light of day. Alec reined in his horse and let go a heartfelt sigh. "It's beautiful country, Matthew, no denying that."

Drysdale rode on a bit; then realizing that his friend had stopped to admire the scenery, he halted as well. "You'll be able to enjoy the likes of it every day if you decide to buy old Bristed's place."

Alec did not reply. He seemed to be regarding the landscape closely, as though he were considering Drysdale's words. At that precise moment, a pale young man came into view on the opposite bank of the creek. He was clad in a well-cut gray frock coat and trousers; and although he was not close enough for his features to be clearly discerned, he was bareheaded, and so one could not help but notice that his hair was a brilliant shade of red.

"Look!" Drysdale cried out, pointing out the apparition. "Over there!"

At the sound of his voice, the mysterious young man turned away from them, gliding on in silence as he headed for a thick grove of trees that stood several yards off. With his back to them now, the awful horror of the vision became apparent. The man's skull appeared to have been smashed in. His thick curls were clotted with blood, which was dripping down to leave a spreading stain upon the shoulder of his coat.

Drysdale's voice dropped to a strangled whisper. "Dear God, what can this mean?"

"What's the matter with you, Matthew?" Alec asked, coolly feigning surprise.

"Can't you see him? Over there, beyond the creek. That . . . man. All that blood. He's been injured. He looks pale enough to be a corpse."

"I don't find your humor the least bit amusing." Alec's reply was sharper now as he stared off in the direction Drysdale had indicated. "There's no one here but the two of us, leastways not that I can see."

Drysdale's grip on the reins was so tight that his knuckles blanched. As if he were mesmerized by the grisly sight, his eyes continued to follow the man until he had disappeared into the shadows of the trees, and then a violent shudder ran through him. "Are you sure that you saw nothing?" he asked Dalton again, a rising hysteria threading through the words.

"We are quite alone, I assure you."

"Well then," Drysdale concluded, his voice hushed and solemn, "it must have been a ghost."

Mrs. Potter regularly spent a quiet hour before supper in the evening reading in the hotel parlor. On occasion, John Andrews would join her there, and they would pass the time together. Of course, Kate and Alec had made this arrangement beforehand in order that they might exchange information without arousing any suspicions. But to the rest of the hotel guests, it only seemed that Mr. Andrews had taken a special interest in the attractive widow, and there was nothing at all odd in that.

On this particular evening, Kate was carefully perusing the copy of *Macbeth* that she'd purchased before leaving Chicago. She had never read the play before, but Pinkerton had made her curious. She wanted to discern its connection to what he had in mind for Mr. Drysdale. Now finally, after hours of wading through the obscure language, she understood.

"Banquo's ghost," she muttered to herself, "of course."

"Good evening, Mrs. Potter. May I join you?"

A faint southern drawl flavored the familiar baritone, and Kate looked up, surprised to see Alec Dalton's tall frame filling up the doorway. She'd been so absorbed in the words of the play, she hadn't even heard him approach. He cut a dashing figure, dressed for riding—with his frock coat of deep forest green, fawn-colored waistcoat and breeches, and tall, polished boots. In a few long strides, he'd crossed the room, swept off his wide-brimmed planter's hat and tossed it on the nearby table, looking more than a little pleased with himself.

No sooner had he taken up Kate's hand in his and brushed his lips over her skin than a tingling warmth began to course through her veins, and Kate caught her breath. She could not help herself; she was affected, even if it was only because of the role he was playing. Carefully, she tucked the volume she'd been reading into the folds of her skirts, lest he realize what she'd been doing. Somehow she didn't want him to know that until now she'd been wholly ignorant of the works of William Shakespeare.

"Mr. Andrews, how nice to see you again. Do sit down," she replied for the benefit of anyone who might have been listening, and then promptly lowered her voice. "Where have you been these past three days?"

Dalton made a place for himself beside her on the sofa. "Socializing with Matthew Drysdale," he replied.

Kate drew a carefully measured breath when Alec stretched his arm out behind her on the sofa back. As he edged near enough to her so as not to be overheard, the hard length of his thigh pressed against hers. "We rode out and spent some time on his cotton plantation," he continued. "He suggested that I have a look at a property nearby that's for sale. In fact, he thinks I ought to buy it."

Kate was impressed. "You two have certainly become fast friends."

"It wasn't hard. Drysdale's a likeable fellow, and he seems in need of a friend right now."

Dalton had been watching the doorway as he spoke, but now he met her eyes. Kate noticed his distress at once—as if he were vexed to have discovered that Drysdale was not the monster they'd expected him to be—and then all too soon his gaze fell away. She was so close that she could feel the hesitation in him; it was wholly out of character. Was there something about this case? she wondered. Only one possibility presented itself.

"You're not certain of Drysdale's guilt, are you?"

"I'll admit he's not what I expected," he told her, "but Pinkerton's seldom wrong about these things."

"Well then, what is it?"

Since he'd come into the parlor, Alec had been endeavoring to keep his mind on the subject at hand; but Kate made such a fetching picture perched there on the edge of the sofa in her yellow evening dress, with silk roses twined in her upswept hair, and the heady scent of her perfume was distracting. Against his will, his mind conjured up vivid memories of a darkened alcove and her soft body pressed against his, her mouth warm and willing.

"It's you, Kate," he admitted before he'd even realized. "You muddle my thinking sometimes."

Alec watched as the color drained from her face, and she began nervously smoothing the creases from the fabric of her skirt. He knew at once that he'd gone too far. It was one thing to be troubled by secret imaginings, but it was quite another to give voice to them. What the devil had come over him?

Oh, it was not hard to understand why he found Kate attractive. She was young and vibrant, and from the first he had admired her for her strength of purpose, even when they'd disagreed. In time he'd learned to appreciate her talents, too, for she had wasted no time in proving his equal as a detective. Lately, though, he'd begun to realize that his feelings ran far deeper than friendship, and God help him, he longed to discover if she felt the same.

But he knew it was a question that must remain forever unanswered if they were to continue to work as a team. Pinkerton would never condone a relationship that might distract his operatives and jeopardize the case, and who could hope to hide the truth from Allan Pinkerton?

"To be quite honest," he began slowly, all the while knowing that honesty was the one thing he could not offer her, "I guess I'm not so certain of Drysdale's guilt after all. As I said, he's such a likeable fellow. But you seem so sure of yourself—"

Kate had been holding her breath in wait for his reply and now expelled it slowly. She appeared to accept his explanation. "That may be because of what I've discovered," she said and went on immediately. "The ladies have noticed a change in Mr. Drysdale. They tell me that he's become positively unsociable lately. But when I proposed to them that he might be worried about business matters, they insisted that he is a wealthy and successful gentleman."

"So it would appear," Alec agreed. He was greatly relieved that the focus of their conversation had gone back to Matthew Drysdale. "Or he may only be trying to salvage his reputation. He wouldn't be the first gentleman in financial straits to put on a convincing show for the neighbors."

"The concensus among the ladies is not that he has money problems, but rather that he's suffering from religious doubts."

"Religious doubts? Whatever would make them think that?"

When Kate cast him a sidelong glance, Alec knew that she was about to reveal an important clue. "Drysdale hasn't been to church in months," she said pointedly, "in fact, not since before George Gordon's funeral—from which, by the way, he was conspicuously absent. Only a coincidence, do you think?"

Alec felt his confidence reasserting itself now, at least where this case was concerned. Neither he nor Kate believed in coincidence. Drysdale *must* be involved in the murder. "Well, if he is entertaining doubts," he told her, "then perhaps we've helped him out. He's just now undergone a significant 'religious' experience."

Kate grinned mischievously. "Banquo's ghost, I presume?"

He nodded, but his own amusement was tempered by the memory of the cold fear he'd seen in Drysdale's eyes.

"How did Drysdale react to Green's performance?" she wanted to know.

"At first he was convinced he'd seen a ghost," Alec explained, "but then after some deliberation, he changed his story and decided that the reason he'd been frightened was because he thought he'd seen a black man in the woods, carrying a gun."

"A sight certain to strike fear into the heart of any slave holder," Kate remarked irreverently. "It seems far more likely, though, that our Mr. Drysdale has something to hide."

"You ought to have seen his face when he spotted Green crossing that pasture with blood dripping from his hair. It was a ghastly sight. I'll admit that this approach Pinkerton has decided on is a bit too macabre for my tastes, but it may yet get results."

"I don't doubt it," Kate agreed. "I'm ever astounded by the man's knack for knowing just the right method to achieve his ends."

As Alec went on to describe, in vivid detail, Drysdale's reactions to the scene they'd set for him, he was feeing much more at ease. He and Kate worked so well together. Maybe he'd been wrong to imagine his affection for her was anything more than honest camaraderie. Maybe they could be only friends.

"And now it's time, I think, to begin the second phase in our operation," he told her. "Have you devised a way to get yourself invited into the house yet?"

Kate's mouth curved into a sly smile. It seemed she was not ready just yet to give up her secrets. "Pinkerton's not the only one with clever methods," she told him. "Just you watch and see."

Chapter 11

In addition to the cotton plantation, which was half a day's ride from town, Matthew Drysdale kept a modest dwelling in Atkinson, where he, his wife and two young sons resided during the spring and winter months. It was a comfortable two-storied house, situated along the main road in a spot not far from the banks of Rocky Creek, where the scenery was pleasingly picturesque. As their friendship developed, Drysdale often invited Dalton, in the guise of John Andrews, to dine with his family.

It had been less than a week since his encounter with the "ghost," and but for occasional nervous moments, Drysdale appeared to have recovered his vitality. He seemed in particularly good spirits on the evening that he and Dalton sat watching the sunset from the verandah, enjoying their after-dinner brandy, but this changed abruptly when a long, shrill cry cut the air.

Drysdale's glass slipped from his hand and shattered as it struck the porch floor, strewing shards of glass and amber liquid across the boards. Perhaps he was not so calm as he pretended to be. "Dear Lord! What was that?"

The sound had taken Alec by surprise, too, but he reacted with guarded calm. "It came from that grove of trees, down by the road, I think."

Both men got to their feet and hurried down the walk to the gate. They'd only just reached the spot, when a plump, middle-aged lady appeared. Alec recognized her as Mrs. Robbins, one of the guests he'd been introduced to at the hotel. She was dressed for riding, but was leading her horse by the reins now, and she rushed up to the gate, clutching at the pickets.

"Please, Mr. Drysdale, you must help," she pleaded breathlessly. "There's been an accident!"

"What is it, ma'am. What's happened?" Drysdale seemed a trifle less anxious now that he had discovered that the cry he'd heard had been real, and not yet another product of his imagining.

"It's my friend," Mrs. Robbins replied. "She's been hurt!"

The gentlemen followed her as she hastened back in the direction from which she'd come. "We were riding and lost track of the time," she explained. "We wanted to be home by dark. I suppose we might have set the horses too fast a pace. I was several yards ahead. I heard her cry out, and when I looked back, she was lying in the road. Oh, do hurry!"

As Alec came around the bend in the road, he saw first the riderless horse, casually grazing on a patch of grass that was growing along the embankment. And there, just beyond, lay the still body of a woman.

At first glance, she looked like a rag doll, with limbs bent at awkward angles beneath a tangle of lacy petticoats. There was no blood visible on her dark blue habit, only streaks of dusty, red clay from the road, but she was so still that Alec feared she must have broken her neck. He knelt down beside her and brushed aside the veil from her tall-crowned hat and and the wave of glossy brown hair that had fallen across her face. But when he saw the profile, he was sure his own heart had ceased beating for an instant as his body went numb.

"Why, it's Mrs. Potter," Drysdale exclaimed just then, over Dalton's shoulder. "My wife's new friend. Is she breathing, Andrews?"

Cold with trepidation, Alec reached to lay a trembling hand upon her breast, and a tight, anguished sob caught soundlessly in his throat. If Kate were dead, what would he do?

But no, he could feel the rhythmic rise and fall of her breathing, and as if in response to his touch, she stirred and moaned softly. "Oh! What's happened?"

"You've had a fall, my dear," Mrs. Robbins put in. Rapidly regaining her faculties now, Kate attempted to rise, but the firm pressure of Alec's hand on her shoulder kept her in her place. "Lie still," he ordered. "You may have broken a bone."

"Nothing's broken," Kate insisted, and determined, she struggled to rise, with Alec only begrudgingly offering his assistance.

She had barely gotten to her feet, though, before her brow creased in pain, and uttering a sharp cry, she collapsed. Alec had anticipated her fall and in one swift move lifted her up into his arms.

143

"Now, you must listen to reason, Mrs. Potter," he said, rather too harshly, for his nerves were jangled.

He did not intend to set her down. He suspected that Kate would be just foolish enough to attempt to rise again on her own, if she could. "This is a serious fall you've had; the doctor must have a look at you in order to see how much damage has been done."

As if on cue, Kate moaned, effectively silencing his protests.

"Oh, my dear, are you feeling faint?" Mrs. Robbins inquired, anxiously wringing her dainty gloved hands.

"It's only my knee," Kate assured her. "I think it's twisted, but I'll be fine."

"Nevertheless," Drysdale told her, "if Mr. Andrews will be good enough to carry you into my home, I shall send for the doctor—just to make certain."

Retrieving the reins of Mrs. Potter's horse, Drysdale headed up the procession back to his home—with Mrs. Robbins fretting to herself as she led her own mount, and Alec in the rear, carrying Kate in his arms.

Alec was constrained by the circumstances. He could not speak freely to Kate, as he would have liked, for the others might overhear, and yet he needed her assurance that she was indeed all right.

Drysdale called to his wife as he headed up the walk, and as soon as she appeared on the verandah, he began spouting instructions. "There's been an accident, Susannah. Mrs. Potter's fallen from her horse. Have Cleo prepare the guest room and send Old Tom for the doctor at once."

The following hour passed amid a whirl of

144

activity; but once Dalton had done his duty and carried Kate upstairs and settled her on the bed, the ladies took over, and he and Drysdale were relegated to Drysdale's study to await the doctor's report.

When he joined them finally, Dr. Hutchins informed the gentlemen that Mrs. Potter had been fortunate. She had sustained a contusion of the knee and likely some internal injuries as well—but nothing that could not be cured by a period of rest and quiet convalescence.

Despite Mrs. Potter's insistence that she be taken back to the hotel so as not to inconvenience the Drysdales, the doctor instructed that she not be moved, and Mrs. Drysdale assured her that she would be a welcome guest in her home.

Alec feared it likely that he'd not be allowed to see Kate again that night. So far as these people knew, he was no more to her than a polite acquaintance, naturally concerned for her welfare, but no more. And so he was greatly relieved when Mrs. Drysdale came to him shortly after the doctor's departure to inform him that Mrs. Potter begged a moment of his time—to thank him for all he'd done. Even in her pain, Kate had not forgotten her duty, or her partner.

As he climbed the stairs, Alec thought of all the things he might say to her when they were at last alone, but he found himself oddly speechless once he'd entered the guest room and shut the door behind him.

Kate was propped up on a mountain of pillows in a high, testered bed, the quilts drawn up to her chin. Still, she looked far too healthy to be an invalid. As he drew nearer to her bedside, Alec noticed that her skin

145

was flush with color, and there was a dangerous glitter of excitement in her blue eyes.

"How are you?" he asked cautiously.

"Wholly undamaged," she assured him.

"But the doctor says—"

"He's an old fool, who gladly followed my lead when I described my symptoms to him and grimaced at all the proper times. Now, would you kindly open the window for me? They've got me wrapped up like a mummy, and it's hotter than blazes in here."

Alec grinned at her burst of temper and went off to do as she bid, but when he turned round, he was startled to see that Kate had crawled out from beneath her counterpane prison and was now across the room, examining her surroundings, and wearing nothing more than a thin, silk wrapper she'd thrown carelessly over her chemise and drawers.

Alec felt the color rise in him; but he was more angry than embarrassed. "What are you doing out of that bed?" he demanded in a gruff whisper, and then it struck him. "You're not hurt at all, are you?"

"I told you that I wasn't," she retorted, keeping her own voice low, "and I've managed to get into the house, haven't I? The doctor says that I can't be moved for several days at least."

Alec saw now that it had been pretense—her fall from the horse, her supposed injuries—all carefully orchestrated. He had to admit it was clever, but as he recalled the moments of anguish she'd put him through, his temper flared.

"When I saw you lying in the road, I thought you were dead," he hissed. "I thought that—that—"

And then he could contain the rage no longer. "If

you ever put on such an act again," he said and aimed a threatening finger at her, "I'll break your bloody neck myself."

Kate paled at the force of his fury and appeared genuinely contrite as she crossed the room to stand before him. "I am sorry, Alec. I didn't know that you'd be in the house tonight. If I had, I'd have warned you."

His eyes met hers, then drifted lower to the lace-edged neck of her chemise and the spot where the satin ribbon that tied it lay. In his mind, he reached for it.

"Get back into that bed at once," he ordered, more harshly than he'd intended. "Or do you want to spoil these well-laid plans of yours?"

Kate obliged him, but she was not pleased by his ill humor. What was wrong with the man? She'd have thought he would be more impressed by her little ruse. She had gotten into the house, and wasn't that the object of their game, after all?

Oh, he may have had a few uneasy moments before he'd caught on to what she was up to, but that was hardly her fault. All in all, the ends justified the means, Kate told herself as she climbed into bed and gathered the bedclothes around her once more, and then she stopped short. She was beginning to sound like Pinkerton. That was precisely the sort of logic he always used.

Perhaps Dalton realized that he'd gone too far, for he wiped all trace of emotion from his face as he came to stand by her bedside. His manner was business-like . . . and distant. "Do you have everything you require?"

Kate was surprised to find herself stung by the change in him. There was no denying that she'd been irritated by his attitude, but still she'd felt, well, almost comfortable with him all the while they'd been arguing. Now that feeling was gone, though, and she followed his lead, keeping her conversation impersonal. "Mrs. Robbins was kind enough to offer to have my trunk sent over from the hotel. Once it arrives, I shall have all that I need."

"Good," he replied, then hesitated, with furrowed brow, as though he intended to say something more.

But he did not. Bidding her a cool good night, he quit the room, leaving Kate more confused than ever.

Within the hour, Alec was seated at a corner table in Atkinson's local saloon. An open bottle of whiskey stood at his left elbow, but his hand was shaking so badly that he could scarcely bring the glass he'd poured to his lips. When finally he did, he swallowed it down and swiftly poured another, hoping the liquor might burn away the fear that still pulsed through his veins.

But even as his body began to relax, Alec couldn't seem to blot out the memory of Kate lying still and lifeless in the red dust of the road and the terror that had gripped his heart when he'd thought she was dead.

He'd broken his own cardinal rule and gotten too close, and this was the result. Proud, fearless Alexander Dalton, who made it a point never to touch mind-dulling spirits except in the course of his duties, was sitting here now trembling like a child, gulping down whiskey as if it were mother's milk and scarcely able to string together two coherent thoughts. He had to get hold of himself.

"Evenin', mister. You look as if you might be in need of a friend."

Alec raised his eyes from the rim of his glass to see a woman standing before him. He'd noticed her earlier, watching the card game at a nearby table; but she must have lost interest in that, for now her sights were set squarely on him.

She might have been young or old; it was hard to see much more than the illusion of her painted face in the dimly lit saloon. She was tall and rail thin, and the bodice of her cheap taffeta dress was cut far too low to be respectable. But her upswept hair was a familiar shade of chestnut brown, and so as she pulled up a chair and sat down close beside him, Alec managed a half-hearted smile for her.

Her dark eyes settled on the bottle, and the pink tip of her tongue slipped out to wet the thin line of her lower lip.

"Help yourself," he said, offering her his empty glass. "It doesn't seem to be doing me much good."

She wasted no time in pouring out two fingers of whiskey, then greedily swallowed it down. "Nothin' better to warm the blood," she explained as she set down the glass, "and there's a powerful chill in the air tonight. Can you feel it?"

With this, her arm coiled, snakelike, around Alec's, and she sidled closer against him to afford him a better view of the enticing swell of her breasts.

Alec was struck instead by the vision of Kate as he'd seen her earlier this evening, standing near enough to

149

touch and wearing nothing more than a silk wrapper thrown over her chemise. There was no denying now that he wanted her, and not just as a friend. But as he knew well enough, that was something that could never be.

He found himself studying the woman beside him: the practiced moves, the emptiness behind the beguiling expression. To her, this was business, pure and simple. There was no talk of ties, no emotion on either side—merely an exchange of favors for financial consideration. That was how he himself had managed all these years, and there'd been order in his life.

Yes, he told himself, maybe what this woman was offering was precisely what he needed to stop behaving like a rutting stag where Kate was concerned. After all, one woman was as good as the next in the dark.

"How much?" he inquired.

His companion tittered softly, but there was triumph in the sound. "My, my, aren't we anxious?"

Alec coolly repeated the question.

"Oh, not to worry, dearie," she said. "You can well afford it. I've got a room next door. Why don't we go up there and have our drinks in private?"

Dragging her shawl up over her shoulders, she got to her feet, wrapped one hand around the neck of the whiskey bottle and placed the other firmly under Alec's arm. "Come along, then."

He allowed her to lead him out of the back door, but as soon as they were alone in the darkness of the deserted alleyway, he took control. With his sensibilities lost in a whiskey-laced fog, he backed her up against the weathered clapboards of the building and thrust his body close to hers, crushing her mouth with his, wanting to purge himself of the uncontrollable beast raging within him. But it didn't seem to help.

"Easy now," his companion entreated, as she drew back from him and pulled a ragged breath. "My room's right up those stairs over there."

When she'd regained her composure, she regarded him with a sidelong glance that was full of promise and took him by the hand. They crossed to a rickety wooden staircase that ran up the back of a shabby boardinghouse, but as she started up the stairs, Alec had to pause to slow the whirling in his brain. Looking up after her, he saw the tall figure and the upswept chestnut curls, and for a moment, he was confused. "Kate?"

The spell was broken as soon as she turned back to him. "It's Ruby," she told him, "but you call me whatever you like, dearie, I don't mind."

One woman was as good as another in the dark, he'd told himself, but much as he'd wanted to believe it, it just wasn't so. With his mind made up, he reached to retrieve his whiskey bottle from her. Then, peeling a bill from the roll in his pocket, he folded it in two and tucked it down the front of her dress. "I'm sorry I wasted your time," he said and turned to walk away.

Tonight he'd been sharply reminded of the danger in caring too much, and he'd been forced to admit that the need he felt for Kate was far more than physical. But there was something else, too, that he hadn't wanted to face. Tonight he'd seen just how

151

good Kate was at deception, and perhaps it was that which frightened him most of all.

When at last she heard the clock in the downstairs hall chime twice, Kate threw back the bedclothes and got to her feet. Surely it would be safe now; the entire household was asleep. And so she padded across the room to where her trunk lay yet unpacked. The servant who'd carried it in had left it on the floor beside the bureau. Kneeling before it, she lifted the lid.

There was only a sliver of moon for light, but Kate knew what she was after. She rummaged through to the bottom, her fingers feeling about for long strands of knotted fringe. When she'd located what she sought at last, she drew out the bundle and carefully unwrapped the glass bottle that she'd concealed within the folds of her paisley shawl. As she held it up to the light, the liquid within glowed a garish crimson.

The cool night breeze that swept in by the open window seeped through the thin fabric of her nightdress, raising gooseflesh across her skin. Kate tossed the shawl over her shoulders and wrapped it around her, but it did little to quell the tremors that ran through her; they were caused more by nervousness than chill.

Once she'd opened the door and stepped out of her room, though, her purpose was fixed. She crossed the upstairs hall, her bare feet treading lightly over the smooth, polished boards, and hurried down the stairs, pausing for a moment to draw breath and listen to the sharp click-click of the tall case clock in the foyer as its pendulum swung back and forth, marking off the seconds.

She left the house by way of the front door, which was unlocked, and hoped that the faint squeal of hinges, which seemed to her to carry on the air like the sharp cry of a night bird, would not wake the sleepers within. Curiously, once she was outside, Kate felt safe. It was a comfort to be enveloped by the shadows of the night and to listen to the wind soughing gently through the tall pines that stood just beyond the road like dark sentinels. There was nothing evil out here in the dark; the evil lay within.

Only when she reached the gate by the road, did Kate pause at last to draw the cork stopper from the bottle she'd been carrying. Spilling drops of liquid from the bottle into the dry dust of the path, she began to make a trail that led from the gate back toward the house. As she stepped up on the verandah and watched the crimson droplets splash onto the painted boards, a shudder ran through her. She understood now what Alec had meant; this was rather too macabre an approach for her tastes as well. But she mustn't forget poor George Gordon, the innocent young man who'd been so brutally murdered. There was justice yet to be served.

Across the threshold and into the foyer, up the staircase and along the upstairs hall, Kate laid her gory trail, until at last she stood before the door to the Drysdale's bedroom, her hand wrapped around the knob. Without pausing to think how she could explain all of this if she was caught, she let herself into the room.

Her host and hostess were both fast asleep, their breathing deep and even. Scattering a trail of droplets along the floor, Kate moved to Drysdale's bedside and studied his face for a moment while he slept. There was no strength in the jaw or the brow. It hardly looked like the face of a murderer, pale and pasty in the moonlight.

Dismissing the thought, Kate returned to her purpose and upturned the bottle she held in her hand, watching as the remainder of its contents spread out in an unmistakable stain on the man's pillow, his nightshirt and the bedclothes as well. Then, taking care to keep clear of the droplets she'd already spread on the floor, she left the room.

"It will have blood," Mr. Drysdale," Kate intoned ominously, quoting a line she'd remembered from *Macbeth* as she shut the door behind her at last, *"'blood will have blood.'"*

Chapter 12

Just after sunrise Kate was awakened by a sharp cry from the room directly adjacent to hers—the room shared by the Drysdales. Although she had been expecting it, she was not ready when it came. The sound startled her too suddenly into consciousness, and her heart beat a frantic rhythm in her breast even after she'd raised herself upright on the bed and gotten her bearings.

Remembering her business here, Kate quickly tossed aside her bedclothes and crossed the room to put an ear to the adjoining wall, but it was a wasted effort. All she could make out was Drysdale's doleful moan, followed by the soft tones of his wife as she sought to soothe him. Several minutes later, she heard Mrs. Drysdale go out, shutting the door behind her.

Kate had only just resettled herself in the bed when the young black maidservant came in. Her name was Cleo, Kate remembered, and this morning she wore a scarf over her dark hair and a faded, brown calico dress. As she put a fresh towel on the rack and filled

155

the ewer on the washstand with hot water, Kate watched her closely, looking for some sign that the girl was aware of the commotion that had so recently transpired in the room next door. But after acknowledging Kate with a shy "good morning," Cleo went on blithely about her duty.

"Did you hear someone cry out a short time ago?" Kate inquired, when her patience had finally given out. "I thought I might have been dreaming, but now I'm not sure."

"It must have been the master," she replied. "He's feelin' poorly this morning."

"Oh, I do hope it's nothing serious."

Cleo did not intend to stay around long enough to indulge the new houseguest's curiosity. She was already heading for the door, but hesitated there for a moment, deciding to explain.

"I don't 'spect so, ma'am, but Missus tol' me he had the nosebleed somethin' terrible in the night. There's blood all up and down the front hall stairs and out on the verandah, too."

She left Kate to absorb this information in silence. So they'd attributed the blood to a nosebleed, had they? No talk of spectral visitors, of victims reaching out from the grave for revenge? Kate was disappointed.

Soon after the maid had gone, Susannah Drysdale appeared in the doorway, balancing a breakfast tray. She was very near to Kate's own age, but with copper-colored hair and a face as pale and pretty as a china doll's. In spite of the upset this morning, she seemed thoroughly composed.

"Good mornin', Mrs. Potter," she said as she came

156

to set the tray down on the bed before her guest. Her southern drawl was as thick as molasses, but pleasant on the ear. "I trust you slept well."

Kate assured her that she had, and her eyes widened as she examined the carefully prepared meal set out on the tray: toast with marmalade, sausages, eggs and coffee. "I fear you've gone to too much trouble on my behalf, Mrs. Drysdale," Kate protested, feeling more than a little guilty now. "I don't wish to be any bother."

"Please, you must call me Susannah, for I want us to be good friends. I've already explained that I shall be glad of your company. As you know, I don't get out much. There are the boys to take care of, and they are quite a handful these days."

All at once, a faint moan interrupted their conversation; it was Drysdale, same as Kate had heard earlier. Susannah's attention strayed toward the sound, and two bright patches of color rose in her cheeks.

Kate made good use of the opportunity. "Has something upset you? The maid has told me that Mr. Drysdale is ill."

The woman seemed to consider for a moment, then perched herself on the edge of the chair which stood beside the bed. "This mornin' when we woke, there was blood all over Matthew's pillow, his nightshirt, and the floor besides," she confided, a frown marring her pale brow. "I told him I would send for the doctor, but he forbade it. He said he'd only had a nosebleed."

"But I can see that you're worried nonetheless," Kate said. "It's understandable. Has he experienced any other symptoms? Anything at all unusual?"

"Well, he has been nervous lately," she offered, "and he's had trouble sleepin'."

As the woman's distress increased, so did Kate's feelings of guilt. She had already convinced herself that Susannah Drysdale knew nothing of her husband's actions outside their home. If he was found to be a murderer, the woman would suffer enough. Kate did not feel comfortable adding to her burden just yet, and so she conjured a smile to reassure her. "I'm sure it's nothing serious. Men, especially successful businessmen, always seem to have far too much on their minds. I imagine that's your husband's problem. You mustn't worry yourself over nothing."

"Yes," she agreed. "Matthew always claims that I worry too much, and perhaps I do. Oh, but here I am troublin' you with my problems when you have your own to worry 'bout, and you must have your rest. Do forgive me."

She rose to leave, but Kate reached out to catch her hand and grasped it firmly, secretly hoping she might impart some of her own strength to the woman through her touch.

"Nonsense, Susannah. I'm glad to be of some help to you, after all you've done for me. I only wish that I could do more. Perhaps later if one of your servants will carry me downstairs, I can entertain the boys for you for a while—read them a story or something. Would that be all right?"

Susannah seemed doubtful. "The doctor said you needed rest and quiet—"

"I'm not the sort to keep still," Kate told her. "If

I'm to be confined to my bed in solitude, I shall go mad. You'd be doing me a favor, believe me."

"Well, if you're certain you'd be up to it. . . . All right, then."

Mr. Drysdale's condition had improved so rapidly that by afternoon he was able to keep an engagement he'd made with Mr. Andrews to go riding. Meanwhile, Kate did her penance in trying to entertain Susannah's rambunctious boys. Once she'd been installed upon the wicker settee on the verandah, she supervised their game of checkers, read to them from the Grimms Brothers' *Fairy Tales*, and played peacemaker as they nearly came to blows over the ownership of a bedraggled hobbyhorse.

Susannah kept herself busy with her domestic chores, directing Cleo in her work and supervising the cook, who was preparing supper for the family and their guests. Of course, Mr. Andrews had been invited to join them at the table, but as it turned out, the meal had to be put off nearly an hour, for the gentlemen did not return until just before dark.

When they came up the road at last, it was apparent that something unpleasant had occurred. Alec was cool as ever, but Drysdale's face was colorless, his eyes vacant and staring, as if there were some invisible scene unfolding before him. Now and again he reached up to nervously tug on his long moustache.

Kate watched as they turned into the drive and dismounted in the stableyard. Old Tom and a tall, gangling lad came out to tend the horses, going

159

quietly about their business until Drysdale's shrill voice cut the air. "It *was* a ghost, I tell you. It stood right there on the banks of Rocky Creek, pale and dripping with blood, and it looked straight at me."

"Get hold of yourself, Matthew," Alec said sternly as he followed him through the side gate. "And for God's sake, lower your voice. You're scaring the wits out of the servants."

Sure enough, Old Tom was staring at his master, the whites of his eyes standing out in bold contrast to the wizened brown face. He and the younger boy exchanged anxious glances before they turned to lead the horses back toward the barn.

Kate knew that Alec would be pleased with Drysdale's outburst, in spite of his words to the contrary. She predicted that it wouldn't take more than a few days for the story of the ghost at Rocky Creek to spread through town. The slaves had their own grapevine, and it was a remarkably efficient system for passing on information amongst themselves. Soon everyone would be whispering. The more people who knew about this "ghost," the more rumors it would generate, causing increasing pressure to bear on Drysdale's already jangled nerves. If the detectives could not unearth enough hard evidence against the man, then perhaps they could prompt a confession from him. That was Pinkerton's plan.

Drysdale was crossing the yard when his sons caught sight of him and left off the game they'd been playing to scamper to his side. The younger boy attached himself to his father's coattails, entreating him to join in their game, but Drysdale only scowled and shook him off as if he were some pesky mongrel.

Kate felt a stab of pity for the child, even as Alec, who'd been following a few steps behind, ruffled the lad's hair and lifted him easily up onto his broad shoulders while the elder brother tagged at his heels. "Your papa's tired," she heard him say to them both. "We've had a hard ride today. Now I think it's time that you boys went in and washed for supper."

Drysdale passed Kate on the verandah without so much as a glance. He went into the house, and she heard him climb the stairs, muttering to himself. At Alec's insistence, the boys went back to the kitchen to wash, leaving Alec alone with Kate on the verandah.

"What's happened?" she asked, as he pulled up a wicker chair for himself and sat down beside her.

"Drysdale's convinced he's seen a ghost."

"Do tell," Kate remarked and cast him a sidelong glance.

"His behavior's been odd all afternoon. We rode into town, intending to have a drink at the saloon, and on the way, the banker, Mr. McGregor, stopped us and invited us in for a chat. Matthew wouldn't so much as set foot over the threshold, though," Alec explained, sarcasm heavy in his words. "I can't imagine what's got into him."

"It seems the poor man's had nothing but trouble today," Kate replied. "This morning he woke to find a pool of blood on his pillow. In fact, it was trailed all over the house. As I understand it, he had an awful nosebleed."

Alec's heavy brow rose a fraction. "Nosebleed?"

Kate nodded, and he grinned at her, finally giving off all pretense of innocence. "By the way, I've

161

brought a fresh bottle for you," he said, lowering his voice as he drew a flask wrapped in brown paper out of his pocket.

"Wait a day or so before you make use of it," he advised. "By then he'll have let down his guard."

Kate took it and slipped it into her basket of knitting. From beneath the balls of brightly colored wool, she withdrew an envelope, which she handed over to him. "My report," she explained. "See that it's posted to Pinkerton, will you?"

Alec winked at her as he tucked the envelope into his jacket pocket. For a moment as her eyes met his, Kate's thoughts strayed. She couldn't exactly say when the war between them had ended, but it had. Perhaps it was this case that had made them allies. Alec might not always agree with her methods, but he had come to accept her as an equal, and amazingly, Kate had begun to trust him. She'd never have believed she could trust another man after Henry. Now if only she could manage to keep her heart unentangled—

Ah, but it was already too late for that. As she read the unspoken emotion in those green eyes of his, Kate could deny it no longer. She'd fallen in love with Alec Dalton, long before their war had ended and even before the confession he'd nearly let slip that evening in the hotel parlor. She knew what he'd meant to say to her then, even if the words had not been spoken, but there was scant comfort for Kate in this knowledge. To allow herself to contemplate a future with Dalton was to give up all that she'd worked for—and no matter what her heart told her, it was a sacrifice she was not prepared to make.

*　　*　　*

In the days that followed, Matthew Drysdale suffered through yet another spectral visitation and several more episodes of chronic "nosebleed." The entire neighborhood was soon abuzz with talk of the Rocky Creek ghost. Several people claimed to have seen it themselves, although none could agree upon precisely what form the apparition took. It was discovered that the latest trail of blood, which Drysdale had attributed to his nosebleed, extended all the way to Rocky Creek—to the very place where the ghost had been sighted—and there was speculation that perhaps the trail led not *from* the Drysdale house, but *to* it, and the mysterious ghost might, in fact, have some personal score to settle with Matthew Drysdale.

It was not pleasant to watch as the man's nerves slowly disintegrated. Before long, his appetite had decreased, his color had gone sallow and dangerously pale, and he was liable to start anxiously at the slightest noise. Susannah was quite naturally concerned about her husband's condition and confided to Kate that he scarcely got a good night's sleep anymore, but twisted and tossed fitfully for hours beneath the bedclothes, ofttimes while mumbling unintelligibly.

All the while Pinkerton had kept in communication with Dalton, who informed Kate that their employer was pleased that their efforts were having effect and convinced that they would soon have their confession. Kate, however, was not so sure.

She had been with the Drysdales three weeks when

the doctor informed her that her own recovery was nearly complete and lent her a walking stick with which to hobble about. Then he proceeded to turn his attention to Drysdale himself, who was feverish and bedridden, his condition worsening by the day. The doctor's diagnosis was nervous exhaustion, the prognosis uncertain.

That night Kate lay in bed, unable to sleep as she struggled with her doubts about this case. Were Drysdale to die or to be driven hopelessly insane, the money that had been stolen from Atkinson Bank would never be recovered—if indeed he was guilty of the crime. And if by some chance Pinkerton was mistaken in his interpretation of the evidence, then the detectives themselves would be guilty of destroying an innocent man.

The clock in the hall had already struck two when Kate heard the footfall on the stairs. She nearly ignored it as a product of her imagination, until the stillness was pierced by the familiar squeal of the front door hinges. Tossing aside the bedclothes, she rushed to the window in time to see a silvery blur of movement below on the walk. Her heart beat a painfully insistent rhythm as, for the merest instant, she thought she was seeing a ghost. Closer inspection reassured her of her sanity. It was Drysdale, risen out of his sickbed. He was barefooted and clad only in a long, white nightshirt, which had been illuminated by the shimmering light of the full moon, and he was going out by the gate.

Kate considered rousing Susannah, but resisted the urge. She knew she must follow him. There was no time to dress. She slipped into her mules, reached

164

into the wardrobe for her heavy cloak, and tossing it over her nightgown, hurried out into the night after him.

Careful to keep to the shadows and maintain some distance between them, Kate followed along as Drysdale plodded down the road at a sluggish pace. What was he up to—out walking in the middle of the night, wearing nothing more than a nightshirt—and where was he headed?

It was not the chill of the night air, but a sense of uneasiness that caused the prickling that crept along her spine as Kate watched him turn off onto a narrow dirt path. She knew this path well enough; she had walked this way herself more than once in the past few weeks. It led down to Rocky Creek.

Drysdale trod onward, and she lost sight of him briefly among the dark swaying branches of the trees. But when she reached the clearing, she spotted his figure again, reflected by the moonlight as he made his way along the banks of the creek. He headed upstream a few hundred yards until he came to a place where the creek was at its widest, and here he stepped off into the swirling waters.

Kate rushed forward and sank down on all fours, concealing herself within a thick clump of shrubbery near the bank, her breath coming hard and fast. Had they finally driven him over the edge? Did Drysdale intend to drown himself in the waters of Rocky Creek, without giving up his secrets?

Still crouching in her hiding place, with thorny twigs scratching her face and pulling at her hair, Kate dug her nails deep into the dusty, red earth beneath her palms, momentarily paralyzed by indecision. What should she do? There was no time to go back to the house for help. If she were to confront Drysdale on her own, who could say how he might react? If he was truly bent on self-destruction, she was hardly capable of stopping him.

But then again perhaps suicide was not his aim at all; perhaps his nervous state was no more than a clever act. If Drysdale had somehow discovered that there was a traitor in his midst, he might have lured her out here with malice in mind. Kate remembered, with a cold shudder, poor George Gordon, whose skull had been split open by a vicious blow from behind that was most likely dealt him by this man. Suddenly sobered, she kept to her place.

She was somewhat relieved as she turned her attentions on Drysdale once more. Surely he could not mean to drown himself here, for as she saw now, in the place where he stood the creek was scarcely knee-deep. But he bent over at the waist and reached down, as if he intended to lift something out of the waters, then straightened up at last—empty-handed. With this odd ritual completed, he waded toward the bank.

Kate edged forward, watching Drysdale closely in order to put some purpose to his actions, when she felt something hard and smooth beneath her palm. Brushing a hand over the spot, she caught a glimmer of metal reflected by the moonlight and dislodged a twenty-dollar gold piece from the dust and then another, which lay directly beneath it.

Curiosity got the better of her, and with her treasure clutched tight in one fist, she picked up a stray branch with her free hand and feverishly swept the area clean. But there was no sign of any more coins, nor any indication that the hard-packed ground had been disturbed at all.

All at once, Kate looked up to realize that Drysdale was gone. Clambering to her feet, she hurriedly retraced their steps, hoping to catch up with him, but he was nowhere in sight. By the time she reached the main road again, she was angry with herself. Though the coins might prove an important clue, she had allowed them to distract her from the matter at hand. Drysdale. Where was he?

She had almost decided to go back to the house, when she heard a heavy footfall behind her, and whirling around, she saw him, only a few yards distant. Somehow she had gotten ahead of him . . . or had he intended this all along. Flight was her first instinct, but as she turned to run, she caught her foot up in the hem of her cloak and tumbled head over heels onto the ground.

With the wind knocked out of her, Kate was momentarily stunned and realized as she struggled to untangle her garments and rise that she had no hope of outrunning him. Although he had not altered the speed of his approach, he was already nearly upon her. So she collected herself and, with growing dread, got to her feet to face him.

But when the time came, he brushed past her without so much as a glance—as if she deserved no more notice than a rock or tree or some other part of the midnight landscape. Kate's blood ran cold to see the empty look in his dark eyes. They were wide open and staring, and it struck her as he passed her by that these were very much like the eyes of a dead man.

Chapter 13

It was late when Kate finally returned to her bed and so not surprising that she did not awaken until ten o'clock the following morning. The persistent chimes of the hall clock startled her out of a heavy slumber, and when at last she perceived the hour, she quickly put on her clothes and made her way downstairs, clinging to the handrail like a drunken sailor as she descended—the fog still thick in her brain.

So much had happened last night, but she was still shaken by the fright she'd received and in no condition to sort out the facts on her own. She needed to speak with Alec, to tell him what had happened and ask his opinion about Drysdale's midnight ramblings and odd behavior and the two gold coins.

The dining room was empty, of course—breakfast had been served and eaten hours ago—but as she passed by, she could hear the sweet, accented tones of Susannah Drysdale's voice carried in through the open window. Leaning heavily upon her walking stick, Kate adopted a halting gait and headed out to the verandah to join her hostess.

Keeping a gentle rhythm to and fro in her rocking chair, Susannah was reading to her sons from the thick volume of fairy tales. The youngest boy was nestled on her lap, his curly head resting on her bosom, and the elder sat cross-legged at her feet, peering up at her through thick, dark lashes, even as his thoughts were focused on the tale about a faraway land.

It was a touching tableau, and Kate stood for a moment watching them from behind the screen door, loathe to disturb the peace of the scene. A wistfulness possessed her, a bittersweet longing. . . .

Perhaps Marcella had been right; perhaps there was no more important choice a woman could make than that of wife and mother, but try as she might to imagine herself in Susannah's place, a serene madonna with a child on her knee, no such vision would form in Kate's mind. Worse than that was the realization that if her purpose here was successful, she would be at least in part responsible for destroying this little family.

Kate pushed open the screen and went out quickly, to avoid any more thoughts in that vein. As soon as Susannah caught sight of her, she set down her book on a nearby table and spoke to her sons. "We'll finish this later, boys. For now, you may run along into the kitchen and have some biscuits and strawberry jam. And ask Gemma to bring Mrs. Potter's breakfast out on a tray, will you?"

Following a polite chorus of "Yes, mama," the boys scampered off in search of their treat, leaving the

170

two women alone.

"Good mornin', Kate," Susannah said, and rising, she moved to usher her invalid guest to a seat. "Come sit down here on the chaise. Do you need a blanket? It's still quite cool in the shade."

"No, thank you," Kate replied, allowing Susannah to help her settle onto the wicker chair. "I do apologize for sleeping so late, but I'm afraid I had a rather restless night."

"Nothin' serious, I hope. Shall I send for the doctor?"

"Oh, no," Kate insisted and promptly changed the subject. There was no need to waste the doctor's time on her spurious illness. "Where is Mr. Drysdale this morning?" she asked. "Is he still keeping to his bed?"

"No, he's feelin' much better, actually. His friend, Mr. Andrews, came by early this mornin' to take him down to the plantation. He suggested that the change of scenery might be good for him, and I'll admit I'm inclined to agree."

Kate, however, was distressed by this news. with all that had happened, she'd completely forgotten Alec's intention to take Drysdale to his plantation. He'd explained that the last time they'd visited there Drysdale had seemed calmer, as if he thought the place a refuge from his troubles. So Alec had decided that if the ghost was to pay him a visit while he was there, Drysdale would come to believe that his tormentor intended to pursue him no matter where he might hide, and this might be enough to push him into a confession.

But because she had so carelessly overslept this morning, Kate hadn't been able to speak with Alec.

171

He was not aware of Drysdale's midnight wanderings, nor of Kate's fears that the man was no more than a hairsbreadth from losing his hold on sanity. She had to get word to Alec!

"I was just thinking myself how pleasant a change of scenery would be," Kate began cautiously. "It's presumptuous of me, I know, but you have mentioned that we might drive down to see your plantation one day. Do you think, so long as the gentlemen are there anyway, that we might take the carriage down this afternoon and join them—for one night at least?"

Susannah had a devilish glint in her eyes. Kate knew that her hostess suspected that the reason she was so anxious to make the trip was because she had set her cap for the handsome Mr. Andrews, and it seemed by her expression that Susannah approved. "It *would* be fun," she admitted, "just Matthew and I and you and the charming Mr. Andrews. I could leave the children with the servants. If we set out soon enough, we could be there in time for supper."

And so after packing their bags for a short stay, the ladies set out on the road south to the Drysdale plantation. Susannah handled the carriage reins and pointed out places of interest along the way, leaving Kate with nothing more to do than admire the scenery.

The day was mild and breezy, the landscape picturesque, but as they left the feral forests behind and started through the acre upon acre of open field which would soon be planted with cotton, Kate got a vastly different view of this country.

Scattered across the land she saw the black, brawny

172

field hands, barefooted and shabbily dressed in homespun, who were busily tilling the soil to prepare it for planting. Some had seen more than a few such seasons, for their frames were bent, their skin faded and weathered by the elements. There were women in the ranks as well, wearing kerchiefs and sun-bleached calicos, and girls who looked too young to be mothers, carrying infants in slings over their backs as they wielded their hoes.

As Kate watched them at their labors, Susannah proceeded to describe, with pride, the particular qualities of the Drysdale plantation—its prime acreage and impressive harvest in years past and the great number of servants for whom they had to provide.

But, as Kate was beginning to realize, these were not servants; they were slaves, and there was a difference. It was not that she was witness to any particular maltreatment on the journey that day that changed her perspective; the overseers had no cause to use their whips, and none that she observed were beaten or fitted with heavy chains. But now and again as the carriage jounced along the road, she would come across an upturned face whereupon was fixed a cold, dull stare. Little wonder in that. These people's lives were not their own. They could hope for no more for themselves and their children than to live out their lives working upon another's plot of land. And Kate Warne prized her own freedom far too highly not to have been affected.

The trees were casting long shadows upon the road when the ladies' carriage finally turned into the gravel drive of the Drysdales' plantation house. The building, a spreading structure of white clapboard, had twin chimneys, long windows bracketed by dark green shutters, and a deep verandah which ran along its facade and was supported by half a dozen tall columns. The inside of the house was as tastefully decorated as the Drysdales' house in Atkinson, though its appointments were far more elegant: thick, French carpets, fine-woven tapestries, rosewood furniture and crystal chandeliers. The modest appearance of their city house had misled Kate about the Drysdales. But, as she saw now, it was merely their winter retreat; this was the place from which the family conducted their social activities and entertained some of the finest families in the county.

Even with the distraction of such magnificent surroundings, Kate had not forgotten the purpose behind this sojourn and was plainly disappointed to learn that Alec had gone off hunting with Drysdale. Susannah, on the other hand, proclaimed it an ideal turn of events. Now they would have ample time to bathe after their dusty journey and make themselves "presentable" before the gentlemen arrived for supper.

Kate was instinctively wary of that word and her hostess's motives, and with good reason, for as it turned out, Susannah had determined to play matchmaker for her invalid friend and the eligible Mr. John Andrews. She began by sending Kate a maid to help her dress, a frail slip of a girl with coffee-colored skin whose mother, it was claimed, had once been ladies' maid to a French heiress in New Orleans. Kate could not deny that the girl knew her business, and when afterward she stood before the glass, she found herself perversely pleased with her efforts.

Supper proved a frustrating affair. Even with the fresh-cut flowers and soft glow of candlelight and Susannah's well-intentioned attempts at pointing out Kate's finer qualities—"Don't you think that Mrs. Potter looks particularly lovely in that shade of lavender, Mr. Andrews?''—Kate knew, even as she sat across the table from Alec, that she would not be able to get a word alone with him until much later, and that might be too late.

Something in Alec's expression told her that a plan was in the offing. No doubt Mr. Green was hiding in the shrubbery outside even now, waiting for the proper moment to play his ghostly role yet again.

Throughout the meal, Kate kept a close eye on Drysdale. He seemed perfectly lucid now, although his eyes were a trifle bloodshot and his complexion too pale to be healthy. But Kate could not forget his actions the night before. There was trouble in this if they kept on; she could feel it.

In this house, though, surrounded by luxury, she had trouble summoning sympathy for Matthew Drysdale. If indeed he was guilty of the murder of George Gordon and the theft of the money from the Atkinson Bank, he had not turned to crime because he'd been in dire straits—his motive could only have been to foster continued support of this expansive lifestyle.

When Alec suggested that they all take a walk after supper, Kate thought she might at last have her chance to speak with him alone; but when he made no move to take her arm, and instead preceded his host out through the French doors at a brisk stride, her throat went dry, and her heart began to hammer in her breast. Clearly, he meant for Kate to keep Susannah Drysdale distracted. Unable to stop the plan that was already in motion, Kate had no choice but to oblige. Gathering up her walking stick and leaning heavily on it to support her "injured" knee, she followed Susannah outside and managed to keep some distance behind the gentlemen.

By the time they'd crossed the lawns, dusk had streaked the landscape with smudges of gray, and crickets were chirping their courting songs. Just ahead, the gentlemen had only just disappeared into the shadows of a leafy grove, when—not unexpectedly—Kate heard a scream.

Susannah rushed on ahead, and when Kate reached the grove at last, she found her friend kneeling over her husband, who was lying upon the ground, unconscious.

"What's happened?" she asked.

"I'm afraid he's had another one of his visions," Alec explained. "It's caused him quite a shock."

With this, he sprinted off toward the house to alert the servants so that they might carry their master inside. In the meanwhile, Kate knelt down carefully beside Susannah, who had taken up her husband's head in her lap and was smoothing back his hair. "It's some disease of the brain, I fear," the woman said, her voice trembling as her eyes filled with tears. "The nosebleeds and all these strange visions—oh, what am I to do, Kate? What am I to do?"

Drysdale had regained consciousness by the time

he was settled in his bed. He was pale and trembling; but the glass of brandy that Alec proffered seemed to do him a world of good, and despite his wife's pleading, he refused to send for the doctor, insisting that he only needed to rest.

For his part, Alec was satisfied with the outcome of this evening's drama. He remained firm in the conviction that by chipping away, a piece at a time, at Drysdale's resolve, they would eventually gain his confession. He did not miss the look of distress that Kate had been trying to conceal all evening, though, and once they'd left Mrs. Drysdale to fuss over her husband, he caught her by the arm and squired her out into the garden and away from the house so that they might confer in private.

They settled in a quiet spot, on a low marble bench sheltered by a row of boxwood hedges, but to his dismay, when he turned to Kate, Alec found himself tongue-tied. He was unable to stop staring at her. Somehow she looked different tonight . . . fragile.

The lavender silk dress was luminous in the moonlight, and her soft brown hair had been fashioned into looped plaits, entwined with ribbons and delicate sprigs of fresh lilac. The temperamental blossoms had already begun to fade, but they filled the air around her with their fragrant perfume. Alec inhaled until he felt his lungs would burst.

Kate was twenty-six years old, nearly ten years younger than he was, but she had a sharp tongue and even sharper wit that for most of the time made it difficult to think of her as either young or vulnerable. Yet tonight she seemed both.

"What is it, Kate?" he asked, not daring to touch

177

her, much as he longed to. "What's wrong?"

She looked up into his eyes, and the words fairly tumbled out. "It's gone too far. We're robbing the man of his sanity and shattering an entire family in the process. Poor Susannah is at her wit's end. You can put a stop to this, Alec. Pinkerton left the case in your hands."

"There's no other way," he replied. "Justice must be served. Matthew Drysdale is a thief and a murderer. You know it, and I know it, and we can't let him forget."

"How can we know for certain?"

There was a wild note in Kate's voice so wholly unlike her that the sound sent a chill through him.

"Pinkerton might have made a mistake," she persisted. "We could be destroying an innocent man. Even if Drysdale is guilty and we keep on pushing, who knows what he may do, or who may be hurt next? And we haven't even considered what this will do to Susannah and the children."

All at once, Kate's blue eyes went wide with shock, and she raised a trembling hand to cover her mouth. "My God, listen to me! I sound . . . hysterical. A minute more and you'd have had to slap my face to calm me."

Kate was ashamed to find such weakness in herself and even more ashamed that Alec Dalton should be witness to it. "Maybe you were right," she told him. "Maybe a woman can't think the same way about some things as a man; maybe I'm not so capable as I thought—"

Without even thinking, Alec grasped her by the shoulders, her skin whitening under the pressure of his fingers. "Don't believe that, Kate. Don't ever believe that! I was a fool to say what I did. I never doubted your abilities, but you were so damned confident, so impetuous that I feared you'd be hurt—".

When he saw the pained look in her eyes, Alec loosed his grip, but he did not release her. He'd gone too far now to pretend that he didn't care. He wanted this woman, more than he'd wanted anything in his life.

Kate caught her breath as his fingers began to play lightly over her bared shoulders, and before she knew it, she was in his arms and he was kissing her. Desire warmed her blood, threatening to leave her uselessly giddy and weak. It was tempting to give way, for the pleasure in the sensations Alec wrought seemed to ease all her anxieties, but still Kate struggled for control. If he truly cared for her, then why couldn't he see the danger in this?

Alec's thoughts were pressed by other worries, though. He took care to be gentle as his mouth sought hers, persuading her to let go, yet even so he felt resistance. Drawing back, he cradled her face in his hands and forced her to look into his eyes, but could read no emotion there. Kate was far too good at concealing it. Was the truth that she did not care for him at all? Or were her thoughts yet consumed by this case they were both entangled in? Alec chose to believe it was the case.

"You mustn't be so hard on yourself," he told her. "Anyone would be uneasy—living at close quarters with a murderer. But there's no need to worry about Susannah and the boys; they'll be provided for

179

whatever happens. She has family to go to. There's a sister in Vicksburg. I inquired."

"You inquired?"

Alec was wounded by her surprise. "I've considered the fate of those little boys, too. I'm not so cold as you'd believe, Kate."

"I never thought that of you," she insisted, and, as if to prove herself to him, reached out to trace the outline of his squared jaw with a gentle hand.

Alec needed no more prompting than that. He drew her against him, and again his mouth found hers. This time as they clung to one another, emotions neither of them had dared express in words were revealed with each labored breath, each charged touch.

"You must know how I feel, Kate," he whispered against her ear. "Before you came, my life was uncomplicated. I thought I'd made my choices, that I'd never need anything except my work, but now—"

"Alec, no," Kate pleaded. "Don't say anything more. We can't think about such things. It's too dangerous."

He dropped his head, and a shock of sandy hair fell across his brow. He knew full well that she was right, and obliging, he released her, but caught up her hands in his, as if he felt the need to maintain some physical contact between them. "All right, no more talk about us . . . for now. But there's more behind your apprehension about this case than you're saying. I can feel it, Kate. Something else has upset you. Please, tell me."

Kate did as he bade, relieved to turn the conversation away from what had just transpired between

180

them. She didn't want a chance to consider the choice she'd made. "Last night, I couldn't sleep," she began. "I heard someone moving about in the hall, and when I got up to investigate, I saw Drysdale going out of the house; so I followed him."

There was no longer any denying the depth of Alec's feelings for her. Now, though, his concern was manifest by a fierce flare of anger at her carelessness. "Damn it, Kate, I've warned you against going off on your own!"

"There was no one else," she replied simply. "I had to go. And it seemed so peculiar. Drysdale was barefooted and wearing only his nightshirt, as if he hadn't planned to go out, but was compelled to."

"What happened then?"

Kate proceeded to relate in detail the events of the night before, about Drysdale's wandering and the strange scene at Rocky Creek. Alec was thoughtfully quiet as he digested the information.

"I'd hidden myself," she explained. "I was kneeling in the bushes not far away from the place where he stood when I felt something in the dust beneath my hand."

Alec watched in silent fascination as Kate reached to slip a thumb and forefinger into the low-cut bodice of her dress and slowly withdrew a lace handkerchief, which had been tucked between her breasts. When she'd unknotted it, two twenty-dollar gold pieces were revealed within the fabric resting in her palms.

Carefully, Alec took them up to examine them more closely, but at first he was only aware of the fact that the metal was still warm from its contact with her skin. "Much of the money stolen from the bank was in gold coin," he said, his voice rising as he realized what this meant. "I'll send word for Pinkerton to come down at once. Drysdale must have buried the missing money somewhere near the creek. We'll need to search the area thoroughly."

"That's not all," Kate interrupted and went on to tell him how she'd encountered Drysdale on the road. A tremor ran through her as she related the tale, as if the night air had suddenly grown too cold. "I was sure I'd been found out," she told him, "even that he'd planned it, that he meant to harm me—"

"I don't think that's the case," Alec assured her. "From all you've described, I'd guess he was sleepwalking."

Kate realized that very likely Alec was right, and she felt foolish not to have seen it for herself; but even so she could not still the warning voice within her. "Sleepwalking or not, he's half-mad already, Alec. I saw it last night when I looked into his eyes. What good will it do us if he loses his reason?"

"In a few days this will be over," he promised. "Thanks to you, we now have a clue as to what Drysdale's done with the money. Once we have our evidence, we can be done with Matthew Drysdale and Atkinson and this whole business. And then Kate, dangerous or not, we *will* talk about us."

Chapter 14

Matthew Drysdale seemed to have recovered himself by the time they all took leave of the plantation the following morning, but Kate remained uneasy about his state of mind.

A week went by before Allan Pinkerton finally arrived in Atkinson and three days more before she received the summons for which she'd been waiting. Explaining to Susannah Drysdale that the message which had come for her was an invitation to have lunch with one of her lady friends at the hotel, Kate managed to take her leave of the house without arousing suspicion. From there it was a simple matter to make her way, unnoticed, to Alec's hotel room, where the two men were waiting for her.

"Kate, my dear," Pinkerton said, coming forward to take up her hands as Alec shut the door behind them. "Once again you've managed to affirm my faith in you."

The Scotsman was fair to grinning. It was not a usual state for him, and Kate knew that something important must have transpired. "You've found the gold," she guessed.

"Aye, that we have. All but eighty dollars of it, buried in a cheesebox beneath a flat stone in that shallow spot in the creek bed."

Kate breathed an audible sigh. She could feel Alec's presence just behind her, and even though she could not read his expression, she was certain he was smiling and mentally chiding her for her doubts.

Pinkerton released her hands and went to stare out of the window for a moment before taking up his usual habit of pacing while he spoke. "Tonight I shall ask the bank officers to accompany me to Drysdale's plantation. Alec and our young Mr. Green seem to think we'll find the paper money buried out there. But even so, it can only be considered circumstantial evidence to a judge and jury. We need a confession."

By the brisk, unemotional tone in his voice, Kate recognized that he was about to get to the point of this summons, and when he drew the bottle filled with crimson liquid from the pocket of his frock coat, she did her best to remain composed; but her hand was shaking as she reached to take it from him and slipped it into her reticule.

"It's only this one last time," he vowed, as if he sensed how distasteful this task had become for her. "Tomorrow Drysdale's to be arrested, and if we've unsettled him enough, we shall have our confession."

Before Kate had any chance to argue, Alec stepped forward to retrieve a stack of envelopes from his bedside table. "I'd best be on my way," he announced. "Drysdale is expecting me. He asked if I would bring his mail from the office he keeps in town."

Kate ought not to have been surprised to see that the envelopes were stained with splatters of dried blood, yet still she was unable to stifle a gasp when she saw them. "Odd thing, that," Alec said with an evil grin. "There seem to be bloodstains all over his office."

With that, he left them, and as Kate's gaze returned to the place where the letters had lain on the bedside table, she realized that he had left one of them behind. Snatching it up, she waved it before Pinkerton and followed Alec out into the hall, catching up to him just before he reached the landing.

"I knew you wouldn't miss it," he told her, and as she handed over the envelope, he grasped her hand and spoke quietly. "Pinkerton would have you wait for the news, but I don't want you to have to worry about this one moment longer than is necessary. Meet me here tomorrow night at ten, if you can, and I'll let you know what's happened."

Kate promised that she would, and he conjured a reassuring smile for her. "It will all be over soon," he told her, and heedless of the consequences, he leaned to brush a kiss against her lips before he turned and headed down the stairs.

When Kate went back to the hotel room, she found Pinkerton staring out of the window again, dark brow furrowed as he tugged thoughtfully on his beard. "Come sit down, Kate," he said.

She followed his orders, settling into one of a pair of armchairs which stood before the hearth, and

185

before long, Pinkerton came to sit beside her. "You've done an admirable job here," he told her.

For her part, Kate did not think so and shook her head in vigorous denial. "My instincts have interfered every step of the way, Allan. I think you know that."

"I'm aware that you disagree with my methods on this case; it comes through quite plainly in your reports, even if you've never said it outright. But you did the job just the same, and that's what matters."

"There's a confession to be had yet," she reminded him.

"And I've no doubt we'll get one."

As she allowed herself to meet his unflinching gaze, Kate wondered if Allan Pinkerton ever had doubts about anything. She envied him his resolve and single-mindedness. It was surely these qualities that were at the heart of the success of this man, who only fourteen years ago had emigrated from Scotland a penniless barrelmaker.

When he offered her a warm smile, Kate could not help but imagine that his talents extended to mind reading as well. He rose out of his chair as if he'd reached some decision and began to pace the stretch of carpet behind her.

"You've always been a puzzle to me, Kate," he remarked, in a manner that was more familiar than was his custom. "As if you had no life at all before that day you appeared at my office door. You ne'er speak of your past, nor your husband, but he must have been quite a man to have been worthy of such a fine woman."

Kate was too surprised to reply. Pinkerton had

never before inquired into her personal life. The measured tread on the carpet ceased now as his thick hands settled on her shoulders. A peculiar trepidation was rising in her as Kate wondered what he was up to. He was trying to draw her out, of that much she was certain, but what was it precisely that he wanted her to say?

"Aye, well, whate'er the reason, you'll not settle for the sort of life that satisfies other women," he continued. "You prize your freedom highly, Mrs. Warne, and I for one am glad of it. I've a personal stake in your success, you know. This is a not a job for a woman with ties."

Abandoning her chair, Kate crossed to the bureau, all the while avoiding Pinkerton's eyes. This was Alec's room—she'd almost forgotten—and his things lay scattered across 'the bureau top: a brown satin string tie, comb and brushes, a pearl-headed stickpin, a stray shirt stud. . . . Kate reached out to pick up the stud and closed her fingers tightly around it. Could it be that Pinkerton had witnessed her exchange with Alec in the hallway and meant to warn her without accusing her outright?

"I'll always be grateful for the opportunity you've given me," she replied slowly, still unable to meet his eyes.

"I've a business proposition for you, Kate," he said, revealing his intentions to her at last. "'Tis time that I hired more women. I want you to train them, Kate, and oversee their work. Mind you, it will take your total commitment; you'll scarcely have a life to call your own. Well, what say you? Are you willing?"

Kate could not believe what he was offering her. It

was a chance to direct her own staff—a staff made up of women detectives. It was more than she'd ever dreamed possible, and without hesitation she turned to him and accepted his offer.

The following day promised to be a crucial one, yet once it dawned, it seemed to drag on uneventfully—apart from another disturbing discovery by Drysdale of more trailing bloodstains. But to Kate, even this macabre occurrence was becoming routine.

Perhaps Drysdale sensed something of what was to come, though, for he seemed even more highly strung than usual and spent the morning preparing to remove his household to the plantation and close up the town house for the season. It was nearly time for spring planting, he reminded them all.

Susannah had endeavored to convince Kate to come along with them, but Kate could only tell her friend that as she was still unsure of her plans, it would be best if she moved into the hotel for a few days. Then, if she decided to stay on, she'd join them later.

The packing was finished by noon, but an ominous grumbling in the distant hills foretold unpleasant weather for travelling. Drysdale had arranged for Susannah, the children, and the servants to go down to the plantation that afternoon. As for himself, he planned to meet with his good friend Mr. Andrews, complete his business in town and join them all later that night.

Kate's trunk was sent over to the hotel in the morning, but she stayed on to help Susannah with the last-minute details of packing up the household. They said their goodbyes at the gate, and Kate could not help but wonder, as she watched the family's covered carriage and the wagon, crowded with baggage and servants, start down the road, if she would ever see any of them again.

The storm broke soon after Kate had settled into her room at the hotel, and it unleashed its fury upon the town all that afternoon, with wave upon wave of cold rain washing against the windows, fogging the glass and blurring the view.

When it was time, she dressed and went down to supper, where she spent her time in renewing acquaintances among the guests. Try as she might, though, Kate could not keep her mind on the succession of trivial conversations, for she knew that even now, somewhere across town, the case she and Alec had worked on for weeks might be reaching its conclusion. It was a relief when, pleading exhaustion, she could excuse herself finally to return upstairs, but once she was alone in the hall, it was Alec's room she headed for instead of her own.

Eager as she was for news about the case, there was something more on Kate's mind tonight—the remarkable offer that Pinkerton had made her yesterday. Nothing could have pleased her more than such an opportunity, yet somehow she needed to know Alec would be pleased, too.

He'd said ten o'clock, and it was nearly that now; but Kate was disappointed when she let herself in to find that the room was dark and still. There was a damp chill in the air that seeped through the thin fabric of her lavender evening dress. A shiver vibrated through her, and so Kate knelt down before the hearth and busied herself with laying the fire. When at last it started to blaze she rose, brushing off her skirts, and stole a glance at the mantel clock. Drysdale ought to have been arrested sometime this afternoon. Pinkerton would have had plenty of time to question him by now. Confession or no, it ought to be over. Kate could not think of any reason why Alec should be detained, but there was nothing else to do but settle herself in one of the chairs by the firelight and wait.

More than once she discerned the sound of footsteps outside on the hall carpet, only to hear them pass by the door. An hour passed. Kate tried not to think on what might have gone wrong, but a nagging voice within kept reminding her that thanks to their efforts, Matthew Drysdale was near to losing his mind. He had already murdered one man; there was no predicting how he might react when cornered.

With the rain still beating a steady rhythm against the clapboards, Kate alternated her concentration between the second hand on the clock and the dancing flames in the hearth. The effect was hypnotic, and despite her best efforts, she was nearly dozing when the rattling of the doorknob startled her to attention.

She was on her feet by the time Alec entered the room. The first thing she noticed was that his clothes were saturated with rainwater. A wave of brown hair was plastered against his forehead, his face glistening, moustache scattered with droplets as if he'd been standing in the rain and had thrown back his head to let it wash over him. His hat was in his hand, and he let it slip now from his fingers to the floor.

As he stepped into the circle of the firelight, Kate saw that he was ashen-faced, his green eyes dull and glassy, but only when she noticed the dark smear of blood on the sleeve of his 'frock coat and the unmistakable crimson stains on his hands, did she lose her calm.

"You're hurt!" she cried and rushed to him, anxiously stripping off the coat so that she might examine his arm.

To her relief, she found no damage at all, not so much as a torn sleeve. It was then that she realized that the blood was not Alec's. "What is it?" she asked, apprehension rising in her. "What's happened?"

All at once, Alec came to life. His arm flashed out, and catching Kate by the waist, he dragged her against him, his rain-soaked clothes dampening her gown, the blood on his hands staining the fabric. She'd seen the wild, wounded look in his eyes as he'd reached for her and knew the embrace was meant to be purely protective, but his grip was so fierce that she could scarcely draw breath. Still he would not speak. As she slipped her arms around him, though, his shoulders slumped, and she felt the uneven breath he pulled vibrate deep in his chest.

"It's over," he said in a voice half-strangled. "He's dead. Drysdale's dead."

Kate felt as if the blood in her veins had gone cold, numbing her as it coursed through her body. Although she'd predicted that something like this might happen, she hadn't expected it would have such an effect on Alec. She drew back so that she could see his face. All along he'd seemed so sure of what they were doing.

"How?" she asked.

Pain creased his brow, and he reached to press a hand across his eyes as if it might block out his visions. Taking charge, Kate broke free of him and went to fetch a whiskey bottle and glass from the bedside table. "This will help," she said.

Returning to his side, she poured him a drink, then watched as he downed it swiftly and took the bottle from her trembling hand to pour himself yet another.

"You'd best get out of those wet clothes," she prompted him, "or you'll catch your death."

Fortified by the liquor, Alec seemed to have regained some of his vigor. He went to the washstand, filled the basin, then stared absently into the glass. Ignoring Kate's presence entirely, he stripped off his sodden waistcoat and shirt all in one rough move. Buttons bounced across the floor. He slung the sodden clothes over a chair and concentrated on washing the blood from his hands. As he finished undressing, Kate turned away from him and clutched at the carved back of the armchair where she'd been sitting when he came in. She needed to know all that had happened, but in his present state, she dared not push him.

When he returned to her side, he was barefooted and wearing a dressing gown of gray figured silk. "I've ruined your gown," he noticed now as he looked on the sorry state of her dress, which was now water-marked and bloodstained. "And more than that, I've frightened you, haven't I? I'm sorry, Kate, but this has shaken me through and through.''

Kate motioned him into the chair. When he sat down, she settled herself on the hearth rug at his feet. ''Tell me about it,'' she said.

Outside the storm had begun to rage once more, and Alec's words were punctuated by cracks of thunder so startlingly intense that they rattled the windowpanes. ''I was with Drysdale, in his office, when they came to arrest him,'' he began. ''To have seen the look of astonishment on his face, you'd have thought he was an innocent man. But he couldn't hold up when they took him into the bank and Pinkerton brought forth his evidence—especially not after our Mr. Green came out of the vault, made up to look like the dead man.

''Oh, it was theatrical, but it did the trick. Drysdale confessed on the spot. His motive was common enough. He'd come to call on his friend George Gordon one evening at the bank, after hours, in order to draw out the remainder of his savings. He had debts to pay; he was painfully strapped for cash, and there sat Gordon, the only obstacle between him and the thousands of dollars in the open vault.''

''So, he was guilty after all,'' Kate said and breathed a light sigh. ''I suppose I shouldn't have doubted it. Pinkerton's scarcely ever wrong about such things.''

But Alec had not yet reached the crucial part of his tale, and she could see that he was still deeply troubled by the memory of it. She reached to take up his hands in hers. ''Please, tell me the rest,'' she entreated.

Alec nodded, focusing his attention full on the fire burning in the hearth before he resumed his tale so that she could not read his expression. His voice sounded hollow and distant. "Drysdale asked then if he might have a word with his 'good friend,' Mr. Andrews, and so they left us alone in one of the private offices. He seemed calm enough. He asked me to break the news to Susannah to tell her that he was sorry. Then he shook my hand and bid me goodbye.

"I'd scarcely reached the door when I heard him whisper: 'God help my wife and children.' As I turned back to him, I saw the gun in his hand. He must have had it hidden in his coat all the while. I met him eye-to-eye, thinking for a moment that he'd somehow discovered that I'd betrayed him and meant to kill me for it, but he looked too helpless, too pitiful. And then I watched as he pressed the barrel to his temple. I wanted to cry out, to rush him and wrest the gun away, but I felt as if I were paralyzed. He only fired one shot, and by the time I reached him, he was dead."

Kate squeezed her eyes shut, as if she were seeing the scene played before her and needed to block it out. "Oh, God," she said, the words hushed and solemn. "Oh, my God, Alec. It must have been awful."

Alec freed his hands from hers and strode impatiently to the window, where he stared through the rain-spattered glass to the empty street below. He'd intended to spare her the worst of what he'd seen tonight, but then how could he possibly expect her to understand the effect it had had on him?

"I know that Drysdale got no less than he deserved," he told her. "He'd have been hanged for murder at any rate; but as I stood there, staring into the eyes of a dead man, I felt a chill so cold that it cut clear through to my bones."

Kate came to stand behind him now and laid a calming hand on his shoulder. He turned to her. "We never know when it will be our turn. Do we, Kate? I'd hate to think of dying without letting you know . . . without telling you how I—"

"Hush," she soothed, pressing her fingers against his lips. "You're upset by what's happened, that's all."

"No!" he replied, catching her hand in a painful grip. "It's made me see what's important. We can't go on ignoring the truth. I love you, Kate."

Kate let his words hang on the air, savoring the sound. A part of her wanted to hear them, wanted to believe that love would be enough.

After all he'd been through tonight, Alec needed her. Just meeting his eyes, Kate could feel how much, and yet she hesitated. It was not fair to let him believe that there was a chance for them. She had to tell him of Pinkerton's offer, and of the future she had already decided upon, but when she started to speak, the words caught in her throat.

"I love you, Kate," he said, more insistently this time. "I know that you love me, and I won't let you leave this room tonight until I've made you admit it."

"You ask too much of me," she barely managed to say, "more than I can give."

Alec's lungs ached as he pulled an unsteady breath. He was still suffering from the shock of all that he'd witnessed tonight; he needed Kate in his arms to

195

make him forget. In one swift move, he drew her against him, burying his face in her perfumed hair.

Kate put her hands to his chest in a halfhearted effort to keep some distance between them, but as she did so his dressing gown gaped open. She was very much aware of the crisp mat of hair beneath her splayed fingers and of his heart, beating an insistent rhythm against her palms. "Give me tonight, Kate," he whispered. "I swear I'll ask no more than that."

Without waiting for her reply, Alec began his assault. His breath was warm on her skin. It ruffled the tendrils of hair resting on her nape, and as his open mouth slid along the soft line of her jaw, the brush of his moustache heightened the tingling sensations that spread through her, fuelling an all-too-familiar urgency.

Kate gasped as his mouth descended on hers, ruthlessly demanding her response. And all the while his hands were ranging across her back, fingers fumbling with the row of tiny hooks that fastened her bodice. After he'd undone them all, one sleeve slipped down. Alec brushed aside the other impatiently, regarding her in breathless triumph as she took a half-step back and dropped her arms at her sides so that the silken fabric fell away, leaving her standing there in corset and petticoats, her skin gilded by firelight.

Kate never had a chance of escape. She'd been helpless from the first, betrayed by her own body, which had responded to his with a frightening intensity. Where was the harm? she asked herself, as reason finally gave way. She wanted this as much as he. It was one night—only one night. . . .

Reaching out, Kate laced her fingers behind Alec's neck and drew him down to her, allowing his mouth to capture hers once more. His kisses overwhelmed her, filling up her senses and promising pleasures yet to come.

The room was spinning in a blur of shadows and amber light as her heart drummed a violent rhythm in her breast, competing with the incessant patter of the rain as it beat upon the roof. And all the while, Alec busied himself in unpinning her chignon, unbinding the heavy coil of hair, and carelessly scattering pins across the floor.

"You ought to wear it loose," he said, his lips softening against her cheek as he combed out the curls with his restless fingers until they tumbled in a thick, dark wave over her shoulders. "It suits you."

"I'm no china doll, Alec," Kate said, amused by his efforts. "You ought to know by now that I'm too plain and practical to be pretty."

Alec scowled and looked her square in the eye. "I don't know that. I don't know that at all. Beauty isn't only gold curls and pink cheeks, Kate. It's spirit and fire and intelligence. And to me, at least, it's an impossible woman with sapphire eyes."

Alec had been cradling her head in his two hands as they spoke, breathing of her clean, sweet scent, and revelling in the feel of her body molded against his. But it was a struggle to stem the passions rising within him, and when he could bear it no longer, he turned his efforts upon the lacings, tapes and ribbons that kept Kate still bound up in yards of fabric.

When she was free at last, he lifted her from the pool of clothing, carried her to the bed and set her down gently upon it. Kate shivered as a chill swept through her. She drew up the quilt, wriggling beneath it, but as the sensation was caused more from anticipation than cold, it did not subside until Alec had at last cast off his dressing gown and lay down beside her. Kate turned into his arms, thrilling at the heated touch of his skin against hers, and before she knew it, he had rolled her beneath him.

"Say it, Kate," he urged, breathing the words against her parted lips. "You don't need to be afraid."

Looking up into those eyes of his, those eyes as clear and green as bottle glass, Kate saw his love reflected. She knew that this was right, and she wanted to tell him so. He needed some pledge from her, especially tonight.

Propped on one elbow with Kate trapped beneath him, Alec regarded her through half-closed lids, but there was a glittering intensity behind them which belied his languid smile. His free hand trailed along the arc of her extended arm, exploring with an aching slowness the rises and hollows of her body before finally coming to rest possessively on the full curve of her hip. His lips settled on the arch of her throat, then slipped lower as he began to scatter feather-light kisses across her skin, before returning to capture her mouth once more.

He tasted of whiskey, but Kate was the one feeling its effects. She shut her eyes to slow the whirling in her brain, but it only made her more aware that her skin was melting beneath his persistent fingers.

When the time came, Alec gave her no warning. A soft moan broke from her lips as he took her. So perfectly did their disparate forms fit together that it was not hard for Kate to imagine they had been meant for one another all along. Instinct took over then, guiding her frenzied hands as they explored the taut planes of his back, her hips meeting his in perfect rhythm. Each touch was sweet ecstasy, each kiss fanned the flames higher and hotter.

"I love you," she cried when she could bear it no longer. Overwhelmed by one last, exquisite surge of release, she buried her face in his shoulder, amidst the cascade of her own dark hair. "I love you, Alec Dalton, and God help me, I'm sure to be lost because of it."

They lay together in silence for a long while; the only sounds in the room were the faint roll of thunder as the storm ebbed away in the distance and the crackling of the fire still burning in the hearth.

"Not lost," Alec said to her at last. "Never lost. You'll be here with me, here in my arms where you belong."

Kate shut her eyes; she could feel the words vibrating deep in his chest. She wanted to believe him, but the chill was returning, even as she lay there beside him.

She had won the heart of a good man, an honest man. It ought to have been the ultimate prize. Indeed, it would have been for most women, but not Kate Warne, who had known only disappointment when she'd placed her happiness in someone else's hands. She dared not give up her independence, not ever again.

Of course, Alec wouldn't understand that what he wanted of her was impossible. A man did not have to choose between love and ambition, but for a woman it was something else entirely. Kate had agreed to sacrifice her personal life when she'd made the choice to work for Allan Pinkerton, and she had reaffirmed that vow only yesterday when she'd accepted the promotion he'd offered. She saw now that tonight had not solved her problems, only complicated them by showing her just how much this man meant to her when, in truth, there was no chance for them, no chance at all.

The urge was strong to lose herself in the comfort of Alec's embrace, but Kate knew what she must do. When the sound of steady breathing beside her told her that he was asleep, she slipped as quietly as she could from his arms. Gathering together her clothes, she dressed hastily and was crossing the room headed for the door when he stirred. Noticing that Kate was not beside him, Alec raised up in surprise.

"Kate? What are you doing?"

Kate turned back to him, looking like a guilty child before her mask slipped in place and she regarded him coolly. "I'm going to pack a bag and go down to the Drysdale plantation," she explained simply. "Susannah will need a strong shoulder when she gets the news."

"But you don't have to leave this minute," he protested. "It's late. Wait until morning. Come back to bed."

As he reached for her, Kate's desperation increased. "No. I can't," she told him.

Losing her calm, she backed into the chair as she tried to keep a distance between them. If he touched her again, she might not be able to resist.

200

"I'm sorry, Alec. I was wrong to think that we could . . . that you and I. . . . You swore you'd ask no more of me. If you care for me at all, you'll forget what's happened between us tonight."

Alec was stunned by her words, but when he looked into Kate's eyes, swimming with unshed tears, he knew that she was serious. Tonight he'd been overwhelmed by his own need; he hadn't considered how much an admission of love would cost her.

There had to be some way to convince her that they belonged together, he told himself, but he could not bear to argue with her, not now. There was no denying that in the throes of passion, he had sworn not to ask any more of her, and so he had no choice but to agree.

Chapter 15

Chicago, Illinois
1859

The sultry summer's heat had pervaded the city for more than a week now, heightening discomfort and shortening tempers. Kate tried to concentrate upon the stack of reports on her desk, but when she could stand it no more, she put them aside and got up to pace the length of her office, hoping to stir up the heavy air. She strayed to the open window, staring out over the rooftops toward Lake Michigan, where in the distance a bank of gray clouds was forming. The faint grumble of thunder sounded promising, at least, if only the east wind would pick up and blow the storm ashore.

All at once, a shiver coursed through her, in spite of the heat, and Kate was assailed by memories—sweet, painful memories. Ever since that night so long ago, that night she had sworn to forget, Kate had not been able to look on the signs of an approaching storm without remembering the night that she and Alec had made love. For a moment, she closed her eyes and allowed herself to dream.

Two sharp raps upon her door brought a swift end to her reverie and signalled the approach of Allan Pinkerton. When the door swung open, he was standing there in waistcoat and shirtsleeves, his face flush with color. He strode into the room, and Kate turned to him, but kept her place by the window, resting herself on the ledge.

"I've a personal favor to ask, Kate," he announced. "Some valuable merchandise arrived for me last night, and I was wondering if you would take receipt of it for me, until other arrangements can be made."

Kate shook off the last remnants of her musing and focused her thoughts on what he'd asked her. "Yes, of course," she replied. "How many packages are there?"

"Four altogether. Two large and two small, but I think you'll be able to manage."

"You needn't worry," she assured him.

"Now on to business," Pinkerton continued, resuming his usual brisk business manner. "The Sumner case. Do you recall it?"

Kate did, indeed. James Sumner, a retired sea captain, had consulted Pinkerton some weeks ago. He was concerned about his younger sister, Anne—an attractive but rather empty-headed female—who had been carrying on a love affair with a married man by the name of Alonzo Pattmore. Captain Sumner had considered Pattmore a dangerous, despicable character from the first, but when Pattmore's wife died under suspicious circumstances, he was sure of it. He feared that his sister might be involved, and so he'd enlisted the agency's help, hoping to prove that Pattmore alone had murdered his wife, and thereby remove his sister from the influence of this evil man.

"I sent Grace Seaton to the boardinghouse where Miss Sumner is currently residing and instructed her to strike up a friendship with the lady," Kate told him. "She has been sending daily reports, which I've had copied and put in a file on your desk."

Pinkerton pulled thoughtfully on his beard. "I've just now read through them," he said. "Frankly, I didn't think we'd have much need for this, once we'd got Mrs. Pattmore's body exhumed for autopsy."

"The results were not conclusive?" Kate surmised.

"Worse than that. Our Mr. Pattmore seems to be all that Captain Sumner had feared. And he is a man with great political influence as well. At first, he attempted to have his wife's body switched for another before the coroner could get hold of it. We anticipated he might try something of the sort, though, and were on watch in the graveyard to dissuade the body snatchers from their purpose. Failing in that attempt, Pattmore persuaded the coroner to appoint men who were friends of his to the coroner's jury. The verdict, not surprisingly, was death by natural causes."

After working for Pinkerton for all this time, Kate ought not to have been surprised by this kind of corruption, but it disturbed her nonetheless. "So, in the eyes of the law, there was no murder," she said, shaking her head. "What is there left for us to do now?"

"Our cause is not wholly lost," Pinkerton assured

her. "The sheriff had his own suspicions about the progress of this investigation, and I managed to get hold of the body before it was reinterred. I arranged for a doctor-friend of mine to take the necessary samples. If the results of his analyses show poison, we shall have evidence enough to prove that a murder was committed."

"And how do you wish Miss Seaton to proceed in the meanwhile?"

"Instruct her to continue to play the devoted friend to Anne Sumner. Have her watch the woman closely and report on every encounter she has with Pattmore, and see to it that we obtain copies of any correspondence that passes between them. What we need is evidence to tie Pattmore to the murder, and we need to discover just how much the girl knows."

Kate nodded solemnly, and then Pinkerton seemed to hesitate. "Miss Sumner has been too wary to confide in our Miss Seaton," he explained, "but we have learned that she is a superstitious young woman and easily led. Now, I know that you have more than enough to keep you busy, but for what I have planned, I need you on this case, personally; no one else will do."

"Me? But, Allan, you've just said that Miss Seaton is—"

"Miss Seaton is fine just as she is, Kate. I've another role in mind for you."

With that, he handed her a book. As she studied it, she read the title aloud, and her brow creased with a puzzled frown. *"The Mysteries of Magic and the Wonders of Astrology* by Dr. Roback?"

* * *

After Pinkerton had explained his plan and outlined the part Kate was to play in it, he suggested that she take the remainder of the day off to make the necessary arrangements. It was not hard for Kate to leave behind the stifling office and the paperwork cluttering her desk. She quit the building feeling free, for the moment at least, as she crossed Washington Street, heading for home.

When first he'd formulated his plan to hire women, Pinkerton had decided that for propriety's sake, as well as their own protection, the lady detectives ought to be housed in a dormitory of sorts—with Kate acting as their matron. Although Kate could hardly argue with his logic, she thought such an arrangement sounded cold and institutionlike. To her surprise, she found the reality a great deal more pleasant.

Home was now a two-storied, white clapboard house just down the street from the agency offices, with comfortable furnishings and lace curtains, a sitting room with shelves for her collection of books, and a flower garden out back. It was a lively household, with a cook and a maid and a trio of young lady detectives for company.

The walk seemed longer this afternoon. As she trudged along the dusty boardwalk, Kate did her best to ignore the prickling of heat that spread across her shoulders from the blazing sun. She tried to concentrate instead on the preparations that must be made for her part in the Sumner case, yet all the while found herself anticipating the cool shade inside the house and longing for a bath to wash away the dust and perspiration that clung to her skin.

Once she'd dragged herself up the front steps and

let herself into the house, Kate breathed a sigh of relief. She had scarcely removed her bonnet when Cora the maid, a buxom young Irish girl, appeared in the hall. The girl was dishevelled from her chores but wearing a cheery smile nonetheless. "Afternoon, ma'am."

"It's awfully quiet," Kate remarked at once. "Where are the ladies this afternoon, Cora?"

The girl took Kate's bonnet from her and hung it by its ribbons from one of the pegs on the wall beside the door. "Miss Emma and Miss Carrie have gone shopping, I believe, and Miss Grace is off on business. But I expect you'd know more about that than I."

"Miss Seaton will be away for another week at least," Kate informed her. "But I need to speak to Mrs. Baker and Miss Reynolds. I'm going up to change now, and afterward I'll be in the sitting room. Would you please send them there as soon as they return?"

As Cora nodded, a stray wisp of auburn hair slipped out of her starched cap and was at once dampened by the glittering beads of perspiration on her brow. "Yes, ma'am. Dulcie's just mixed a fresh batch of lemonade. Shall I bring a pitcher in for you? It's powerful hot today."

"Lemonade would be nice. Thank you, Cora."

With that, Kate started up the stairs to wash and change her dress. "I'd say as how we need a fine thunderstorm to wash away all this heat, ma'am," Cora called after her, "but I know how much you hate those storms. Why, last time we had one, I lay in my bed and listened to you pace the floor for half the night."

Kate stopped short on the landing, feeling the blood drain away from her face. She didn't realize that anyone else was aware of her peculiarities about thunderstorms. "We all have some childhood fear that we can't let go of," she replied in the way of an explanation, although the truth of the matter was something else entirely.

Half an hour later, Kate was settled in an easy chair by the open window in the sitting room, engrossed in the odd volume that Pinkerton had given her and making notes of all that she'd need to play her new role.

When the ladies joined her at last, she bade them sit down and poured them each a glass of lemonade before getting to business. They seated themselves side-by-side on the sofa and gave her their full attention.

Emma Baker was, like Kate, a widow. She was close to Kate's age, as well, but there the similarity ended. Emma was pale and petite, with sable ringlets and flashing dark eyes. She had been born to a Virginia family of comfortable means and had married a Chicago businessman; but after her beloved husband had died, she'd needed a different sort of life, and Pinkerton's advertisement for lady detectives seemed to offer just the thing.

Carrie Reynolds, by contrast, was a mere child of nineteen, but with a perception far beyond her years. She was fair-haired and willowy, with an ethereal quality that gave no hint of her hard-headed nature. But, like Kate, she had known a life of poverty, and when given the chance, she'd grasped at Pinkerton's unusual offer with both hands.

"Ladies, I need your help," Kate began. Setting

down the lemonade pitcher, she went to retrieve the papers upon which she'd been writing and handed one to each. "This is a task for which I know you are both amply qualified. In the next few days, we need to acquire as many of the items on this list as we can."

"Shopping?" Emma cried, and it was hard to tell if she was more surprised or amused. "Our assignment is to go shopping?"

Meanwhile, Carrie busied herself in studying the list. "One pair of skeletons," she read aloud, "two Oriental lamps, incense burners, astrological charts. . . . Just what are you up to, Kate?"

"They're props for our latest case," Kate explained. "As I've said, we need them as soon as possible, but let's try and be economical, shall we? The agency will be footing the bill, and Mr. Pinkerton will have my head if I run up the expenses."

Just then, there was a knock on the sitting room door, and Cora came in, carrying an envelope. "This just arrived for you, Mrs. Warne," she explained, "by messenger. He's waiting for your reply."

Kate's brow furrowed as she took up the envelope. She wondered if it might be yet more instructions for her from Pinkerton, but then she saw her name on the envelope and recognized the hand. It was not Pinkerton's.

A flush that was caused by more than the summer's heat spread from her collar to the roots of her hair, and Kate was very much aware of the three women watching her as she drew out the letter. She wished she could send them all away and be alone when she read the words on the page, but the messenger was waiting. She had to keep her calm; then they'd think that it was no more than a business matter. Yes, that's what she had to do.

Kate,
I have only just got back to town and write to you in the hope that you have had a change of heart and will agree to meet me somewhere so that we can speak openly. We cannot go on as we have been for so long, denying the truth. I beg you not to ignore my request yet again. My messenger awaits your instructions.
                                        Always,
                                        Alec

Kate's heart hammered fiercely against her breast-bone. Her eyes were dangerously bright, but she swallowed her emotions and forced a smile upon her face.

"Cora," she said, in a voice that bespoke a calm indifference that she hardly felt, "you may tell the messenger that there is no reply."

It was all very convincing. No one seemed to notice that Kate's hands had dropped into her lap, nor that she had crumpled the page and was now twisting it tightly between two whitened fists.

It was well after midnight when Kate left the house by way of the kitchen door, her head and shoulders enveloped in a black silk shawl, despite the fact that the night was too warm to warrant it. She traversed the narrow alleyways, where the stench of rotting garbage was ofttimes overwhelming, but where the dismal darkness afforded more protection to those who wished to pass unseen. And more than once, her hand edged toward the handle of the revolver she had tucked into the waistband of her skirt, when she thought she heard a stray footstep or a skittering noise in the shadows.

At length, she came to Dearborn Street, where she hurried on past the pools of light cast by the street lamps until finally she'd reached her destination: the home of Mr. John Jones, a free black man, who ran a prosperous tailoring establishment and was one of the most effective abolitionist leaders in Chicago.

It was Allan Pinkerton's request that had brought her here tonight. All his talk this afternoon of "merchandise" and "packages" meant that another group of runaways had arrived in the city. And he had asked her to take charge of them.

For as long as Kate had known him, Pinkerton had been a fervent abolitionist. When the opportunity presented itself, he had gladly taken on the task of aiding runaway slaves from the South in their escape to freedom in Canada, and for some months now, Kate herself had been helping in small ways where she could.

The work she'd committed herself to was strictly against the law. The penalties for infraction were severe, so great care had to be taken to maintain secrecy. And there were slave catchers to contend with as well, men whose only thought was of the reward money they'd receive for returning their quarry to its master.

For her own part, Kate was willing to take the

risks. It was no more dangerous than the work she did for the agency, after all. How could any caring human being refuse? Besides, Kate had a special regard for freedom, and she had seen more than enough of slavery when she'd visited the plantations of Mississippi to convince her that something needed to be done to end it.

Kate let herself into the yard by the gate and went around the house to the kitchen door, where she rapped sharply three times, paused, then rapped once more. Within seconds, the door opened slowly to reveal the slender figure of Mary Jones, who, despite the lateness of the hour, was still dressed in a fashionable gown of white linen and wore a lace cap over her shining black curls.

"Mrs. Warne, do come in," she bade warmly as she stepped aside to allow her to enter.

Kate walked through to the dining room, where a light was burning. As she entered, Mr. Jones, who'd been seated at the head of the table, rose to greet her.

"Thank you for coming, Mrs. Warne," he said, taking up her hand in his own sturdy grip. "We'd not have called upon you, except that we've more 'guests' ourselves than we can handle at present."

"I'm glad to help, whenever I can," she told him.

Kate could feel several pairs of dark eyes gazing upon her. Directly beside Jones, there was seated a brawny young man, dressed in rough homespun. As she turned a reassuring smile on him, she noticed for the first time the small boy who was sitting on his lap, clutching at a thick slice of bread. In the chair at his side was a weary-looking girl, who looked no more than seventeen, and cradled in her arms lay a tiny babe.

"This is the Price family," Mr. Jones told her. "Caleb and his wife, Rachel, their son, Ben, and baby girl, Alva. They've come all the way up from Missouri. If you could take them for a few days, until I can arrange passage for them to Detroit, I'd be more than grateful to you."

"Of course," Kate replied. "We'd be happy to have them."

"Caleb, you must take your family and go with Mrs. Warne," Jones instructed. "Mind you do exactly as she tells you, and we'll have you safe in Canada in no time."

Putting down his son, Caleb rose and shook the hand of the man who'd given him shelter. "Yes, sir, I'll do that, and we thank you, Mr. Jones, sir, we surely do."

Mary Jones came up behind Kate then and tapped her on the shoulder. When Kate turned around, she handed her a parcel wrapped in brown paper. "This is a suit of clothes for Mr. Price, and something for the boy as well. They'll need more than what they've been travelling in. I was thinking that perhaps one of your ladies might have an old frock that might fit his wife—"

"Of course," Kate said as she took up the parcel.

And with that, she gathered up the little family and began to retrace the circuitous path that would lead them back to the house on Washington Street.

Chapter 16

THE WORLD RENOWNED SIBYL
MADAME LUCILLE
HAS ARRIVED IN CHICAGO

She has cast horoscopes for all the the crowned heads of Europe, Africa and Asia, and will do the same for all who consult her. Who loves you? Who means to do you harm? Madame Lucille knows your past and will divine your future. Visit and learn your fate.

Fee: $10.00
The Temple of Magic
540 South Clark Street

Alec narrowed his eyes against the glare of the afternoon sun as he reread the handbill, mopping the sweat from his brow with a kerchief he'd pulled from his pocket. He'd been away, working on a case in Memphis for more than a month, but as soon as he'd returned to the city, he'd sent word to Kate. When she didn't reply, he went to the agency looking for her, only to learn that she wasn't in her office. And when he'd asked where he might find her, George Bangs had only laughed and given him this handbill.

Alec had already seen several of these this morning. They were posted all over town, and by asking a few questions in the right places, he soon learned that the celebrated Madame Lucille was attracting quite a following among those wealthy enough to afford her consultation fee. Although he couldn't credit that a sensible woman like Kate would resort to visiting a fortune-teller, he needed to see her, and so that was where he headed.

Ever since the resolution of the Drysdale case, Kate had avoided him, steadfastly refusing to see him alone and treating him with cool civility whenever their paths were forced to cross at the agency. All that was left for Alec was to relive the one night they'd spent together, seeking solace in those memories as he tried to discern the mistakes he'd made.

Perhaps he had asked too much of her while promising nothing in return, or perhaps the truth of it was that in his overwrought state, he had forced her down a path she'd never intended to take.

Alec swallowed hard as he confronted that painful possibility. He had always known that Kate was fired by a great ambition; one had only to see what she had already achieved to know how dedicated she was to her work. But he had to believe that she'd meant it when she told him that she loved him.

For most all his life, Alec had held fast to his

solitude. It had been his strength, his armor, but now somehow he'd changed. He wanted more of life; he wanted Kate, even if it meant risking everything. Maybe now that some time had passed, he told himself, and she had accomplished what she'd set out to, there might be a chance for them. He had to try.

Madame Lucille's Temple of Magic was located on the second floor of an unassuming red-brick building on Clark Street. Alec climbed the stairs, knocked on the door and was promptly met by a fierce-looking fellow, swarthy-skinned with a flowing moustache, who was appropriately clad in a turban and colorful Oriental robes. Without speaking, the man ushered him into a large reception area where several young ladies, with faces veiled in spite of the heat, were awaiting their audience with the fortune-teller.

Alec seated himself in an armchair in the corner. After several minutes of discreet observation, he had assured himself that none of these ladies was Kate. She must already be inside. But it was a fair-haired young gentleman who emerged from behind the closed door at the head of the room shortly thereafter, and then Alec decided that Kate must not be here after all. This had to be George's idea of a joke, though Lord knew he'd never shown much of a sense of humor until now.

An elderly couple came knocking then, followed by yet another young lady and a middle-aged man wearing a diamond stickpin in his striped silk cravat. All were duly escorted in by Madame's silent sentinel, who afterward took up his place beside the door, arms folded stiffly across his broad chest.

Alec had nearly tired of waiting. He no longer expected to find Kate here, but his curiosity had gotten the better of him. What sort of powers did this "world-renowned sibyl" possess that she could attract such a well-heeled crowd? he wondered as Madame's door opened and her latest client departed. The sentinel approached him. He was about to find out.

Alec entered the inner sanctum, and the door shut firmly behind him. Heavy curtains had been drawn across the windows, blocking out both air and sunlight, but the room was faintly illuminated by a pair of swinging brass lanterns that hung on chains from the ceiling. The air was thick with a pungent incense; the heat in the small chamber, nigh on unbearable.

As his eyes adjusted to the dimness, Alec noticed that the walls were hung with representations of mystical symbols, and a chart bearing the signs of the zodiac lay upon the table in the center of the room. Madame Lucille certainly had a flair for the theatrical, he thought as he sat himself down in one of the chairs by the table.

Suddenly, she appeared. So fluid were her movements that one might have imagined that she'd emerged from the center of the full-length mirror that hung in the far corner of the room, but Alec was quick to note that she had merely entered by way of a door hidden behind the draperies that hung alongside it.

Noting that her presence had been observed, Madame struck an attractive pose. Her dress was of a soft white fabric, draped artfully in ancient Grecian style, with a filmy train that lent her a wraithlike appearance. Her arms were bare, but for a pair of wide silver bracelets, marked with the mystical symbols that were her stock-in-trade.

Alec was impressed. Even her face was carefully painted to heighten the angle of her cheekbones and give the eyes an exotic slant. Those eyes were blue: a vivid, sapphire blue. At last, realization swept through him like a chill breeze. He recognized this woman. The fortune-teller, Madame Lucille, was Kate.

So she'd been here all along. Alec saw this grand charade for what it was now—yet another of Pinkerton's odd schemes for solving a case. No doubt if he looked closer, he'd find that the swarthy Turkish sentinel was one of the office boys done up in disguise, and of course, George Bangs must have assumed that Alec knew the particulars of this case. Indeed, Alec told himself, he ought to have suspected something like this, and he would have—if his thoughts had not been otherwise occupied.

But none of this was important to him now. What was important was that he would finally have the opportunity to speak to Kate alone. He had the advantage, for her eyes had apparently not yet readjusted to the darkness in the room. "What knowledge do you seek?" she asked in a voice that was deeper and more solemn than her own.

Alec dared not speak, lest he give himself away, but he reached into his coat and withdrew a roll of bills, from which he peeled a ten-dollar note to lay upon the table. Kate swept closer, and he knew that his time had nearly run out. She recognized him as soon as she sat down. There was a flash of fear—and something more—in her eyes, but Alec was ready and caught her arm before she could flee. A sharp pain pierced the heart he'd kept protected for so long as he realized that she could scarcely bear to be in the same room with him.

"I'm a paying customer, Kate," he said, his grip tightening on her arm. He needed her to feel the same hurt that he was feeling. "So look into your star charts and tell me what you see in *my* future."

Kate did not fight him, only sat very still, her face paling beneath the makeup. Her gaze dropped to the table as she sought to escape his accusing eyes.

"You're so damned good at this that I can't help but wonder if you've been deceiving me, too," he revealed, his voice harsh with hurt. "Was it all a lie, Kate? You and I . . . what we shared? Or was it that you only felt sorry for me?"

"Please," she pleaded softly. "Pinkerton will be here any minute. We're expecting someone. If you persist, you'll jeopardize this case."

Chastened, Alec released her, and she rose quickly, too quickly perhaps, for she swayed on her feet and had to clutch at the chair back for support. Alec sprang up at once and caught her up.

"It's the heat," she insisted, before he could even ask. "It's only the heat."

But Alec would not release her. He'd waited too long to feel her in his arms again. He had to make her understand. "You're wearing yourself down. You've committed yourself, body and soul, to the success of the agency and to this dream of Pinkerton's—"

"It's my dream, too," she protested.

Alec knew that he'd erred as soon as he saw the hurt in her eyes, but he had no choice but to press on. "Just hear me out," he pleaded. "Until I met you, I was content to let the agency be my whole life. But now there are times when I think that you and I and all the rest are little more to Allan Pinkerton than tools that he uses to achieve his own ends. You mustn't ever forget that you're a woman, Kate, flesh and blood. You need a life of your own, outside of all this. *We* need to build a life together."

Kate dropped her head, and a wave of dark hair swept across her face and prevented him from reading her expression. "Impossible," she whispered.

"I won't believe that," he replied firmly and brushed aside her hair as he cupped her face in his hands, "and I won't let you believe it either."

The moment his lips touched hers, she responded, seeming to draw strength from his kiss, pressing nearer to him, her hands clutching tightly at the fabric of his coat. Alec felt some of his dissipated confidence returning, and when he drew back, his expression mirrored his triumph. "You see," he whispered, "you do love me, Kate."

At that, she slipped easily from his arms, as if she were more shadow than substance, and edged toward the curtain that offered escape. "It doesn't matter," she told him, the words breathless and unsteady. "Don't you understand? Love isn't enough, Alec, not this time. Please, please go."

There was no time to argue with her now. It would be disastrous if Pinkerton should catch him here like this. But his faith had been restored when he'd held

221

Kate in his arms and felt her need, as strong as his. He would regroup to plan his strategy, he decided, and then he'd be back to try again.

"I've not given up," he told her as he quit the room. "One way or another, I *will* change your mind."

Kate withdrew behind the curtains, sank down into the chair that stood before her makeshift dressing table and buried her head in her folded arms on the table top as she sought to stem the tears burning in her eyes and quell the tremors that shook her body.

She was tired and hot, and she'd been breathing that damned-awful incense all morning long; there was nothing more to it than that. All she needed was a bath and a good night's sleep, and she'd be fine. Lifting her head, Kate inhaled deeply and reached for the cloth beside the washbasin. She dipped it into the tepid water, wrung it out and wiped the sheen of sweat from her brow and her palms and the back of her neck.

The face in the mirror was no longer that of the exotic Oriental mystic whom Kate was supposed to be portraying. Heat and tears and perspiration had melted it into a grotesque mask which was neither Kate nor Madame Lucille. She went to the basin, splashed her face and hurriedly scrubbed away the remnants of her makeup.

Yet even as she busied herself with practical matters, Kate's thoughts strayed traitorously back to the encounter with Alec. He'd told her that they

222

needed to build a life together. God knew it was a tempting proposition, but one that she could not accept. Pinkerton had warned her once that hers was not a job for a woman with ties. And in this, Pinkerton was right. Kate could not give Alec the kind of life he wanted and still have the freedom to continue her work with the agency. And she would never give up her work. Better that Alec should find himself a woman who could devote herself fully to him. He deserved nothing less.

There was no more time to waste on personal concerns, Kate chided herself; she had a job to do. The waiting room was filled with people seeking the counsel of Madame Lucille, and Miss Sumner could be among them, even now. She had to prepare herself.

Pinkerton arrived, by way of the back stairs, before she had finished applying the last touches of paint to her face.

"You look like a wilted flower," he remarked offhandedly, as he came up behind her, with hands thrust in his pockets.

"If you'd spent hour upon hour sweltering in that horrid little room with naught but acrid smoke to breathe, you'd wilt, too," she shot back sharply. "I'm doing my best to repair the damage."

Pinkerton's dark brows rose in surprise, but he did not respond. Kate realized at once that she'd given more credit to Alec's observations about Pinkerton than she meant to. Surely that was why she'd lashed out at him. She turned to apologize. "I'm sorry, Allan. The heat has sharpened my tongue."

"What you're doing here is important, Kate,

believe me," he told her earnestly. "I wouldn't have you waste your time."

"I know that. I've told you it's only the heat," she explained once again, and then sought to lighten the mood. "As for the work I'm doing, you may be surprised to learn that Madame Lucille has spent the morning hobnobbing with some of Chicago's most elite citizens. They seem to put great stock in this astrology business."

"Have you taken down all the particulars?"

"You'll find a list of Madame's clients on the table beneath the charts."

"I've assigned two men to this duty. They ought to be able to uncover enough background information about your clients to make you sound like a credible fortune-teller. As for the future predictions, we'll leave those in your hands."

Just then Madame's costumed attendant appeared between the draperies. "Miss Seaton arrived a short time ago," he informed them. "She has Miss Sumner with her."

"Thank you, Jack," Kate said. "Please see to it that she remains in the waiting room. I shall need to speak with Miss Sumner alone."

"Yes, ma'am."

As Jack's turbaned head disappeared behind the draperies, Kate prepared for her entrance.

"I'll watch the performance from here," Pinkerton told her. "Are you sure you're ready for this? You've committed all of the information from Miss Sumner's file to memory, haven't you?"

Kate cast him a reproachful glance. "Just you watch and see."

224

The outer door opened, and Kate peered through the curtain as a veiled woman was led in. When the door closed behind her, the woman shrank back; then gathering up her courage, she stepped farther into the room. "Is anyone here?" she called out in a light, breathy voice.

Kate chose that moment to make her entrance. "What is it you seek?" she demanded as she swept into the room.

Anne Sumner's reply was barely audible. "I—I wish to know my future."

Kate came to stand with her two hands resting lightly upon the table, astrological charts spread before her. "Then, come here and sit beside me, miss, and I will tell you what you wish to know."

For a moment, the girl seemed rooted to her spot, but then she rushed to the chair which Kate offered her and sank down in a soft rustle of petticoats.

"Throw back your veil," Kate instructed, as she took her own seat. "How can I tell the fate of one whose face I have not seen?"

Miss Sumner obliged, and Kate took the time to study her carefully. Her hair was a froth of auburn ringlets, some of which lay prettily dampened against her brow. The heart-shaped face was as pale as fine porcelain, and she was staring unashamedly now at Kate through an overlarge pair of soft brown eyes. With a beauty such as this as his prize, it was not hard to imagine why Alonzo Pattmore might have been tempted to poison his wife.

"I will need to know the date and hour of your birth in order to cast your chart," Kate informed her.

"Yes, yes, of course. I was born near midday on

November twelfth in 1832. But is there nothing you can tell me now, Madame?''

"You are impatient," Kate replied sharply. "I can tell you that much. Very well, give me your hand, then.''

The girl held out her hand, and Kate snatched it up and examined it closely, running her finger along the lines in her palm. She fixed a look of deep concentration on her face and began: "Your parents are dead. You have one brother, an older brother who cares very much for you. And now I see water, a great body of water, a patch of sail. At one time your brother was a sea captain, but presently he lives on land. He has retired, no?''

Miss Sumner was clearly amazed. "Why, yes. It's true, all of it. But this is remarkable, Madame. Please, do go on.''

"You have quarrelled lately with your brother, haven't you? Yes, I can see that you have. He wants only what is best for you, though; believe me when I tell you this.''

By now, Kate had the woman's undivided attention. "There is another man in your life, one who claims to love you. But I see trouble with that one," she intoned ominously.

"What sort of trouble? Tell me more.''

With this, Kate dropped the woman's hand and settled back in her chair as if exhausted by the effort she'd just expended. "I cannot say now; I will know more once I have looked at your stars. You must come back tomorrow if you wish me to tell you all.''

Miss Sumner was fairly squirming in her chair, eager now for any word of her lover, Pattmore.

Pinkerton was right; she was a superstitious little thing. "Please, Madame. Oh, please try."

Kate brought a hand to her temple and squeezed her eyes tightly shut as she muttered an unintelligible incantation. "Danger, danger hangs over you like a heavy, black cloud," she continued, then paused for a moment to heighten the effect. "I would not trust this man if I were you."

"But he loves me; I know that he loves me," Miss Sumner protested, her agitation growing. "Perhaps the danger has already passed, Madame; perhaps you are mistaken."

Kate shook her head fiercely. "There is a woman, an older woman, who stands beside this man of yours; she will not let him go. The darkness takes her now, but wait, she speaks to me."

Miss Sumner's pretty face had gone quite pale. "What? What does she say?"

Kate leaned forward and grasped her by the wrist her blue eyes flashing. "Murderer!"

The girl let out a shriek and fainted dead away.

Chapter 17

"Mrs. Warne? Please, Mrs. Warne, you've got to wake up."

Reluctantly, Kate opened her eyes and reached out to still the hand that was tugging at her bedclothes. "Cora? What is it? What's wrong?"

"It's them 'guests' of ours. Their little boy's come down with the fever."

Kate threw aside the blanket and got to her feet. The sun had scarcely risen. The room was tinged with ruddy orange light, but Cora was already dressed for the day. Retrieving her wrapper from the bedpost, Kate struggled into it as she slipped on her mules. "How bad is it?" she asked, following the maid out of the room and down the hall.

"Bad enough," Cora replied. "His ma says he's been thrashin' and moanin' all night. Poor thing don't know what to do; she's practically a child herself. Shall I fetch the doctor, ma'am?"

Kate swiped back the dark wisps of hair that had escaped her braid and shook her head. "We can't afford to involve a doctor in this unless we've no other choice. It would be dangerous for all of them. I'll take a look at him first."

The Price family was ensconced in the guest room at the back of the house. Even at this hour, the tiny room was stifling. When Kate went in, she found Caleb sitting in the rocking chair, staring vacantly out of the window, baby daughter cradled in his hard-muscled arms, sweat glistening on his dark skin. Rachel stood beside the bed, fussing over her son.

"Oh, ma'am," she cried, as soon as she saw it was Kate. "Our boy's took sick. Maybe it's a punishment from the Lord—for runnin' away from our master."

"Hush now, Rachel," Caleb ordered. "You know that ain't so."

"The Lord does not side with slaveholders, Rachel," Kate said to her as she came to lay a hand on the boy's forehead. "You may take my word on that."

The child lay very still now, nearly buried in a mound of quilts. It seemed as if he scarcely breathed at all. His eyes were only half-opened and glazed over, his face and forehead hot and dry. Kate's heart sank. The extent of her medical knowledge was a combination of common sense and what little she'd learned by experience, but she knew enough to recognize that this was serious. If it were her child, she'd want a doctor to tend him, but under the circumstances, she dared not take the risk.

"Well now," she said, drawing a deep breath as she turned on those assembled in the room, all of whom were silently awaiting her judgment. "The first thing we need to do is open that window and take off

230

some of these blankets."

"But, ma'am, with the boy as he is, he'll take a chill," Rachel protested, her black eyes brimming with tears. "Please, ma'am, I don't want my boy to die."

"Then, you must do exactly as I say, Rachel," Kate replied firmly. "The fever's too high. We need to bring it down at once. Cora, bring up the washtub and fill it with cool water. When you've finished with that, run down to the ice house and fetch a block of ice, if there's one to be had. As soon as I've dressed, I'll go down to the druggist and see if I can't get a tonic."

Rachel had already begun removing the blankets and was folding them neatly before setting them on the foot of the bed. Kate went to her and grasped both her hands. "Listen to me now. I want you to dampen a cloth in the washbasin and bathe his face and arms and chest with cool water. As soon as Cora's filled the tub, put him in it. Let him soak in the water for a while. That ought to bring down his fever some. Then you're to dry him off, put him back into bed and cover him with the bedsheet—only that, do you understand?"

"Yes, ma'am. I'll do just as you say."

"Good. And try and get him to drink some water if you can. It's important."

Kate left them then and returned to her room to dress. Afterward, she went down to the kitchen, drank two strong cups of coffee to fortify herself while she explained to Dulcie, the cook, all that was going on, then put on her bonnet and started for the druggist's. He was out on the boardwalk, just rolling out his canopy when she arrived.

231

"Good morning, Mr. Henderson."

"Mrs. Warne," he replied, acknowledging her with a slight nod of his head.

"It's a fine morning, but I don't think we'll see any relief from the heat, do you?"

"Not likely."

With this, he turned and went back inside. Kate followed him in, her brow furrowed in puzzlement. Mr. Henderson was usually such a loquacious old gentleman. He always had a tale to tell and never failed to relate the latest gossip to her whenever Kate came into his shop. Yet this morning he was oddly reticent. Perhaps he wasn't feeling well.

"My maid has taken ill with a fever," she explained once he'd installed himself behind the counter. "Is there something you could recommend?"

"Tincture of aconite," he replied tersely, then reached for a small brown bottle and set it before her on the counter, all without meeting her eyes. "It will increase perspiration and reduce the fever. Give her one drop in water every half hour until the fever breaks."

Kate took it up and studied the label. "Thank you. The poor girl hardly slept at all last night."

"Maybe you ought to call the doctor, then." Mr. Henderson cast her a sidelong glance that left Kate feeling markedly uncomfortable.

"She can't abide doctors," she told him. "She made me promise I won't send for one. I'll just try this."

She paid him for the medicine and turned to go. As she was walking to the door, she heard him mutter beneath his breath. "Quite a high and mighty attitude for a maidservant, if you ask me. But I expect she's one who knows how to shut her eyes and hold her tongue about certain goings-on."

Kate might have attributed Mr. Henderson's behavior to illness or an odd bout of foul temper and let it go at that, but when, on the walk home, an acquaintance passed her by on the street without speaking and two neighbors frankly ignored the greetings she offered, she was more than a little suspicious. Had word somehow gotten out that she was harboring fugitive slaves? Surely something had happened to alter the world's opinion of her—or this little corner of the world, at least—and Kate did not care to think what that something might be.

Drawn by the tempting aromas, Kate came into the house by the kitchen door and discovered Dulcie, with sleeves rolled halfway up her meaty arms, the knot of her silver hair slipping down low on her nape. She was in the midst of frying ham and eggs and baking biscuits enough to feed an army. Dulcie was pleased anytime the ladies entertained guests, even "unexpected" guests such as these, for it meant more people to appreciate her superb cooking, and the woman fairly thrived on flattery.

When Kate went upstairs, she found young Ben still soaking in his tub. It did not seem as though he'd improved at all since she'd left him, though, and so, after helping Rachel to towel him off and put him to bed, Kate measured out his medicine—a little less than half of what the druggist had recommended for an adult—and saw that he drank it down.

Cora came up soon after, carrying a small cake of ice in a pail, but breathing heavily from the exertion. "This was all I could get," she told her mistress.

"Paid a pretty penny for it, too."

Kate took it from her and went to work at once with the pick, chipping off glittering shards of ice, which she then wrapped in clean cloths and packed around the boy, beneath the bedsheet. "Caleb," she said, while she worked, "if you and your wife will go downstairs to the kitchen, Dulcie will see to your breakfast. And don't you mind about the children; Cora and I will sit with them."

The young man nodded. "Thank you kindly, ladies. We do appreciate all you've done for us."

While Cora took the babe from its mother's arms, Kate sat down on the bed and reached to place her hand on Ben's brow. She was relieved to find beads of perspiration forming there. All the while, Rachel Price lingered in the doorway, scuffing at the floor with the toe of her well-worn shoe.

"He's a little better, I think," Kate said to reassure her. "You go along now. You must eat to keep up your strength, else how will you care for your family?"

Satisfied, the girl left them then to join her husband in the kitchen, where doubtless Dulcie would see to it that both were well-fed.

"We've done all we can for him." Kate sighed, stroking the boy's round cheek as he drifted off to sleep. "But a prayer or two wouldn't hurt."

"Yes, ma'am," Cora agreed. "Oh, and by the by, ma'am, a package come for you after you left this morning. I took it up to your room and set it on the bureau."

Kate raised a brow. "A package?" she queried. "What sort of package?"

"You go along and have a look at it, if you like, and then go and have your breakfast. I'll keep an eye on the children."

Kate looked from the boy on the bed to the infant in her maid's arms. Both of them were sleeping now; perhaps she could slip away for a while. "Do your best to keep the baby quiet, Cora," she told the girl, as she rose and moved toward the door. "With a houseful of unmarried women, we would be hard pressed to explain a crying child to the neighbors."

"Don't you worry none about that. If she starts to cry, I'll make her up a sugar teat; that's what Mam always did to keep the little ones happy."

Satisfied that Cora had the situation well in hand, Kate made her way down the hall to her room and and saw that there was indeed a small, square box, wrapped in brown paper, lying on the bureau. She stood there, staring hard at it, as the practical voice in her head reminded her that it was likely only something that she'd ordered through the mail and then forgotten: a packet of pills or bottle of perfume. . . . But it had been a long, tiring morning, and for now at least she wanted to recall what it felt like to be a child at Christmas. Snatching up the package, she hurried to the windowseat, dropped down on the cushions and tore at the wrappings.

Beneath them was a velvet-covered box. Kate wasted no time in opening it, and when she had, she drew out a long, braided silver chain from which hung a pendant: a snowflake, wrought of silver, glittering brightly as it twisted in the sunlight. It brought back a vivid rush of memories . . . of the first case she'd worked on for Pinkerton and the masquerade ball at the Tremont Hotel. On that night, her hair had been dressed with fancy hairpins from whose heads had dangled delicate ornaments just like this one. There was a note inside the box, too, and she unfolded it to find that the words were written in a familiar hand.

Do you remember this? I picked it up in the alcove, that night of the ball, after you'd gone. Call me a fool if you like, but I kept it. That night was your triumph, you know. You proved to all of us what you were made of. I never meant to fall in love with you, Kate, but I knew even then that we belonged together. It seems now that you need the reminder more than I, so I've strung it on a chain for you. Wear it and maybe you'll remember, too.

Kate clutched the necklace so tightly in her hand that the sharp points of the pendant cut into her palm. As if she could forget. . . .

If only he would heed her pleas, but he didn't understand. She could never be the woman he needed. He asked more of her than she could give.

Just the same, when she went down to the dining room to join Emma and Carrie for breakfast, Kate had fixed the silver pendant around her neck and was wearing it beneath her bodice. What harm would it do to keep this token and her memories? It was likely all she'd ever have of Alec.

Taking her place at the head of the table, Kate noted that with her entrance, the conversation had suddenly ceased. The ladies seemed so innocent in their pretty linen dresses, china cups poised daintily in the air. But Kate had seen the furtive glances they'd exchanged, and now they were regarding her almost warily.

"Well?" she prompted, wondering what the trouble could be.

Carrie made the first attempt. "It's only . . . well, you ought to have told us the boy was sick, Kate."

"Yes," Emma piped in, "we might have been able to help."

But that wasn't at all what Carrie had started to say, and Kate knew it. "There was no need to disturb either of you. Cora and I have done what we could to bring down the fever. The child is resting quietly for now."

With that out of the way, Kate levelled her gaze on her fair-haired friend, who was less prone to equivocate. "Now, I know that something else has happened, and there's no use in the two of you trying to keep it from me. What is it?"

Carrie sighed and reached across the table to where the morning paper lay. "There's something in here that perhaps you ought to see," she said, and pointing to the editorial page, which had been folded over, she handed it to Kate.

Beneath a small headline that read "FEMALE DETECTIVES" was the following report:

It has been learned that the celebrated local detective, Allan Pinkerton, founder and director of Pinkerton's National Police Agency, has

237

taken into his employ a number of unattached young women with the avowed purpose of training them as detectives. These women have been placed under the direction of Mrs. Kate Warne, who was the prototype for this unusual experiment and has been Mr. Pinkerton's special "protégée" for the past several years.

No doubt Mr. Pinkerton wishes to put to the test the adage that it is possible to "catch more flies with honey than with vinegar"; but while few would deny the power of feminine wiles, there is no doubt that even the most chaste young woman cannot remain long in the company of thieves and murderers without being perniciously affected. The skeptical among us cannot help but suspect that the canny detective has an altogether different future planned for these unfortunate ladies.

Kate closed her eyes, but it did not help shut out the hateful words. Three years of her life she'd worked, and for what? To be accused of being nothing more than Allan Pinkerton's mistress? The paper slipped from her fingers as she got to her feet.

"No one will believe it, Kate," Emily offered, trying to sound cheerful for all their sakes. "Not our friends, not the people who know us. Why, I'll bet scarcely anyone will even read it at all."

But people had read it, and they'd believed it, too. Kate understood now why Mr. Henderson had been so brusque this morning, and why her neighbors had stared right through her as if she were made of glass.

The stress of maintaining her composure under

238

the scrutiny of her two companions was wearing on Kate. She knew that they expected her to call up all her strength and laugh off the vicious attack, but she could not. This had been a bitter blow, and Kate was wearied, with scarcely enough strength to stand on her own. Turning on her heel, she quit the room.

Chapter 18

A slight breeze rustled the lace curtains in the sitting room and carried in the sweet fragrance of the roses that Kate had planted in the bed outside, just beneath the window. They were yellow roses, like the one she'd pulled from Alec's lapel that very first night at the theater. He was not the only one with memories to cherish.

As she stood there, Kate pressed a trembling hand to her heart and felt the silver snowflake, cool against her skin. Alec had warned her from the first about the press and what they would make of a woman detective, but she'd not given his words the attention they deserved. She had been too arrogant, believing that she could show the world that a woman could be something more than a man's possession. But she'd been wrong.

Even with all her success, nothing had changed. The report in the paper had made that abundantly clear. In the eyes of the world, any woman not content with those roles society set out for her was little better than a whore.

She did not turn around when she heard the knock upon the door, nor when Carrie entered, calling her name.

"Kate? Come back and have your breakfast."

Kate stood her ground, folding her arms tightly across her breast. "You needn't wait for me. I've lost my appetite."

But Carrie would not be put off. She came up behind her and lay a hand on her shoulder. "It's none of my business, I know," she said gently, "but you mustn't let this weigh on you. In a few days, no one will remember what's been written. What *is* important is what you've accomplished. I've always admired you for your strength, Kate. If not for you, where would Emma and Grace and I be?"

"Better off, by most accounts," Kate replied in a bitter tone that was wholly out of character. She paced the length of the room, then dropped down onto the sofa in a rustle of skirts. "What am I, after all, but a kept woman, who is introducing you to a life of debauchery?"

"None of us believe that," Carrie insisted, following her. "You've trained us far too well. We've become excellent observers—if nothing else—and rest assured, if there were something more than business going on between you and Mr. Pinkerton, we'd have discovered it by now. He's fond of you, yes, and he's pleased by your success because it enhances his own, but nothing more than that."

Kate was grateful for Carrie's cool sensibility. It kept her from sinking still further into a mire of self-pity. Feeling a little better now, she expelled a long sigh. "I've too much on my mind, I suppose, else I'd be laughing over the whole affair."

"There's no mistaking the change in you these past few days," Carrie remarked as she settled beside her. "If there's something troubling you, if you need a friend, I'd be happy to listen and to help if I can."

Kate considered the offer. She'd not had a friend to confide in since she'd came to Chicago. Perhaps she'd worked for Pinkerton for too long, for it made her uneasy to think of sharing her secrets. Still, just now she was feeling so utterly exhausted and overwhelmed that friendship seemed a comforting proposition.

"You know, I think we're very much alike, you and I," Carrie confided, as if sensing Kate's hesitancy.

At last, Kate managed a smile. From the first she'd felt a kinship with this plucky young girl. Oh, yes, she could see that they were very much alike.

Carrie was silent now, as if weighing her words carefully before she spoke again. "It's a man, isn't it?"

"Whatever would make you think that?"

Although she'd endeavored to sound lighthearted, Kate was amazed by the girl's perception and—she could not deny it—somewhat unnerved. Were her feelings so transparent?

"In all the time I've known you, I've never once seen you flustered," Carrie went on to explain. "You manage your work and your life with a calm efficiency that makes the rest of us feel . . . well, inadequate, to say the least. But yesterday as I watched you read the letter that the messenger had brought, I saw a softness in your eyes and a hint of regret. What could it be but a man?"

"There *is* someone," Kate admitted at last. Surprisingly, she felt relieved to unburden herself. "It's not Allan Pinkerton, I can tell you that, but—well, his name isn't important. He is very determined, very persistent. He wants me to marry him."

Carrie's pale brow rose slightly, but she gave no other hint of surprise. "He knows of your connection with the agency?"

Kate nodded. "He claims it will not matter, but I know that it will. He is a man, no less."

"And do you love him?"

The question was unexpected. Kate felt her cheeks warm and promptly turned away, pretending to focus her attentions on the movement of the window curtains, lifted gently by the breeze. "That doesn't matter."

"Oh, but it does," Carrie replied fervently. "You cannot give your whole life to your work. Even Mr. Pinkerton hasn't made such a sacrifice. He has a wife and children to go home to at night. If this man loves you and you love him, you will find a way."

Kate's heart was pounding vigorously. Carrie's enthusiasm was infectious, but she dared not even contemplate such a suggestion. "Surely you can see that it's different for a woman," she protested. "For now, he may say that he understands the importance of my work, but when the time comes, he will still expect me to run his household, to be there at home when he needs me, to bear his children, and I cannot—"

"You think too far ahead, Kate. None of us knows what the future will bring. If happiness is offered you today, then take it and worry about tomorrow when tomorrow comes. That's what I would do.''

It was sage advice, indeed, from one so young, and with all that had happened, Kate could not help but consider.

To Kate's relief, young Ben Price's fever had begun to wane by the time she was ready to leave for work. She gave instructions for his care to Cora, then headed for the fortune-teller's studio on Clark Street, where she spent the remainder of the morning going over the reports that Pinkerton's two detectives had delivered to her regarding the clients whom Madame Lucille was about to entertain.

One by one they came to her, and one by one she sent them away with mouths agape, marvelling at her amazing powers of perception. Pinkerton had arrived in the midst of the performance; Kate noticed the slight flutter of the curtain as he took up his hiding place. She was kept so busy, though, in her shadowy, sweltering sanctum that there was scarcely time for them to speak. He was only able to poke his head between the curtains once, shortly before Miss Sumner's anticipated arrival, and remark in surprise that this fortune-telling venture was well on the way to paying for itself.

Madame Lucille's silent sentinel made certain that Anne Sumner was the last of Madame's clients to receive her audience, and by the time she was shown into the darkened chamber, she had already spent half an hour in the reception area, pacing the carpet in nervous contemplation.

245

"Ah, my dear," Kate said as she rose to greet her. "Your chart has been cast, and your future is set out here before me."

Miss Sumner lifted her veil and hurried to take up the chair at Kate's side. "Please tell me, Madame," she urged.

"I have warned you of the danger and grave troubles ahead. Your life, your very soul, is in peril, but you may yet be saved, if you heed my warning and follow the path I set out for you."

As Kate revealed the dire premonition, Miss Sumner's pretty face went ashen, and her lower lip began to tremble. "Oh, tell me what to do," she entreated. "I shall do whatever you say."

With great flourish, Kate drew up the chart, which was done up in curious markings, and studied it carefully. "It is this man, the one who is your lover," she began, "he has murdered his wife that he might be with you. I know this now, and very soon others will learn the truth. They will hold him accountable for this horrible crime, and if you keep silent, you, too, will be made to pay."

"How can you ask me to betray him?" the girl asked, pitifully wringing her tiny white hands all the while. "I love him, and he loves me. His wife was very ill; he told me so. She was dying and would have suffered greatly anyway. He only wanted to spare her from the pain, Madame. That's all."

"She was not ill," Kate insisted, "not until he began to give her poison. She was growing older; that was her only crime. He wanted her out of the way so that he might take him a new wife, a pretty young thing for him to pet and fondle."

Miss Sumner put her face in her hands and broke down in tears, but Kate had very little sympathy for her, even if her brother was the agency's client. This girl had been amply graced by Fate. Beauty, wealth, a loving family, all had been hers. She might have had any number of fine young men as suitors, but she'd foolishly allied herself with Pattmore: a lecherous, married man, twenty years her senior, a liar and murderer, who'd all-too-easily convinced her that his victim needed to die.

"He loves me," the girl said yet again, as if to reassure herself.

"Oh, he loves your pretty face, your shining curls, your milky white skin, that's all true, but when your beauty begins to fade with age, his affections will fade, too. Mark my words: He'll find another to replace you, and then he'll slowly dose *you* with poison until you are too weak to help yourself. You'll lie there in your bed while he explains to his new lover that you are ill and in so much pain that it would be a mercy to end your life."

"No! Stop it! I cannot listen to any more of this," Miss Sumner wailed, pressing her hands tightly over her ears.

"Do you doubt that he is capable?" Kate demanded, her blue eyes blazing. "Has he not already murdered one wife?"

"Oh, what shall I do? What shall I do?"

Kate eased back in her chair and gave the girl a moment to collect herself. When at last her sobs had diminished, Kate issued instructions in a calm, clear voice. "You must leave the boardinghouse where you are lodged. Go home to your brother at once and confess all that has happened. He will keep you safe from harm. You must speak out when you are asked and tell what you know of the man who has been your lover. Only then will you be free of his evil influence."

"However shall I find the strength, Madame?"

Thus prompted, Kate took up the girl's hand and pretended to concentrate upon the lines in her palm. "I see that there is another man in your future," she said, after a long pause. "He is a stranger to you now, but you will know him when he comes. Trust in what I say; he has been sent to help you."

"But who is he?"

Kate shook her head vigorously. "I do not know his name, but I see him as clearly as I see you sitting here before me. He is not a tall man, but his shoulders are broad enough to carry all your troubles. His hair is dark. He wears a beard, and his eyes are a clear gray in color. Yes, he is the one. He will show you the way. Only through him can you escape this cloud of evil which hangs over you."

Sighing deeply, Kate released Miss Sumner's hand and sank back in her chair, as if drained by this latest effort. "I can tell you no more. The choice is now yours to make."

Miss Sumner got quickly to her feet. "Thank you, Madame. I will do just as you say. I will go home to my brother at once."

Replacing her veil, she quit the room, leaving Kate to struggle wearily to her feet and seek refuge from the stagnant air and stifling heat in the back room that was hidden behind the curtain.

"A brilliant performance," Pinkerton announced

as she joined him.

Kate did not acknowledge his remark immediately. She made straight for the washbasin and splashed her face with cool water before addressing him. "I'm only thankful that it's over. I'm sorry, Allan, but I haven't the patience for Miss Anne Sumner. She's just the sort that gives all women a bad name: spoiled and selfish and seeing only what she wishes to see."

"I can't say that I blame you for your opinion," he replied, a wry smile tugging at the corner of his mouth. "She is an intolerable female. But I don't think you'll need encounter her again. That performance you gave will have all but convinced her to testify against Pattmore."

Kate sank down into the chair before the mirror and began to remove her makeup. "I take it that this means Madame Lucille is officially relieved of her duties."

"Aye, that it does. Unless, of course, you feel that you're making a greater success of this venture than at your detective work."

Kate's amusement died away instantly. "To be frank, I'm not feeling successful in any capacity today."

Pinkerton came to stand behind her, soberly studying her reflection in the mirror. "You've seen the editorial in the *Times*, haven't you?"

"It's naught for you to worry over," she said, a wry twist to her words. "It will likely serve to enhance *your* reputation."

"I'd not want it so, Kate, not at your expense," he replied earnestly. Kate had never thought to see Allan Pinkerton wounded by mere words, but that was

249

indeed what she saw when she regarded him now. "I shall write a reply, denying it all, if you like."

Kate only shook her head. "People will believe what they will. We can't change that. It's best if we let it all be forgotten quickly." The little speech was meant to convince him that she hadn't been affected by this, but Kate's voice faltered as soon as she broached the subject that had been on her mind all morning. "But—what must your family think?"

"You needn't worry yourself about that," he assured her. "My Joan's a sharp woman. She knows what's what."

A long silence ensued, as if Pinkerton was contemplating further, and then he turned his back on her and crossed to the opposite end of the room, preventing her from reading his expression. "I do fear the children might not understand, though. They're at an impressionable age, and I'm away from home for so much of the time that they're liable to believe that it's not always on account of business . . ."

Kate scowled and tossed her washcloth into the water, creating a wave that sloshed over the basin and across the polished surface of the dressing table. "I don't like this role I'm being made to play."

Irritated now, she got to her feet and reached to mop up the spill with a towel.

"You've known all along that something like this could happen," Pinkerton reminded her. "It's only a wonder they've waited this long to launch their attack. But it's always seemed to me that—well, I never thought you cared what anyone thought."

"I've never been accused of being any man's

mistress before," she retorted. "I told myself it wouldn't matter, but now that it's happened— it's . . . degrading, Allan. Why does everyone choose to believe that if a woman achieves any measure of success, she must have bartered her body to get it?"

"Because that's been the way of the world for thousands of years—and likely will continue to be so."

Clearly Pinkerton considered this only a philosophical question; but to Kate it was quite personal, and his reply cut her deeply. "Then, all along I've been wasting my time," she shot back. "Maybe it would be for the best if I resigned."

"What?" He turned on her now, surprised and angered by her attitude. "If you're going to give up because one newspaper printed the opinion of one evil-minded gossip, then you've not half the strength I've given you credit for, Kate Warne. What about all you've accomplished? What about all the good you've done?"

But Kate was not to be goaded by his gibes. She turned away and settled once more into her chair. "You're right. I haven't the strength, Allan. Let someone else take over. You don't need me; you've Carrie and Grace and Emma. Any one of them can do what I do. I'm tired of being the pioneer, the *woman* detective."

Kate was thinking of Alec now and the life that they could have together. There was nothing standing in her way, except her own childish fear of being hurt. But Alec Dalton was not at all the same man as Henry Warne had been. She and Alec were friends. They'd worked together, learned to trust one an-

251

other, and much as she'd tried to deny it, their love was a powerful bond. If she wanted, she could be a wife to him, raise their children. She hadn't realized before how badly she wanted it.

As if he sensed that he was losing the battle, Pinkerton returned to her side. Catching up her hands, he drew her to her feet, making her face him. "Aye, lass, you're bound to get tired," he said, his tone soothing now, "if you insist on dragging the whole of womanhood along whene'er you take a step. You ought to have seen enough of the world by now to know that most women don't care. They're content with their lot, and they'll be your most vicious critics if you don't choose to conform. Do what you do for your own sake. Let the others follow if they will, but in the name of heaven, don't let them hold you back!"

Pinkerton's grip on her hands had tightened, and his gaze cut through her like a knife. In that instant, Kate was convinced that he could read her thoughts, that he knew what she was contemplating, but still she could not look away.

"I need you, Kate," he insisted. "The first time you walked into my office, and I saw the fire in those blue eyes of yours, I knew that you were different. No other woman could do what you have done for me. You must promise me that you'll never talk of leaving again."

It took all the strength she could muster to shut her eyes against him. "Please, Allan," she implored, "please don't press. I'm hot and I'm tired and I can't promise you anything right now."

Reluctantly, he released her and stepped back

awkwardly, clearing his throat as if he'd realized that he'd gone too far. "I'll leave you to change your clothes, then. Go home and get some rest. You'll feel better after a good night's sleep, and we'll talk in the morning."

Kate watched him leave by the back door and breathed a sigh of relief when she was at last alone.

Chapter 19

"I need you, Kate. The first time you walked into my office, and I saw the fire in those blue eyes of yours, I knew that you were different. . . . No other woman could do what you have done for me. . . . You must promise me that you'll never talk of leaving again."

From behind the heavy draperies, Alec listened to Pinkerton pleading with Kate, and the knot in his stomach twisted tighter all the while. He cursed his hand for reaching out to separate the curtains, so that he might peer inside. He cursed himself for drawing nearer that he might spy upon them. And when he saw them, hand-in-hand, eyes locked in an intimate exchange, he still could scarcely believe it.

He let the curtain fall back and turned away as his mind sought out the words he'd read in the article in this morning's *Times*. He'd never really believed that there was any truth to it. In fact, that was why he'd come here—to offer comfort to Kate. But how could he have mistaken what he'd seen with his own two eyes?

Stunned, Alec sank into one of the chairs that stood before the table and sat there for a long while with his head resting heavily in his hands. It was as if for all this time he'd been walking through a heavy fog, unsure of everything around him, and now finally that fog had lifted, making it all painfully clear.

Kate had been putting him off for months, telling him that there was no hope for them. He'd suspected that she was hesitant to give her heart for some private reason. She had been married before, after all; and she never spoke of the husband she'd lost. Then, too, as he himself had pointed out to her, her job with the agency left her too little time for her personal life. But with all that they'd shared, Alec would not have believed that Kate's heart was engaged elsewhere. He'd never have imagined that she and Allan Pinkerton—

Rage welled in him, and unable to contain it any longer, he smote both his fists heavily upon the table. This careless action upset the tall brass vase that stood in the center, and he watched in dull surprise as it rolled lazily across the scattering of astrological charts, then clattered onto the floor.

He lifted himself out of the chair and bent down to retrieve it. He was still on one knee when he looked up to see that Kate had come in and was standing before him, looking painfully fragile, yet lovelier than ever. She had put up her hair and changed into a summery frock of pale blue linen, and her face was flush with color.

"Alec?"

The question was plain enough. She had not expected to see him there, but he offered her no explanation, only got to his feet and stood silently—with the vase in his hand and the look of a guilty schoolboy written across his face.

She conjured up a pensive smile for him. "I'm glad you've come. We need to talk."

For a moment he was pleased, but the memory of what he had seen and heard just a short time before rushed over him and soured the feeling. He returned the vase to the table, drew a steadying breath and turned to meet her.

"There's nothing left to say, Kate. You needn't worry about me badgering you any longer. I understand now why you've been putting me off. You see, fool that I am, I imagined that I was the only man fortunate enough to enjoy your favors. I see now that I was mistaken."

Kate felt a numbness spread through her as the realization set in. "You've seen the newspaper," she said, her voice scarcely more than a strangled whisper.

She hadn't thought this day could get any worse, but as she looked at Alec, she knew that the worst was still to come. His face was that of a stranger, with accusing eyes that glittered like two hard emeralds. His words were hard and hurtful. "Oh, more than that. I arrived here in time to hear Allan's touching little speech."

She shut her eyes, reaching inward for some source of strength to sustain her, but there was nothing left. A small, tight sob caught in her throat as she regarded him.

"You could have told me, Kate," he said, seeming to soften. But then his lips flexed into a hard line, and the muscles in his jaw went taut. "Then he and I might have compared notes."

He let go a harsh laugh, and Kate shuddered convulsively, as if she'd been struck, clutching at the draperies behind her for support with two whitening fists. "But h-how . . ?" she stammered wearily. "How can you believe . . . that I—"

The question died on her lips.

Whatever the truth was, it didn't matter anymore. Alec had found a reason to close himself off again, and the instincts that had motivated him for so long before Kate Warne appeared in his life seized control. "No matter," he replied, careful to keep his voice even, all trace of emotion buried deep within. "I concede to the better man."

As he turned and headed for the door, Kate cried out wildly. "Alec!"

With his hand wrapped tightly around the knob, he hesitated, looking back to see the desperation in her paling face and one silver tear, which had slipped out and was slanting across her cheek.

She was so good at deception. He couldn't forget that. If only she'd say the words, if only she'd say, "I love you." He had to hear it from her, before he could risk any more.

"Tell me not to believe it, Kate," he begged her, letting down his guard for an instant. "Tell me it's a lie."

Kate would not deny it. She'd been prepared to give up everything for him, but tonight he'd proven that in spite of all they'd been through, he did not trust her. She remained silent, closing herself off from him

258

as completely as if she'd quit the room.

Alec dropped his head, turned and walked away.

The dawn was a murky one, obscured by the fog, which had come in with the tide off the waters of the lake. A fine gray mist softened the landscape and made the summer air almost too heavy to breathe. The city was as still as a churchyard.

Kate woke with a throbbing headache, and the pressure only increased as she tried to lift her head from the pillow. Nevertheless, she dragged herself out of bed, dressed hurriedly, and swallowed two cups of coffee along with a packet of headache powders before making her way across Washington Street to the agency offices. If she kept busy with her work, she told herself, her mind would not be tempted to stray to yesterday's painful encounter with Alec.

As she climbed the stairs to the office, it struck her that there was every chance he would be there. She did not relish having to confront him again. There was nothing more to be said between them. And yet—although she would never have admitted it—there was still, buried deep within her, a small kernel of hope that she would arrive to find him waiting there to apologize for all the awful things that he'd accused her of. To her relief—and dismay—she found his office darkened and empty as she passed it by.

Once Kate had settled in, Pinkerton did not wait long to approach her. She'd only just opened the file on the Sumner case that was sitting in the center of her desk and begun to peruse the papers when he knocked briskly and entered, shutting the door behind him.

"You'll be pleased to know that the doctor's analyses have shown that Mrs. Pattmore was poisoned," he began, "and we've obtained a sworn statement from Miss Sumner attesting to Pattmore's guilt."

Kate managed a weak smile. "That is good news. I shall send a note at once recalling Miss Seaton."

"And I've arranged passage for your 'houseguests' on board a train bound for Detroit and then on to Canada. Have them ready this evening; I'll send a carriage."

Kate acknowledged his instructions with a slight nod, then returned her attention to the papers on her desk, kneading her brow all the while. Although Pinkerton had finished with business, he lingered, regarding her cautiously.

"Are you feeling any better this morning?" he asked, after a long moment's hesitation. "You're not still considering leaving us, are you?"

Kate expelled a deep sigh, and calling upon all the strength she could muster, she met his sharp eyes. "I know I reacted badly to what was written in the newspapers, and I'm sorry for that, Allan. But I'm calm enough now to see that I've worked too hard to give anything up."

"Aye, that's precisely what I thought you'd say," Pinkerton replied. He looked pleased and perhaps just a bit relieved when he turned to leave.

"Allan?" Kate called after him, swallowing hard as she sought to disguise the desperation in her voice. "I neard that Alec was in town—"

"He was, but only for a few days. He came to me early this morning and requested an out-of-town assignment. 'Tis odd, don't you think?"

Why she'd suddenly felt compelled to ask about Alec, Kate couldn't say, but now she was sorry that she had. A dull, heavy ache gripped her heart. "It's been an awful summer," she remarked, not wishing to discuss it further. "Maybe he can't take the heat."

"He seemed cool enough to me—cold, in fact. I've sent him to Buffalo on the trail of a forger, but I must remember to have a talk with him when he returns."

Kate wasn't worried. By the time Alec returned to Chicago, he'd have buried all his personal feelings deep within, just as Kate was learning to. Pinkerton had trained them both too well.

The inhabitants of the city had been waiting for weeks for relief from the summer's heat, and it came at last that evening as storms rolled in from the west across the plains. First came the lightning. No longer protected by the darkness of the sitting room, Kate winced with each brilliant flash and shuddered as the accompanying rumble of thunder vibrated deep in her chest. As raindrops began to spatter against the raised window sash and dampen the lace curtains, she clung tighter still to the soft brown bundle in her arms and hummed snatches of a vaguely remembered lullaby from her own childhood.

The babe in her arms snuggled closer in reply, reaching out to coil her tiny hand tightly around one of Kate's fingers, and all at once, Kate was over-

261

powered by a painful mix of longing and regret. She hated tears. They were a visible sign of a woman's weakness, and she'd always sought to suppress them; but she could do nothing to stem those that spilled out over her cheeks now. Someone had told her once that the most important job a woman could have was as a wife and mother. At the time, Kate had argued the point, convincing herself that she was different, but now she wasn't so sure.

"Kate?"

Kate looked up in surprise to see Carrie Reynolds in the doorway, narrowing her eyes as they slowly adjusted to the darkness within. Kate swallowed the lump that had formed in her throat but still could not reply.

"Oh, there you are," Carrie said, as things finally came into focus. "Whatever are you doing sitting in the dark, Kate? And with the window open and the rain blowing in?"

She hurried in to shut the window and would have lit the lamp, too, but when Kate realized what the girl was about, she cried out, her voice a harsh whisper.

"No! I've only just gotten the baby to sleep," she explained, knowing full well it was a lie. The truth was that she did not want Carrie to see her tear-streaked face.

"Emma's found a travelling dress and bonnet to fit Mrs. Price," the girl announced. "The whole family has already changed into their new clothes. They're waiting in the kitchen for the carriage to come, so I can take the baby back to them whenever you like."

Kate did not move from her spot on the sofa; she

was loathe to lose the warmth of the child, especially tonight.

"Oh, and there's someone waiting to see you," Carrie added, as if perhaps this news might prompt Kate into action.

"Someone?" Kate echoed, showing some interest at last.

"She didn't give her name," Carrie replied. "Cora put her in the parlor to wait."

Kate dutifully rose up from the sofa, aware of the pull of her stiff muscles and the sudden rush of blood through her veins as she did so. She felt old tonight . . . and very tired. She reached to hand the sleeping infant to Carrie, and as she did so, a white blaze of lightning briefly illuminated the scene. Kate knew that in that instant, Carrie had read the desolate expression on her pale face and seen the glistening streaks of tears, but the girl was kind enough to pretend not to notice.

"If you'd rather, I could have Cora ask the woman to come back tomorrow," she offered gently.

Kate shook her head. "No, it's all right. If she's come out in this weather, it must be important. I'll see her now."

Carrie hesitated one moment more, as if deciding whether or not to speak, then went off to join the Price family in the kitchen. Standing alone in the darkness, Kate was paralyzed by the sound of rushing water as the rain began in earnest, cascading over the gutters and blowing in sheets against the clapboards. But there was no good in hanging on to her memories. Alec Dalton was a part of the past.

Gathering all the strength that remained in her, she shut out the sound, drew a handkerchief from her waistband, and swiped at her tear-stained cheeks. With a firm set to her jaw, she went to greet the guest who was waiting in the parlor.

She found the woman busily admiring the room's decor: the whatnot shelf in the corner with its collection of porcelain figurines, the painted landscape which hung on the far wall, and the pair of carved rosewood chairs. She stood before the windows, with her back to Kate—a rain-spattered silk shawl resting in the crook of her arm, the plumes of her bonnet dampened and bedraggled. There was something familiar about her stance, though, and the short, plump frame.

"Marcella?"

The woman turned, and Kate saw at once that she was right. Marcella started forward as if to greet her warmly, then seemed to change her mind and hesitated mid-stride, with a smile frozen on her face. "Kate," she said and then awkwardly began fumbling for words. "I—I—it's so good to see you. You're looking well."

Although her expression did not reflect it, Kate was quite plainly surprised. She hadn't seen her cousin in more than three years, not since they'd argued over Kate's choice of career. Kate bore no malice, though; she'd never expected Marcella to understand. A smile curved on her lips, and she came forward with both hands extended.

"Thank you," she replied warmly, clasping Marcella's two hands in hers. Looking on her cousin's agitated state, Kate grew concerned. "Whatever has brought you out on such a dreadful evening? There isn't anything wrong, is there? Is Cousin Jonathan all right?"

"He's fine. We're both fine. Oh, Kate, I just couldn't wait another minute to come and see you. I've been meaning to come for such a long time. Jonathan is always pointing out the fine things being written about your Mr. Pinkerton and his agency in the newspapers."

"Come sit down and we'll talk," Kate invited. "We've a lot to catch up on."

She rang for Cora, who arrived promptly to take Marcella's bonnet and shawl, and then instructed the girl to bring refreshments.

"Tea and cake, ma'am?" Cora inquired. The usually garrulous maid had put on a freshly starched apron and was standing solemnly at attention with all the enthusiasm of a newly recruited soldier. Apparently Cora had deduced that Marcella was an important visitor, for she was doing her best to impress her.

"Yes, thank you, Cora," Kate replied, "that will be fine."

The girl left them then, and Kate ushered her cousin to the sofa, where they settled down together.

"I want to . . . to apologize for what I said about this job of yours," Marcella began, and then the words came out all in a rush. "I was wrong, and when I heard what sort of accusations they were making about you in the newspaper, well, I realized that no matter what I'd said before, it just couldn't be true; and I had to come and tell you so."

Kate could not seem to meet her cousin's eyes. Her

emotions were too close to the surface this evening, and she was perilously near to losing her composure. She went on staring evenly at her hands, folded neatly in her lap. "Thank you, Marcella. That means a lot to me."

Cora returned with the tea tray and remained just long enough to set it down on the table beside Kate. "You must be good at this 'detective' work of yours," Marcella remarked as Cora quietly withdrew, shutting the doors behind her. "Jonathan and I always knew you had a special talent for handling people, even our most difficult customers. And I can see you've done well for yourself—living in this lovely house with all its fine furnishings—and a maid."

"The house belongs to the agency," Kate explained, as she handed her cousin a steaming cup. "I live here with three other lady detectives. It's an arrangement that was made to assure our safety and to guard against just the sort of thing they're accusing us of."

As soon as she'd spoken, Kate was sorry. She'd never intended to reveal her bitterness; she did not want Marcella to know how much the lies had hurt her. Before Marcella could respond, Kate put a smile on her face and quickly changed the subject as she offered her cousin a plate upon which rested a thick slice of Dulcie's spice cake. "How is business? Does Mrs. Patterson still come into the shop?"

"All too often, I'm afraid," Marcella replied ruefully. "I only wish our other customers were so loyal. We've lost a lot of trade to those fancy new shops on State Street."

"The city's growing so quickly, surely there are enough customers for everyone."

Marcella shook her head. "That's just it. Everything's changing here; it isn't at all the same friendly place it used to be. Jonathan thought it over for a long time before he decided. He's sold everything, Kate. We'll be leaving for St. Louis in a few weeks."

"St. Louis?" Kate echoed, astonished by the news.

"Jonathan has family there. We'll stay with them for a while, and then head west—maybe somewhere in the Kansas territory. We want to find a place that's not so crowded, a new town, just starting out—where the people are friendly and everyone knows who his neighbor is."

"If that's what you both want . . ." Kate replied carefully, as she attempted to gauge her cousin's true feelings.

"It is," Marcella assured her, a serene smile lighting up her round pink face as she set aside her cup and leaned over to pat Kate's hand. "We're getting on in years, and Chicago is moving too fast for us. This change is just what we need. But I couldn't think of leaving without mending the rift I've made between us."

Kate returned Marcella's smile, her blue eyes bright with tears. "I know you've only wanted what's best for me."

"I never truly understood until now what was 'best for you,'" Marcella corrected. "You didn't want to find love again, nor be a wife and mother. It was hard for me to accept that at first, but I told myself that the Lord always has his reasons. Maybe you were meant to suffer poor Henry's murder in order to fire the need

267

in you to see justice done for others. And now just look at all the people you've helped."

Marcella reached out and wrapped her arms around her younger cousin. "You keep on doing the work that you have to do, Kate, no matter what anyone may say about you, and always know that we're proud of you."

Kate remained still and silent in Marcella's motherly embrace—all the while feeling a dangerous swell of emotion rising in her. She drew a long, steadying breath, only to feel it catch sharply in her throat. There was some truth in what Marcella had said. Kate knew how important her work was, but as Alec had once tried to remind her, there was more to be gotten out of life. She had not gone looking for love; but it had found her nonetheless, and if Marcella believed that Kate could not have been content as a wife and mother, she was wrong—very wrong.

Chapter 20

Philadelphia, Pennsylvania
1861

Alec Dalton stepped up onto the depot platform, rubbing his hands briskly together to warm the blood in his stiffening fingers as he took stock of his surroundings.

The hour was late, the depot of the Philadelphia, Wilmington, and Baltimore Railroad all but deserted now, except for the porter who had just gone inside to share a cup of coffee with the railway clerk and warm his hands by the stove.

The eleven o'clock train for Baltimore stood ready on the track within the cavernous shed, its locomotive groaning impatiently as it belched thick clouds of smoke into the chill night air. The passengers had already boarded, but there was a delay tonight. The president of the railroad had directed that the train be detained until a packet of important documents destined for Washington could be brought on board.

All at once, the rear door of the sleeping car swung open, and a woman stepped out. Silhouetted against the square of yellow lamplight that shone from within the car, it was possible to discern no more than that she was tall and slender, for she was clad in a dark mantle and veiled bonnet that effectively masked her features. But Alec would have recognized her no matter the disguise, and a painful longing overtook him as his eyes perused the familiar features. He hadn't seen her in months—hadn't touched her in three long years. Whenever their paths crossed now, they behaved like two strangers.

With gloved hands resting lightly on the railing, Kate Warne cautiously surveyed the dark interiors of the shed, and when it seemed she had satisfied herself that there was no one lurking in the shadows, she turned her gaze on the depot. Alec saw her stiffen as she caught sight of him, and for too brief an instant, their eyes locked—

A clatter of hoofbeats and jangling harnesses broke the stillness, and both turned their attentions on the closed carriage which drew up to the wooden sidewalk on Carpenter Street. As it rocked to a halt, the door was thrown open, and three men emerged.

The first was Allan Pinkerton, with his right hand shoved deep into the pocket of a rough woolen overcoat and doubtless wrapped around the grip of his pistol. His gruff features were creased in a frown as he scanned the depot with a wary eye. Although he did not recognize the next man, Alec surmised that he must be Ward Lamon, the lawyer from Illinois. He was tall, with an athlete's build, keen eyes, and a dark moustache, and he carried himself with prideful assurance.

The last man to step down from the carriage was tall as well, but lank and long-limbed. He would have appeared to the casual observer to be an invalid, for he leaned upon his lawyer-friend as he alighted and was well-protected against the night air. He wore a heavy woolen shawl draped over his shoulders, a plaid muffler tied at his throat, and a soft felt hat with a wide brim, which shielded his face from the bitter winter wind.

As the men started toward the train shed, Kate swept down from the rear of the car and rushed toward the "invalid." Clasping his two hands heartily in hers, she stood on her toes to kiss his cheek.

"My dear brother," she said in a clear voice that rang out on the chill air, "I have arranged things quite comfortably for you. Come along now, and I'll show you to your berth."

Placing her hand upon his arm, she led him toward the railway coach, with the other men following close behind. They all disappeared quickly through the rear door of the car, with most of the passengers on board the eleven o'clock train to Baltimore never even aware of the late arrival of this invalid and his entourage.

From his vantage point, Alec watched as the driver of the carriage that was still standing on Carpenter Street snapped the reins and the rig jerked suddenly into motion. Before it wheeled out of sight, though, yet another man jumped down from the seat beside the driver and headed for the depot, an official-looking package tucked up under his arm. Taking his cue, Alec strode toward the train and mounted the rear platform.

Once the little group was safe inside the railway car, Kate relaxed a bit. Releasing her "brother's" arm, she stepped away and threw back her veil. "I must apologize for my familiarity, sir," she told him, "but I've made special arrangements with the railroad to reserve the entire rear portion of this car for my invalid brother, and all must be as it seems tonight in order that we should not arouse any suspicions."

"I understand, ma'am," he replied, straightening to his full height as he drew off his disguise, "and as I've told Mr. Pinkerton, for this evening I've put myself entirely into your capable hands."

Kate regarded her charge. The visage revealed to her in the lamplight was raw-boned, but with angles softened by a pair of heavy brows and a dark beard. His was not exactly a handsome face, but a kindly one, and was already showing signs of wearying under the weight of reponsibility. Knowing all that she did, Kate did not envy Abraham Lincoln the position that he would soon take up in Washington.

The train whistle blew three short blasts to signal its imminent departure, and after Alec Dalton had come in and secured the rear door of the car, Pinkerton turned to address them.

"Gentlemen," he said to Lincoln and Lamon, "this is Mrs. Kate Warne, and the gentleman there behind you is Alexander Dalton. They are two of my most trusted operatives and will keep close company with you for the next few hours to ensure your safety.

Now, if you will excuse me, I must go out and keep watch for the signals of my other agents, who have been stationed along the line."

With that, Pinkerton gave a curt nod to his compatriots and stepped back out onto the rear platform of the car.

"Please, make yourselves comfortable," Kate said as she drew back the curtains on the two bottom berths at the rear of the car.

The two men did as she bade, settling in with scarcely a word between them. Kate swept by with a crisp rustle of skirts as she headed toward the front of the car, but did not miss the fact that Mr. Lincoln had drawn himself nearer to the edge of his berth to peer curiously down the aisle and catch another glimpse—as if he still found it hard to credit that this young slip of a woman was one of Allan Pinkerton's celebrated detectives.

With the gentlemen comfortably situated, Kate began to shed her gloves, bonnet and mantle. Casting the garments absently into the empty berth beside her, she reached to smooth back the few wisps of hair that had escaped her chignon and allowed her glance to stray to the rear of the car where Alec stood with arms folded over his chest, an impassive look fixed on his face. In that first unguarded moment, though, Kate was sure she had seen a wistfulness in those green eyes of his as he followed the sweep of her hand, and in reply, emotions she'd kept submerged for too long struggled to the surface, generating dangerous ripples that threatened her calm.

Kate's heart was pounding heavily as Alec came forward to join her. "The station was nearly de-

273

serted," he said in a low voice. "I think our passengers have gone unnoticed."

Kate nodded, but she had scarcely heard his words. As he stepped over to warm his hands by the small stove, the lamplight illuminated his features, and all at once her thoughts were consumed by how much he had changed since she'd seen him last. His stride was not so brisk tonight; the stiffness in his gait might even be called a limp. And he seemed pale; the lines in his face were etched deeper than she remembered. Had he been ill?

It took a great deal of effort to turn away from him, to ignore all the questions that were forming in her mind, but Kate could not allow anything to distract her from her purpose here. The president-elect's life was in danger, and it was their duty to see him safely escorted to Washington. There would be no time for personal concerns tonight.

There was a sudden jerk as the train pulled out of the station, but as it began to build up speed, the gentle swaying of the sleeping car and the rhythmic clack-clack of the wheels on the rail seemed to ease the tensions of the travellers within. With the cautious silence between them restored, Kate and Alec settled themselves into berths on either side of the aisle, and almost simultaneously withdrew their pistols, checking to make certain they were ready to fire should they be needed.

It was some hours later, at half-past three in the morning precisely, when the train rolled into the Baltimore station. As Pinkerton promised, his detectives had remained vigilant all the while, and no sooner had the train squealed to a halt than Alec Dalton got to his feet, crossing the car in a few long strides to assure that the curtains on the rear berths were drawn tightly shut. Meanwhile Kate moved forward, where the curious conductor put in an appearance, peering between the draperies that divided this section of the car from the rest.

"Everything all right back here, ma'am?" he inquired.

"Why, we're just fine, sir," she replied in a honeyed voice. "My brother has settled in nicely. I believe he'll manage well enough, so long as he's not disturbed."

Catching his eye, Kate favored the man with a particularly beguiling smile, laid a hand gently upon his shoulder and ushered him back through the drape, taking care all the while to keep her other hand, and the pistol she held in it, hidden within the folds of her skirt.

She returned alone only a few minutes later and expelled a long, uneasy breath. They must be on their guard now. Here, in this hotbed of secessionist fervor, the dangers would be greater than anywhere else along the route.

Alec had spent more than a month in these parts, masquerading as a Southern sympathizer and gathering information about a plan to assassinate Mr. Lincoln. Kate herself had lately taken up residence in this very city, wearing upon her breast the black and white cockade that was the symbol of secessionist sympathies. Once she'd convinced the ladies of Baltimore that she was one of their own, she had become privy to their secrets, including unabashed boasts of the Rebel assassins who were sheltering here. She knew with a dreadful certainty that if these men were somehow to discover the identity of the "invalid" within this sleeping car, they would not hesitate to attempt to carry out the threats they'd been making for months.

Kate would have liked to leave Baltimore behind as quickly as possible, but because of the absence of connecting rail lines, their sleeping car had to be drawn by horses through the city streets to yet another station and the rail line that would carry them on to Washington. By the time this maneuver had gotten under way, Mr. Lamon had come out of hiding and was pacing the car like a caged cat. He was not only Mr. Lincoln's friend, but also his self-appointed bodyguard, and even with the presence of Allan Pinkerton and his detectives, Lamon behaved as if the president-elect's safety rested solely in his hands.

Mr. Lincoln himself seemed refreshed after his nap, and perched on the edge of his berth with his long legs stretched across the aisle, he proceeded to regale them with one of the homespun stories that were so much a part of his character. "You know, Mr. Lamon here has long been known for his abilities as a wrestler," he began. "Isn't that so, Ward?"

He looked for corroboration to the man himself, but Lamon frowned and kept right on pacing. "One day, back when we were both attending the Circuit Court in Bloomington, Lamon had taken on a challenger and was wrestling outside the courthouse. In the course of the fray, he happened to tear out the seat of his trousers, but he was called into court before he could change. So as he stood there addressing the jury, his misfortune became apparent to all.

"One of our more irreverent compatriots started a subscription paper to get up contributions to buy Lamon a new pair of trousers, and everyone had a fine time pledging their help to the 'poor but worthy young man.'"

Finally, unable to ignore his friend any longer, Mr. Lamon turned to them, a smile playing upon the corners of his mouth and pleasantly transforming the hitherto stern countenance. "And what do you suppose Lincoln wrote down beside his name when the paper was laid before him?" he asked, pausing for effect. "'I can contribute nothing *to the end in view.*'"

Kate was amused, but more than that, she regarded Mr. Lincoln now with a growing admiration. She had to admit she'd wondered how a self-educated country lawyer had ever managed to be elected to the highest office in the land, but tonight she was beginning to see exactly how shrewd a man he was. He had quite purposely chosen this lighthearted story to distract them all—and especially his friend Lamon—from the dangers at hand.

The transfer to the connecting train station was accomplished without incident. Fortunately, at this hour most of the city of Baltimore was still asleep. Pinkerton came in from his watch on the rear platform then and instantly captured their attention, for they were eager for a hint of what was transpiring outside.

"They've put us on the siding," he announced.

"They tell me we must wait for the connecting train to Washington."

The tension within the close confines of the railway car increased with this revelation. Lamon took up his pacing once more, and Alec folded his arms tightly across his chest. And all the while, Kate endeavored to ignore the fact that each additional minute they spent in this damnable city only added to the danger of discovery.

Outside she could hear the reassuringly familiar sounds of the railway depot: conversations carried on between the passengers waiting on the platform to board one of the local trains, a conductor calling out boarding instructions, and the hissing and chugging of a steam engine on the adjacent track. There was nothing at all suspicious, nothing out of the ordinary—until from somewhere nearby there came a deep bass voice, stammering out a drunken rendering of the rebel song "Dixie!"

Kate's eyes went at once to Alec. She only caught a brief glimpse of his hardened features, though, as he reached for his coat, pulled his wide-brimmed hat down low across his face, and went out to investigate. With the discordant refrain still ringing in the air, the interior of the coach grew silent. Kate felt the hair on her nape stand on end as she exchanged a wary glance with Pinkerton, and they took up a position on either end of the aisle.

From without came shouts and the unmistakable sounds of a struggle. A gunshot rang out and then another. It was all Kate could do to keep herself from rushing headlong down the aisle and bursting through the rear door to see what had transpired outside, but she had not forgotten her duty. The hand that gripped her pistol was slick with sweat, but she raised a thumb to the hammer, tightened her hold and kept her place.

All the while, Mr. Lincoln was resting easily in his berth, his legs drawn up to fit. He seemed wholly unconcerned with the danger, or else he was very good at concealing his apprehensions. "No doubt there *will* be a great time in Dixie by and by," he said with a thoughtful smile, as he echoed the words of the song.

With this, Pinkerton went out to reconnoiter, and Mr. Lamon promptly took his place, drawing his own pistol from his coat. Kate found her fears multiplying with each moment that passed in silence. What had Alec encountered when he'd gone out to the depot?

Thankfully, she did not have to wait long to find out. He burst through the door a few minutes later, scowling, his hat in hand. Kate winced as she looked on the purplish bruise forming just below his cheekbone and watched him swipe at his bloodied lip with the back of his hand.

"What was it?" Lamon demanded anxiously.

"Some damned, drunken fool with a loaded pistol and no bloody sense!" Alec retorted as he strode down the aisle, tossed his hat into his berth and began to shed his overcoat. "I had to wrestle him to the ground to disarm him, but not before he'd gotten off two wild shots. Naught for us to worry over, though. No one was hurt, and the station master's taking him off."

Kate went to him then, offering up her handkerchief. Alec took it, dabbing at his bloodied lip, but steadfastly refused to meet her eyes. There was a wall between them now, Kate realized with a growing regret, a wall made thick and strong by three years of silence. Noting again how exhausted he seemed, she felt frustrated, helpless, angry . . . and she craved an outlet for all these confused feelings. Hastily making up her mind, she snatched her mantle from the berth, tossed it over her shoulders and went out to confront Pinkerton.

As she drew up beside him, Kate gripped hard on the rear railing as the car shuddered beneath her feet. The Washington train had arrived, and even now their sleeping car was being coupled. Pinkerton seemed to be concentrating his attentions on the process.

"We'll be on our way shortly," he informed her. "How's Alec faring? He certainly made short work of that drunken minstrel on the platform."

When she opened her mouth to speak, Kate found that emotion had constricted her throat. "You're pushing him too hard, Allan," she said tightly. "He's been working undercover in Perryman for months now with no break."

"Nonsense. Dalton has the constitution of an ox. He wouldn't know what to do with himself if he wasn't working."

"Can't you see it?" she protested, irritation rising in her. "He's pale and hurting, and I wouldn't be surprised to find that he's been ill."

"Ill?" Pinkerton echoed in amused disbelief. "No. No, he'd have mentioned that in his reports. Oh, maybe a touch of the rheumatism, but that's inevitable. Like it or not, we're all getting older."

"He's no more than forty years old and—in case you haven't noticed—wholly devoted to you. He hasn't got any life to call his own. But then that's just the sort of abject loyalty you demand from all of us, isn't it?"

Kate faced him with eyes blazing, daring him to dispute the claim. Pinkerton regarded her closely now, as if she were a stranger whom he was seeing for the first time. When he spoke to her, his voice was soft and soothing. "This is more than business to you, isn't it, Kate?"

The car shuddered beneath them once more, and Kate used the distraction as an opportunity to turn her attention from the question in Pinkerton's keen gray eyes. Staring off into the dusky shadows of the winter night, she sought to collect herself. Her heart was hammering heavily. She knew that she'd revealed too much. She hadn't intended to make any sort of confession to him; but her emotions had gotten the better of her, and that had been a dangerous error—one she'd have thought herself too professional to make.

Taking in a steadying breath, she turned back to him, calmly met his eyes and lied. "Of course not. It's just been a long night, that's all, and I'm too tired to be coherent."

Chapter 21

The remainder of Mr. Lincoln's clandestine journey to Washington passed without incident. Given the precarious state of affairs in the nation's capital, Allan Pinkerton offered his services and those of his agency to the president-elect that very night, but it was not until several months later that his pledge was redeemed.

War had been declared between the federal government and the seceding Southern states, the debacle of Bull Run was still fresh in the minds of the people, and Washington was operating under martial law when Kate received a telegram ordering her back to the capital. The address Pinkerton sent her was that of a modest row house in a quiet neighborhood near the center of town, but even as she approached the house, she realized that its ordinary looks were deceiving, for an army captain wearing a solemn frown came out of the door just then, and as he passed her on the sidewalk, he drew himself out of his thoughts only long enough wish her "good morning" and tip his hat in greeting.

No sooner had Kate entered the house than she was met by a fair-haired junior officer, who seemed scarcely old enough to shave. Even with the sultry summer's heat, he was wearing a heavy blue wool uniform, smartly faced with two rows of gleaming brass buttons, and while he appeared unaffected, a telltale bead of sweat trickled down his temple.

"I'm Mrs. Warne," Kate informed him. "Major Allen is expecting me."

"Yes, ma'am. Right this way."

The young man led her into the parlor and then promptly withdrew, shutting the carved double doors behind him. Kate perused the comfortable surroundings even as she went to stand before the wide table in the center of the room, which served as a makeshift desk and was now spread with maps and piled high with paperwork.

"Major E. J. Allen, I presume?" she said to the man behind the desk, who had removed his coat and was working in waistcoat and shirtsleeves.

Allan Pinkerton stubbed out his cigar in a china dish hidden among the clutter and stood to greet her. "Aye, 'tis my *nom de guerre,*" he explained, with a grin that told her he was glad she'd come. "We're operating under military auspices here. Now tell me, how are things in Chicago, Kate? How is George doing managing the office? I trust you had a pleasant journey."

Kate drew off her gloves and straw summer bonnet and endeavored to reply to his barrage of questions in the order they had been asked. "It was odd to see so many columns of Federal troops marching down

284

Dearborn Street, I must admit, but not much else has changed. I've brought a report from George that will bring you up to date on the agency's business, and letters for you from Joan and the children . . ."

Reaching into her reticule, she drew out the packet of papers and handed them across the desk. "As for the travelling, it went smoothly enough until we reached Maryland. The secessionists are still hard at work there—cutting telegraph lines, damaging the roads and burning bridges. I had to change my route twice because of such difficulties."

Pinkerton's heavy brows knit together as he listened. "Aye, we've begun to think of Washington as an armed camp now, surrounded by the enemy on all sides. Sit down and rest yourself," he bade her. "You must be tired after such a journey."

Setting aside his packet of letters, he waved Kate toward a pair of chairs in a shadowed corner of the room. Only then did Kate notice that Alec Dalton was seated in one of the chairs and had been silently observing them all the while. He appeared to be in better health than the last time she'd seen him. The summer's sun had burnished his skin to a warm bronze. His fawn-colored frock coat and trousers were closely cut, accentuating the athletic build that Kate had always admired: the broad shoulders, the hard thew of his arms and long legs.

He got swiftly to his feet as she approached, and even though she had put up her guard, her heart twisted painfully in her breast when he met her with a wistful smile. "How are you, Kate?"

"Well enough," she replied, her voice softening unexpectedly.

From the words that were spoken, a casual observer might have thought this only a simple greeting exchanged between two old friends, but Kate could feel the undercurrents, swift and dangerous, as she allowed her eyes to linger on Alec's familiar features: the tousled shock of sandy hair that had fallen across his brow, the square jaw, and those eyes, eyes as green as bottle glass. . . .

Pinkerton pretended not to notice the awkwardness in their exchange. When Kate and Alec were both seated, he faced off before them and got down to business at once. "I have called you both here because I have been charged by the president with the task of organizing a governmental 'secret service,'" he said and at length fell into his habit of pacing a small stretch of carpet while he continued.

"The city of Washington is rife with traitors. We need only look to the recent disaster at Bull Run as an example of their handiwork. These spies provided their contacts with a complete account of the troop strengths and movements, and so the rebel generals were able to make their own plans accordingly."

Alec leaned forward in his chair, his brow furrowed in concentration. "I suppose, then, that we are being called upon to 'stop up' these leaks of information," he surmised.

"Just so," Pinkerton replied. "It will be a difficult business, though. There are many in this city with Southern sympathies and powerful government connections. We must be certain of our evidence before we act."

"Where are we to begin?" Kate wondered.

"I have been instructed to concentrate my efforts

on Mrs. Rose Greenhow, a wealthy widow who has, over the years, become a fixture in Washington society. She is well-known as a hostess and has entertained the most important men in the government."

"And *she* is our chief suspect?" Alec remarked, brows raised in disbelief.

Pinkerton tugged thoughtfully on his beard and nodded. "Mrs. Greenhow has made no secret of her hatred of the present administration and the federal government," he went on to explain, "and it has been proposed that she is using her social contacts to betray the Union.

"She has also gathered around her a covey of flirtatious Southern belles—women only too anxious to barter their considerable charms for a piece of information. Several of these 'ladies' have been lately observed in the company of young men with access to military secrets: junior officers and government clerks. We can only guess how much damage has already been done by their actions."

"And I imagine you would like me to infiltrate this little circle of spies," Kate piped in.

"I shall keep a close eye on Mrs. Greenhow myself," Pinkerton told her. "But it ought not to be difficult for you to pose as a Southern lady, and make use of those contacts you made during your work in Baltimore to gain an introduction to this circle and see what they're up to."

Alec sighed heavily, but there was no missing the twinkle in his eye. "All that's left for me, I suppose, is to represent myself as an officer willing to be charmed out of his loyalty. A difficult job, but if it will be of service to my country—"

"That wasn't what I had in mind at all," Pinkerton replied, casting him a sidelong glance. "We have already discovered an individual who fills that role: a young War Department clerk named Arthur Stewart. There are indications that he has been associating with 'disloyal' persons. It is possible that he has already passed on some damaging information to the rebels. I want you to befriend the young man so that we may keep a closer eye on him."

"Where do I find this Stewart fellow?" Alec inquired.

"I've been told that he spends a good many of his free hours in Curry's Tavern on Twelfth Street. You've already established a reputation in Maryland as a Southern sympathizer and an important member of their rebel militia. If you can carry on that role here—buy the lad a drink, engage him in conversation and boast a bit—I daresay you'll make an impression on our young Mr. Stewart."

"Boasting, drinking . . . yes, that sounds like an assignment I can handle," Alec replied with a lopsided grin.

Kate had been watching him closely all through his exchange with Pinkerton, and was very much aware of a change in him. Alec was not a humorous sort by nature. Only when he was playing a part did he shed his reserved veneer and become the "good-natured fellow, well-liked by all." He was playing a part for them now, Kate was sure of it, though why she could not begin to guess.

Addressing them both, Pinkerton adopted a sober air. "Understand that if you accept this assignment, it means accepting, as well, a transfer from the agency into government service. In this matter, you will be operating as federal agents.

"Also, while you may be concentrating on separate aspects of the case, there is every likelihood that you will cross paths. You will need to work together. Do either of you have a problem with that?"

The silence that followed was damning. Kate felt a warm flush creep up from her lace collar to the roots of her hair. Her tongue was tied in knots, her mind occupied with wondering what would make Pinkerton ask such a question. She and Alec had worked together in the past without a problem. Why should he think that things would be any different now?

And then her heart dropped heavily in her breast as she recalled what she'd said to him only a few months before on the train from Baltimore. This development was entirely her fault. She had let down her guard that night, spoken without thinking, and because of it, Pinkerton had come to suspect that there was something more than business between her and Alec. She had thought at the time that she'd dissuaded him, but apparently he had not forgotten. . . .

And now, when she needed most to call upon those skills she'd cultivated as a detective, Kate's strength failed her. She could not bring herself to look Pinkerton in the eye, for he would surely read the truth on her face. Instead, she turned anxiously to Alec, who seemed to be unaffected by Pinkerton's query.

"Of course we've no problem," he replied coolly. "Do we, Kate?"

"No, of course not," she said, mustering as much calm as she was able.

"Good." Pinkerton seemed satisfied as he retrieved his frock coat from the chair where it lay and slipped it on. "Then, I'll leave you two alone to work out the details. I've a meeting with the provost marshal, Colonel Porter, in less than half an hour.

"You may send your reports to this address, in care of Major Allen," he instructed as he headed for the door. With a hand on the knob, he paused. "And good luck to you both," he added, regarding them with an enigmatic smile.

When he was gone, Kate sprang from her chair. Foolish as it might have seemed, she felt a desperate need to put some distance between herself and Alec at once. With petticoats rustling crisply, she swept across the room and settled in the windowseat. And as she gazed out of the window, her eyes sought out Pinkerton's retreating figure and remained fixed on him until he'd disappeared around a corner.

Knowing Allan Pinkerton as well as she did, Kate could not help but suspect that he'd planned all of this, leaving them here alone to sort out their problems. But that couldn't be so. Pinkerton was a sharp hand, and if he truly believed that his two detectives were anything more than friends, he'd never allow them to collaborate on this case. Or would he?

"If you'd rather not work together," she said, casually glancing back at Alec as if the subject were not at all important to her, "I'm sure I can manage to make some excuse. . . ."

Alec did not reply, offering her only an unfathomable stare. Kate felt an inexplicable irritation rising in her, and to quash it, she balled her fists tightly, hardly feeling her nails as they bit into the soft flesh of her palms. He did not care for her; he could not—too much time had passed—but then why did he hesitate?

When she could hold her tongue no longer, Kate turned on him. "After three years of silence between us, what's left to think about?"

Alec got slowly to his feet, still keeping his own thoughts well-concealed. "Are you sure *you* can handle this?" he asked.

The solicitous reply only served to infuriate Kate further. How dare he assume that she was still suffering because of what had happened between them! How dare he feel sorry for her! "You needn't spare my feelings," she spat. "I can certainly understand it if you would rather not work with someone that you don't trust."

And with that, all the old wounds were wrest open. Three years melted away in an instant, and Kate was reminded anew of the hurtful words Alec had flung at her when he'd accused her of betraying him with Pinkerton. At the time, she'd tried to convince herself that it didn't matter, that she'd never loved Alec anyway, but her heart knew differently. And now the pain flooded through her as if she were bleeding inwardly.

Alec's expression had softened, and there was concern in his eyes as he took a cautious step toward her. "I never believed it, Kate."

In response, Kate backed herself tightly into the corner of the windowseat. Oh, why couldn't she have left things as they were? She had not realized it before, but the wall they'd built between them had offered her protection, not only from Alec, but from her own conflicting needs as well. Now, though, with that barrier broken, Kate found herself swept into a dangerous maelstrom of emotion. Only one thought kept her from foundering. Regardless of what he now claimed, when it mattered most, Alec had not trusted her. She had to remember that. "Why? Why did you run off, then?" she retorted. "Why did you let me think—"

In two quick strides, he had crossed the room and grasped her roughly by the shoulders, willing her to look into his eyes. "Why wouldn't you deny the newspaper's claims about you and Pinkerton? I begged you to, but you never said a word. You *pushed* me away, Kate . . ."

With that, Alec released his hold and turned from her. His shoulders sagged. "You were so ambitious, too ambitious to give up the work. Marriage wouldn't have been enough for you. God knows *I* wasn't enough for you."

Kate caught a sharp breath, as if she'd been struck a blow and had the wind suddenly knocked out of her. How could he believe such a thing? "It isn't true!" she protested.

But Alec did not seem affected by her denial.

"I know you had a time of it persuading me not to make the work my whole life," she continued, "but you did, you know. And I'd have given it up at the last—all of it—if only you'd asked me."

Alec did not believe it, although deep inside a part of him longed to. After what had happened three years ago he'd convinced himself that Kate did not love him, not enough to be his wife, and he would not abandon that belief now. "I'd never have asked you to give up anything, Kate," he said, his voice tinged with sadness.

As he turned back to her, Alec fell silent, mesmerized by the vision she made, sheltering in the windowseat like a frightened child, the skirt of her summer frock spread round her like a soft blue muslin cloud, her face flush with emotion. He wanted to kiss her then, to take her in his arms and quell the turmoil that raged in the depths of those brilliant blue eyes—the same bitter conflict between reason and desire that he felt himself each time she was near.

But a kiss would solve nothing. And Kate in his arms without the promise of anything more would be torture, no less. So, instead, he pulled in a steadying breath and put out his hand. "Let's forget about the past now and call a truce, shall we? We're both professionals, and there's a job to be done."

After a long moment's hesitation, Kate took his hand. "Yes . . . professionals," she repeated absently, but her brow was deeply etched in frown, and Alec was convinced that her thoughts were not upon the bargain they'd just made.

Chapter 22

Within two weeks, Kate had installed herself in a comfortable suite at Willard's Hotel. Taking on the identity of Katherine Potter, a wealthy young widow from Atkinson, Mississippi—a locale with which she was only too familiar after her work on the Drysdale case—she managed to secure the acquaintance of several Southern ladies who did not bother to hide their rebel sympathies. Chief among these was Mrs. Helena Nesbitt, a shy Baltimore beauty whom Kate had met during her stay in that city, and Sally Bonham, of the Virginia Bonhams, a stiff-spined spinster, whose illustrious family—as she was fond of mentioning to everyone she happened to meet— had settled Fairfax County more than a century ago. With these two ladies as her champions, Kate was duly accepted into the circle, and her patience was rewarded at last when her friends invited her to accompany them to a reception hosted by none other than the celebrated Mrs. Rose Greenhow.

The affair was to be held on an afternoon in early

August, and the guests included some of the city's most distinguished personages: politicians and soldiers and representatives of more than a few old-guard Washington families with ties to the Confederacy.

Mrs. Greenhow's home was located in a fashionable section of the city not far from the White House, and while the two-story brick building presented a modest appearance from without, inside the rooms were spacious and richly decorated. On this particular afternoon, bowls of fragrant summer flowers graced tables in every room, and the heavy, carved furniture had been polished till it gleamed.

The long buffet tables, which had been set up in the formal dining room, were laden with choice delicacies: artfully arranged trays of fresh fruits and pastries, breads and cheeses, and silver platters piled high with fancy sandwiches. The French doors had all been thrown open to allow the guests access to the gardens and the terrace, where a trio of musicians performed a restful string concerto.

Kate had spent the whole of the morning rehearsing her role, mimicking the musical accent of the ladies she'd met while working on the Drysdale case, and taking special care with her appearance—for she had observed that these Southern belles were a notoriously vain lot. With the aid of a ladies' maid thoughtfully provided by the hotel, she had arranged her soft brown hair into a halo of tiny ringlets, weaved through with ribbons. This style, together with the fashionable dress of rose-colored faille which she'd chosen for its daring corsage, camouflaged only by a pretty lace fichu, gave her the look of an attractive but empty-headed belle—precisely what she intended.

Still, in spite of her disguise, Kate felt a chill of apprehension run through her as she and her two friends sought out her hostess. Mrs. Greenhow was a sharp hand; she'd have to be to have accomplished all that she was suspected of. Kate knew she would have to deal cautiously with her, but if, indeed, the woman was funneling information to the enemy, then Kate meant to find out.

Rose Greenhow stood on the terrace steps, lazily stirring the heavy summer air with her fan, as she beguiled a pair of distinguished-looking gentlemen. From a distance, it was difficult to discern her age. Her hair, which was drawn back into a caul of knotted silk, was as dark as a raven's wing—without a single thread of gray. Her skin seemed smooth and flawless, and the bodice of her violet gown clung to a form that was slender and shapely.

But as Kate drew nearer, she could see that Mrs. Greenhow's appearance was more a credit to her skillful practice of the woman's arts than to nature's bounty. A careful application of powders and paints and a tightly laced corset now helped to maintain an appearance that at one time must have come quite naturally.

"They say that she'll bestow her favors 'pon any man willin' to provide information that she can send south," Helena Nesbitt remarked in a hushed voice while they were still out of earshot.

"Surely not," Kate replied, calling up her most convincing drawl. "Why, it 'pears to me that she has charm enough to get what she wants without surrenderin' a thing. Just look how she's bewitched those two gentlemen."

"The taller one is Senator Wilson," Helena informed her, discreetly casting her eye in his direction, "and the other is Judge Willoughby."

With this, Sally Bonham entered the conversation, nudging Kate's arm with a bony elbow. "Don't be naive, girl," she whispered behind her fan. "Rose Greenhow's always been for sale. This time she's found a worthwhile cause for it, that's all."

"Still," Helena said, winding a silky strand of auburn hair around her finger as she contemplated the matter, "my husband John says that we might not have prevailed at Manassas, but for the information she provided to General Beauregard."

"Well, I don't suppose we ought deny her a place among our Confederate patriots, whatever the truth may be," Kate concluded.

Sally Bonham bristled at Kate's generous remark. "Patriot?" She sniffed disdainfully. "Why, I should hardly think so." But Sally's attitude took an amazing turn as soon as they reached the terrace steps, where Mrs. Greenhow stood alone now, her admirers having drifted off momentarily. "Good afternoon, Rose," Sally cooed. "You remember my good friend, Helena Nesbitt, don't you?"

Mrs. Greenhow greeted Helena with a regal inclination of her head that showed off the arch of her graceful white neck to its best advantage. "Certainly I do," she replied. "I must say you look more lovely each time we meet, my dear. You must tell me your secret."

Helena barely managed to thank her hostess before

casting her eyes downward and tittering nervously behind a gloved hand.

"And this is Mrs. Katherine Potter," Sally said, continuing with the introductions, "who's visiting us from Mississippi."

"This is indeed an honor, ma'am," Kate gushed, her words as thick and sweet as maple syrup.

Mrs. Greenhow flashed a warm smile, but Kate felt the woman's dark eyes inspecting her all the while as if, by instinct, she had sensed Kate to be a threat.

"I've heard ever so much about you and your eloquent defense of our Southern cause," Kate followed up quickly, in hopes of putting her at ease. "You're a very brave woman to speak your mind as you have."

"How kind of you to say so, Mrs. Potter," the older woman replied, still cautious. "I've travelled extensively in Mississippi, you know. Whereabouts do you call home?"

Kate met the challenge coolly. "Atkinson. It's a little town near the Tennessee border, not far from Memphis, actually. Have you ever been there?"

"No. No, I don't believe that I have."

"Well, you ought to visit us some time. The countryside is quite lovely: all gently rolling hills and green valleys. I haven't been home myself since my husband died. But only because I simply can't bear the thought of ramblin' about in that big house all alone. It's so full of memories."

Helena, still standing beside Kate, patted her hand sympathetically and sought to ease her friend's discomfort by changing the subject. "We received a letter from John's mama today. Did I tell you? She sent along a newspaper from home, and it says that the Yankees captured a steamer whose cargo, all legally bought and paid for, was meant for our boys—arms, ammunition, quinine—but now we shall have none of it.''

It was precisely the right thing to say to shift the focus of the conversation. Mrs. Greenhow drew in a deep breath, and in a voice that fairly quivered with emotion, she began an exhortation decrying those "shameful, murdering abolitionists" who now controlled the United States government.

Kate took this opportunity to scan the crowd milling on the lawn to see if any of those politicians present to whom Mrs. Greenhow referred had taken offense, but it seemed as if the lot of them were used to such volatile tirades, for they paid her scarcely any mind at all, interesting themselves instead in their own conversations.

In the course of her perusal, Kate caught sight of Alec. They had both been involved for weeks at opposite ends of this case, and so she was surprised to see him here. Still, she was sure she had not mistaken his broad-shouldered frame, even though he was some distance away, in a far corner of the garden beneath the spreading branches of a tall oak tree.

He wore a pale gray suit, closely tailored to his athletic form, and a waistcoat of fancy brocaded burgundy satin—the very picture of a wealthy gentleman of leisure. He was engaged in conversation with a mild-looking young man whom Kate guessed to be Arthur Stewart, the focus of their investigation.

The contrast between Alec and Stewart was

striking. Young Stewart's frock coat seemed to envelop his slight frame, and more than once he reached to loose his collar, as if half-strangled by his silk neckcloth. Clearly he was ill at ease, unsure of himself here in the rarified air of Washington's elite. Alec, however, had adapted himself to his surroundings as if born to this life.

No doubt he'd sensed her scrutiny, for at that moment Alec turned and met her eyes, and as he did so a hint of a smile played across his lips. Kate refused to consider the possibility that the sudden flash of warmth that spread through her might be in response to his attentions. Snapping open her fan, she briskly stirred the air around her.

No one else appeared to pay any notice to their exchange. Kate's companions' attention was held by the irrepressible Mrs. Greenhow, and Arthur Stewart had his eyes fixed on a certain young lady clad in azure blue who, having caught sight of the two gentlemen, was now heading their way.

The woman was pale and blond and petite, a delicate Southern beauty. Kate remembered having been introduced to her at an earlier function. Her name was Betsy Milbourne. She was one of Rose Greenhow's acolytes and a distant cousin of Sally's. All these old Virginia families were related, it seemed.

Kate tried to deny that it was a twinge of jealousy she felt as the beauteous Miss Milbourne drew nearer to Alec. Still, something pricked annoyingly at her calm as she watched them together—Venus and Adonis—surely everyone could see what a striking pair they made.

Kate soon realized, though, to her surprise, that it was Alec's companion, the mild-mannered Arthur Stewart, who had captured Betsy Milbourne's affections. After the exchange of a few pleasantries, Betsy slipped her arm through Stewart's and sidled closer to him. Enticing him with a hint of a smile, she allowed him to lead her back toward the house, leaving Alec standing there alone.

As Kate's objectivity returned, she considered the likelihood that Betsy Milbourne was encouraging Stewart in order to obtain military secrets from him. All at once she felt the familiar rush of blood through her veins that occurred whenever she followed up a promising lead. This was a connection at last, there was no denying it.

Spurred on by the excitement of her theory, Kate proposed to discuss it with Alec at once, and so she excused herself from her companions and sought him out on the fringes of the garden, where she had spied him last. But as she passed through the hedgerow, she saw that he was no longer standing in the shade beneath the green canopy of the oak tree.

"Pardon me, ma'am, but have we met before?"

Startled, Kate turned and came face-to-face with a lanky, dark-haired young gentleman wearing the dark blue dress uniform of a Federal Army captain. His features were drawn in a series of sharp, angular lines that composed a strong and not unattractive visage. Kate's mind raced furiously, and her heart was thumping hard against her breastbone as she tried to put a name to the face and considered where they might have encountered one another—for he, too, seemed vaguely familiar to her. There was always the danger that she had met him some time ago, while she was working on another case, using a name and identity other than the one she professed to now.

She met his probing, dark eyes only briefly before casting her gaze downward and using her fan to discreetly screen her face from his view. The less he saw of her, the less likely he was to remember. "No," she said in her sweetest Southern drawl. "No, I don't believe so, Captain. I'm certain I'd not have forgotten a man like you."

But as she spoke, Kate finally recalled the occasion of their meeting, and as she did so, relief swept over her like a refreshing breeze. It had been no more than a brief encounter. This was the distracted officer who had come out of Pinkerton's lodgings and crossed her path on her first day in Washington; they had never even been introduced.

"Let's remedy this situation, shall we?" she told him and put out her gloved hand, her anxiety allayed. "I am Mrs. Katherine Potter. And you?"

The officer took up her hand and bowed over it. "Captain Robert Ellis, ma'am, at your service."

"And where do you hail from, Captain?"

"I'm a native Washingtonian—the Ellises have made the capital their home now for three generations."

"So Mrs. Greenhow must be an old friend, then," Kate surmised.

"She's my godmother, as a matter of fact. My mother and Aunt Rose have been the dearest of friends for years," Ellis explained, "though I'm afraid that lately neither of them have been too friendly where I am concerned. They don't approve of my choice of uniform, you see."

"My husband always said that a man must follow his conscience, else he cannot be much of a man," Kate replied, keeping her words sympathetic yet noncommittal.

Ellis seemed to be regarding her more closely now, as if her speaking of her husband in the past tense had opened up a whole new world of possibilities to him. "He must have been a very wise man."

His voice had deepened perceptibly, and Kate could not help but follow his dark eyes as he studied her appreciatively—from the arch of her brow to the full curve of her lips, finally settling on the deep décolletage beneath her lace collar. "If I may be so bold as to say, ma'am, he certainly had excellent taste in women."

"You must stop this, Captain, else you'll turn my head."

With this, Kate fluttered her fan in nervous fashion. It was only partially artifice, for she needed to cool the blush that now stained her cheeks. Ellis was certainly wasting no time. Could he possibly be smitten with Mrs. Potter? Or did the men in Washington all think that any Southern woman who had not fled to Richmond with the outbreak of war was for sale?

When she had recovered her wits, Kate realized that she could hardly dissuade Captain Ellis in either case. She had a job to do here, and for now, she must continue to play the role of simpering Southern belle.

"I think I'd like to go in to the buffet table," she

told him. "Would you be so kind as to escort me?"

The smile he bestowed on her was dazzling. "I'd be honored, Mrs. Potter, that is, if you wouldn't mind being seen on the arm of a supporter of those 'shameful, murdering abolitionists.'"

In the way of a reply, Kate laid a dainty, gloved hand on his arm and lifted her chin bravely as she allowed him to lead her across the lawn to the house. She'd go along for now, but if she were to discover that it was his intention to offer an exchange of information for . . . favors, she would see to it that Pinkerton had him arrested at once. That would be one less traitor in Washington at least.

Captain Ellis proved a persistent suitor. He called upon Kate several times the following week: took her out in his carriage to review those troops given to his charge, invited her to lunch at a very expensive restaurant, and escorted her to the theater. She watched him closely all the while, waiting for him to make his move, but on every occasion, he was charming and never less than the perfect gentleman.

As her suspicions about his intentions began to wane, Kate realized—with no small amount of guilt and some regret, for he had proven an entertaining companion—that she could devote no more time to him and would soon have to make a break. In that regard, fate stepped in to aid her, though; for the very next week, his orders came through, and Kate stood by and watched as he and his company marched across the bridge and into Virginia.

Having bid him an appropriately tearful farewell,

Kate returned to her hotel room, wrote out her daily report to Pinkerton, sent it down to the desk clerk to be mailed, and settled in for the night. Only a few hours later, though, she was wakened by the sound of a muffled footfall, and in an instant the blood in her veins turned to ice. Someone was in her room!

There was no moon tonight, no light by which to see, and all that she could make out was the gentle flutter of the curtains as the night breeze swept through the open window. But she could sense an unknown presence in the shadows.

Careful not to make any sudden moves that would alert the intruder, Kate shifted beneath the bed-clothes, slipped her hand under the pillow and wrapped her fingers around the grip of her pistol. But she had no time at all to consider who this nighttime visitor might be, for just then he made his move. Stumbling out of the shadows, he threw himself upon her and clamped a hand across her mouth to prevent her from crying out.

Kate's concern over her vulnerable position might have been greater had it not been for the pistol she now drew from beneath her pillow. Over the rasp of their labored breathing came the definitive click of a hammer being cocked.

"You sleep with a loaded pistol under your pillow?" a voice remarked in surprise; it was a familiar voice. "Rest assured, this is the last time I'll creep into your bed unannounced."

Kate narrowed her eyes, trying to make out the face that was now only inches from hers. They widened in surprise as soon as she'd discerned that it was Alec. He must have seen the flash of recognition in her, yet he did not remove his hand from her mouth.

"You're not going to shoot me, are you, Kate?" he whispered, lips brushing lightly against her ear. "Not after I've climbed that rickety trellis, had my skin damn-near shredded off by the thorns on those vines and torn my favorite suit of clothes?"

Kate seemed to reflect on her position for a long moment before carefully uncocking the pistol and slipping it back beneath the pillows. Alec removed his hand so that she might speak but still kept her pinned beneath him. He seemed to be enjoying his position—too much. He was smug, his grin too broad, and his clothes fairly reeked of whiskey. Kate's temper flared. "You're drunk!" she accused, writhing against him in an effort to free herself.

Her action had an effect that was opposite the one she intended, though. All at once, a wild excitement flooded through her, washing away the anger and leaving her aware only of the weight of his hard body as it molded against hers and the fact that the hand he'd removed from her mouth was now purposefully kneading the tender flesh at the back of her neck.

"Yes, I am," he admitted. "And you'd be, too, if you'd spent half the night in Curry's Tavern, commiserating with Arthur Stewart over the fair Miss Milbourne."

With that, Alec's assault began in earnest. Kate saw the glitter of determination in his eyes as he bent to nuzzle her earlobe, the warmth of his breath on her neck feeding the hunger she'd kept buried deep within her for too long. Shifting his weight onto one elbow, Alec freed a hand and began to work upon the row of tiny buttons that ran down the front of her muslin nightgown. He had unfastened four or more before Kate realized what he was about. Clearly his dexterity had not been hampered by drink.

Kate brought up her own hand to clutch at the gaping fabric. She was feeling dangerously light-headed now and endeavored to redirect Alec's attention before it was too late. "I—I take it Miss Milbourne has not yet given in to his charms, then?"

"Shhhh!" Alec breathed fiercely against her ear. "Can't you see I'm in no condition to discuss business?"

"Then, why *did* you come here tonight?"

Kate knew at once what a mistake she'd made in asking. Alec drew back, allowing her to meet his eyes, and what she read in them both frightened and excited her. In one swift move, his mouth descended on hers, rousing a fury of raw emotion that charged the air around them. Unable to resist, Kate gave over to her senses, returning his kiss with as much passion as he had imparted, sliding her hands beneath his jacket to clutch at the smooth fabric of his waistcoat as if fearful he might slip from her grasp.

It was the most pleasant dream Alec had had in months. Kate was lying beneath him, her hair spread out across the pillow like a dusky silk fan, the air full of the scent of lavender and roses, her scent. He was kissing her, and as her lips parted under his, he wished that the moment might go on forever.

All the while, he had been cradling her face in his hands, but now he let one slip lower, enfolding the slender column of her throat, marvelling at the pulse that beat frantically against his palm. His fingers played over the links of the silver chain that was

308

draped behind her and then drifted lower still to the place where her nightgown gaped open to reveal the soft rise of her breasts. Here, Alec boldly splayed his hand, allowing each uneven breath she pulled to vibrate through him as well.

Kate was not resisting, but doubt pricked at him like a sharp needle. He felt compelled to see her eyes, to see if he could read some of what she was feeling. Almost against his will, he left off kissing her and drew back. Her skin seemed pale and luminous in the scant light, her eyes wide and as dark as the midnight sky. But try as he might, he could not find what he was looking for in them.

"What is it?" Kate asked, her words soft with passion. "What's wrong?"

Alec felt a sharp chill slice through him as at last it struck him. This was no dream. What was he doing? Much as he wanted her in his arms, he had not meant to seduce her. And then quite suddenly he let her go and got to his feet, raising a trembling hand to his temple. "I . . . we can't—"

Alec watched, cursing himself, as her gentle features were marred by a mixture of hurt and confusion. "Why?" She mouthed the word; scarcely a sound broke from her lips.

"I want you, Kate. God knows how much, but not for just one night—not this time. This time it's got to be forever."

Kate let go a shuddering sigh. She was shaken and ashamed of herself for wanting him so much that she'd been willing to forget all that stood between them. Rising up, she drew the bedclothes close around her to cover herself and hugged her knees

309

tightly. As her heartbeat slowed to normal, she collected her thoughts and found her anger increasing.

"Forever?" Her voice broke on the word. "Damn you, Alec Dalton! What sort of game are you playing? You break into my room in the middle of the night, accost me in my bed and then you tell me—"

He dropped his head, contrite as a chastened schoolboy, and Kate noticed, for the first time, his bedraggled state. His hair was sadly dishevelled, there were stains and several jagged rents in his frock coat, and a long, thin scratch slanted across his cheek. "It's the whiskey, Kate. You know I'd never have done such a thing if I were sober. I—I'm sorry. I came here tonight because I need to talk to you about the case, and the next thing I knew . . ."

Recovering her composure, Kate determined that it was left to her to take charge of the situation. There was nothing to be gained in arguing with Alec, and so with a firm set to her jaw, she got to her feet, refastened the buttons on her nightgown, and reached for her wrapper. "Go and soak your head in the washstand basin," she instructed, "and then if you're able, we'll talk business. Much as I'd like to send you back the way you came, I can't let you climb down that trellis in your present state; you'd likely break your neck, and Pinkerton would hold me accountable."

Kate settled herself in the chair by the window, and although she may have looked calm enough, she had to struggle mightily to suppress the torrent of emotion that Alec had stirred up. Meanwhile he did as she'd bade him, and when he returned, his hair was slicked back, and the planes of his face and his moustache were beaded with moisture. Although his eyes looked clearer, Kate doubted that it was solely the cold water that had sobered him.

Planting himself a safe distance away, near the foot of the bed, he began. "Stewart has gotten it into his head that if he can perform one heroic deed for the Confederacy, then Miss Milbourne will have him."

"And that would be?" she prompted.

Alec reached to knead his brow, as if the action would jog his memory. "He won't confide in me wholly, but I suspect he hopes to aid the cause by giving her the military secrets he is privy to. He's been working in the telegraph office lately; he has access to official dispatches before they are sent to our generals in the field."

"When does he plan to see her next?"

"There's a dinner party at Miss Bonham's country house on Saturday."

"And will you be there?"

"I've arranged to accompany Stewart so that I can keep a close eye on him," Alec informed her. "No doubt you'll be there, too, with your attentive escort in tow."

Kate was stung by the sarcasm in his voice. "What do you mean?"

"Well, you have been seeing a lot of that officer—what's his name? Elmer? Elwood?"

"Ellis. Captain Robert Ellis," Kate shot back. Irritated by his tone, she got to her feet and began to pace. "He's been sent into the field, so I'll be spending no time at all with him in future. And you ought to know better than to think that my interest in

311

him was anything but professional."

Alec shook his head wearily. "I don't know much of anything anymore, Kate. All I do know is that I saw you out riding with him yesterday, all soft looks and smiles, and I wondered if anyone could be that good at pretense. As for me, I'm bloody well tired of pretending I don't care."

Kate faced off against him and met his eyes squarely. "That's only the liquor talking again. You tell me that you care, yet when I needed you to, you couldn't trust me. And you've made it more than plain that you still don't. I won't listen to another word. You'll regret everything you've said in the morning."

There was an emerald spark deep within his eyes that touched her heart, threatening her resolve. "I'll never regret loving you," he told her.

Kate shut her eyes against him as she pushed him toward the door. "Good night, Alec."

Chapter 23

Captain Ellis had apparently not been sent too far into the field, for at Miss Bonham's party on Saturday night Alec found himself seated across the poker table from him. And as if that were not enough of an irritation, he had to reckon with the fact that Ellis's good fortune extended to the cards as well, for the man had won the last four hands they'd played.

Alec was cautious by nature and knew when to fold, but his companion, Arthur Stewart, had been losing steadily all evening, and was now busy scribbling figures on a piece of paper, which he'd pulled from his pocket. When he was finished, he signed the note and handed it over to Ellis.

"That's another sixteen dollars I owe you, Captain," Stewart announced. "Check the figures for yourself if you like."

Ellis gave the paper only a cursory glance before slipping it into his tunic. "No need for that, Mr. Stewart. A gentleman is as good as his word."

Alec had lost interest in the game when his own

fortunes had soured, but nevertheless he'd sat there and watched as his hapless young friend compounded his losses. Now, though, Alec had had enough. The aristocratic officer's company was more than Alec could bear, and so, excusing himself, he strode out of the game room to get a breath of air on the upstairs balcony.

Miss Bonham's family seat was located only a few miles outside Washington. It was a comfortable two-storied plantation home constructed of mellow red brick and sheltered by a grove of ancient willow trees. From this vantage point, Alec could make out their shadowy branches swaying against the night sky, the verdant sweep of lawn, divided by a lighter ribbon of curving drive, and in the distance, the neat, white square of a neighboring farmhouse.

Having had his fill of fresh air and scenery, he went down to the drawing room, intending to blend inconspicuously into the background as he leaned against the mantelpiece to observe the crowd. Here, the furniture had all been moved aside, the musicians were ensconced in one corner, and a number of guests were dancing a lively reel.

It was an inexplicable compulsion that caused Alec to seek out Kate's face each time he entered a crowded room. Tonight he knew she would be here, though, and he found her at once, standing within a circle of ladies who were alternately watching the dancers and gossiping behind their fans. A smile twisted on his lips when he regarded them, but faded away as his gaze focused on Kate alone.

She wore a jade green gown with a high-necked bodice that was fashioned of French lace, and her hair was upswept in a simple but elegant style that flattered her sharply etched features. There was no comparing her with the others. She was a thriving, exotic bloom set down in this cottage garden among the daisies and daffodils, and he felt sure that every man in the room could see it.

No sooner had this thought come to mind when Alec caught sight of Robert Ellis—resplendent as a peacock in his uniform, all brass buttons and gold braid. He came up to Kate, spoke a few soft words in her ear and familiarly took hold of her hands. Kate blushed prettily in reply.

An overwhelming rush of possessiveness swept through Alec, and without even thinking, he crossed the room in a few long strides, just as the musicians struck up a waltz.

"Excuse me, Mrs. Potter," he said, interrupting their intimate chat, "but I believe you've promised me the next dance."

Kate met Alec's eyes with mild surprise, the flush of color that rose in her cheeks the only indication that his appearance at this particular moment was unexpected. When she spoke, though, her voice was steady and clear. "Oh, yes." And then to Ellis: "If you'll excuse me, Robert, I do believe this dance belongs to Mr. . . . Dalton, is it?"

Captain Ellis bowed graciously. "It's late," he told her, "and I must be getting back to my men. But I count myself lucky that we're camped so near here, else I might not have seen you at all. Perhaps if I can convince Miss Bonham to invite you out again, before we march south, we might—"

"Perhaps . . ."

Kate averted her eyes shyly, then nodded in farewell as she took the arm that Alec proffered.

Alec met his rival with a triumphant smile. "No hard feelings, eh, Captain? After all, you've had more than your share of luck tonight."

With that, he swept Kate out among the dancers, drawing her closer, perhaps, than was seemly, but tonight he did not care.

"What was all that about?" Kate asked, sounding more than a little piqued.

"The man's insufferable," Alec retorted. "He's just cheated poor Stewart out of two months' pay."

"He cheated at cards?"

"Well, no. But it was clear that the lad had no head for poker, and Ellis took unfair advantage."

Kate cast him a sidelong glance, and then quite suddenly she broke step in the midst of the dance. "Take me for a walk in the garden," she said under her breath, her words taut with urgency.

"What? Right now?"

She was already beginning to squire him toward the French doors. "Have you forgotten why we're here? Your Mr. Stewart has just gone out with Betsy Milbourne, and we'll lose sight of them if we don't hurry."

Alec groaned as shame flooded through him. His mind had not been on the case. With all that had happened tonight, he *had* almost forgotten. There was no time now, though, for recriminations, and once they'd gone out of the doors, Alec's instincts took over. With Kate on his arm, he strolled the brick walk of the formal garden, acutely aware of the heady scent of mignonette and roses on the air, tension rising all the while as he strove to maintain an outward air of calm.

Kate pressed close against his arm. "Do you see them?" she wanted to know.

At last, Alec did catch sight of Stewart and his lady, some twenty yards away. They had settled on a stone bench, and their heads were bent in conversation. "There," he whispered, "on the bench."

Alec watched as the young couple sidled closer together and joined hands. When Stewart looked up, though, and glanced about in nervous fashion, Alec stiffened. Had he spotted them?

What happened next came with only a soft whisper of taffeta petticoats as warning, and then Alec felt the warmth of Kate's body moving against his as one slender arm coiled around his neck, drawing him down to her. Her upturned face was bathed in silver moonlight, her lips parted invitingly. Alec needed no more prompting than that and eagerly accepted the unexpected gift she offered him. How could a kiss given freely in the moonlight be less than wild and thrilling? Still, Alec fought against himself to keep his head; he would not forget his purpose here a second time.

When finally she released him, he exhaled long and low, ushering Kate back into the shadows of the tall, boxwood hedge. "What was that?" he asked her.

"The first useful trick you ever taught me," Kate explained, still somewhat breathless herself. "Stewart will never suspect us of spying on him. Did you see? He handed her a folded slip of paper."

"Which she tucked into her waistband just as she allowed him to kiss her," Alec finished.

"What are we going to do?"

"I'll get word to Pinkerton, and he can make arrangements to have her arrested tomorrow when she returns to her house in Washington with the evidence."

Kate's eyes widened. "But Betsy has told the ladies that she's not going back to Washington," she informed him. "She's decided to go home to join her family in Montgomery, and her train leaves first thing in the morning. We won't have time to contact Pinkerton and set things in motion before then. You don't think she's clever enough to have planned it this way, do you?"

"Not all on her own," Alec replied, his mind racing ahead to consider the options. "But it's for certain she's not working alone in this. Unfortunately, we have no way of knowing whom we can trust here."

"Then, we've no choice but to stop her ourselves," Kate decided. "If I could make the arrest and somehow escort her out unnoticed—"

Alec's grip on her arm tightened. "You'll do nothing of the kind, Kate. Do you hear me? It's too dangerous. This house is full of Confederate sympathizers, and one wrong move on our part will—at the very least—jeopardize all the work we've done."

"But we must do something. We can't just stand out here arguing in the bushes all night. If the Union battle plans reach Richmond, lives will certainly be lost."

Alec ran an unsteady hand through his hair and pulled a calming breath. Kate was only giving voice to what they both knew well enough. Something had

318

to be done. But if their real identities were discovered, their usefulness to the federal government and quite possibly their lives would be forfeit. Still, one of them would have to take the chance. "If I can procure a horse from the stable," he proposed, "then I may be able to stop Miss Milbourne's carriage in the morning before it reaches the station."

"Steal a horse, overtake a carriage, then dispatch the driver and arrest Miss Milbourne, and all without making your true loyalties known in the process?" Kate shot back. "I'm well aware of your talents, Alec, but there's no less danger in that plan."

Alec knew she was right, but he had no new suggestions to offer. He did not say as much to Kate, though. Instead he proceeded to voice his thoughts aloud in the hope that a feasible idea would come to him. "We need to keep a close eye on Miss Milbourne. As she's leaving in the morning, it's most likely that she'll carry the plans south herself; still, we must make certain that she doesn't pass them on to anyone else in the meanwhile."

Kate's head bobbed in agreement. Alec began to sense trouble, though, when he saw the gleam in her eye. "If you can keep watch on Betsy," she said, enthusiasm building, "I'll be able to go after Robert . . . that is, Captain Ellis. Surely he can help us in this. He and his men are camped at a farmhouse nearby."

"Ellis?" Alec repeated the name with a mixture of distaste and dismay as he realized what she was intending. He knew that relying on the man might, indeed, be their only option, but he could not seem to stomach the idea. Robert Ellis was far too smooth.

He might have gotten past Kate with his polished manners, but Alec could not help but be suspicious of any man who was such a sharp hand at poker.

As if privy to his thoughts, Kate put forth her own argument. "He's a Union Army officer, with his own command. For God's sake, Alec, he's gone against his family to wear a Federal uniform. He didn't have to do that. And the first time I saw him, he was coming out of Pinkerton's house in Washington; they're probably well-acquainted." All her points were strong ones, but it was the last that decided him. "We have no other choice."

"All right," he conceded, "all right. But you stay here. I'll go for Ellis."

Kate did not argue this time, only laid a gloved hand on his arm. "You'll still need to ask Sally Bonham for the loan of a horse," she told him, "and at this hour, she'll want to know why. But there won't be any questions if I ask for a mount so that I might slip over to see Robert; she'll assume it's a lovers' rendezvous."

Alec scowled and swore under his breath. He wanted to dispute her, but he knew that she was right.

"I'm not asking for your personal approval of Captain Ellis," she said plainly. "I'm your partner, Alec, and I'm asking you to trust me."

What could he say? For all that his instincts told him to be wary, he saw the need there in her eyes, and it kept him silent. He had disappointed her so many times before; this time he had to prove that he could trust her.

Although the face she presented to the world was that of a tart-tongued spinster, deep within Miss Sally Bonham's breast beat the heart of a romantic schoolgirl. When Kate approached her with her story, related in breathless undertones, a tear glistening in her eye for effect, Sally was only too happy to help Kate arrange one last tryst with her "lover" before he went off to battle. A horse was made ready while Kate discreetly disappeared upstairs to change into a borrowed riding habit. From there, she was escorted by a maid down the back stairs to the stables, where an elderly black groom pointed out the way as he helped her into the sidesaddle.

"The Union 'campment is over the ridge, ma'am, at Langley farm. Jes' follow the road a piece, and you're sure to come upon it. Ol' Firefly here, she knows the way."

Kate whispered her thanks. The groom slapped the mare's flank, and she was off. For a time the road curved gently, cutting through open pastureland, and when she glanced back over her left shoulder, Kate was reassured to still see the cheery yellow squares that were the lighted windows of Sally's house. In a short time, though, the landscape had changed abruptly. Trees rose up on either side of the road, a canopy of leaves overhead obscuring the moonlight, and the air was thick with the smell of damp earth and mosses. Kate was lost in the deep shadows of the forest.

Reflex made her draw up on the reins as she

adjusted her eyes in order to see the way ahead. All the while, Firefly cantered carelessly through the pools of blackness, but Kate's heartbeat quickened to match the horse's gait as she listened to the whining hum of locusts and the brisk rustle of the leaves in the wind and other, more unsettling sounds, which were not so easy to identify.

It took only a short time for Kate's sense of duty to triumph over her caution. The groom had said that the little mare knew her way, hadn't he? Leaning forward in the saddle, she locked the toe of her right boot behind her calf to steady herself and urged her mount into a gallop.

As Kate rode on, her mind was busy working on the problem of how to approach Ellis and how precisely she would find the words to convince him to arrest Arthur Stewart and Betsy Milbourne for their treasonous activities. So intent was she upon her thoughts that she scarcely noticed the wide scattering of tents that now spread across the valley on her left, lit by the amber tongues of a dozen small campfires.

"Halt!"

Kate pulled up at once when she saw the sentries, and their bayoneted rifles, which were now aimed perilously near her heart. She walked her horse just near enough for them to see her clearly.

"Why, look here, Jenkins, it's a woman," the more sturdily built of the two remarked to his partner in surprise and then lowered his rifle.

"Is Captain Ellis here?" Kate inquired.

Jenkins, who wore a corporal's chevrons on his sleeve, put down his weapon as well and drew off his kepi as if only belatedly remembering his manners. "Ma'am?"

"Captain Ellis. I need to speak to him at once," she repeated, this time with more urgency in the words.

The two young men exchanged glances. They had already decided that Kate posed no threat to the camp; now they must have been speculating about the kind of business she'd come to conduct with their commanding officer at this time of the night, for neither of them seemed able to look Kate in the eye.

"He's up at the house, ma'am," Jenkins replied, tossing his head in the direction of the farmhouse that stood some distance away, near the crest of the hill.

Offering them a hurried "thank you," Kate wasted no more time on them, but turned her horse in the direction of the farmhouse. There, she dismounted, tied off the reins on the post and ring in the drive, and crossed the porch to rap on the door.

Ellis himself answered. He was not wearing his dark blue officer's tunic, but apparently he had not yet retired, for he was still in his waistcoat and shirtsleeves. In the darkened room behind him, a single light burned atop a table that he had been using as a desk. When he regarded her, his dark brow furrowed in confusion. "Kate? Whatever are you doing here at this time of night?"

"I need to speak with you, Robert," she entreated. "It's important."

"Come in," he bade, ushering her into the simply furnished parlor, which served as his office. He offered her a chair. Kate refused it, for she could hardly keep still. Instead, she began to pace from the desk to the window and back again.

"There's something different about you to-night," Ellis observed. "Your voice, your whole manner has changed . . ." And then, after a long moment, the revelation came to him. "You're not who you've been claiming to be, are you?"

Kate turned to him. "There's no time for explanations now. Who I am is not important. What *is* important is that vital military information is about to be handed over to the enemy, unless we can prevent it."

If she had told him that the whole of the Confederate Army had just marched up the drive, Captain Ellis could not have looked more astonished—but Kate knew she had to make him listen. "You must take some of your men at once to Miss Bonham's house and arrest those responsible before they can make good their escape."

Ellis's dark eyes went wide, and he shook his head in disbelief. "Now, Kate, be reasonable. Sit down and explain this all to me slowly. There are procedures that must be followed before I can take that sort of action. Surely you can't expect me to ride up there and arrest poor Stewart without any proof."

Kate shuddered, as though an icy wind had just swept between them; it was a harbinger of imminent danger. She was certain she hadn't mentioned Stewart by name. And then her eyes proceeded to scan the room, and she noticed the open saddlebag thrown over a chair with its contents spilling out, as if Ellis had been packing when she'd interrupted and beside it, a plain cloth greatcoat. A disguise perhaps, for a man riding south?

Ellis followed her eyes, and likely her train of thought as well, for taking his revolver in hand, he moved to stand before the door, barring her way. Only then did Kate recognize the cold determination that was written on his face.

"What a shame, Kate, that you couldn't have remained the sweet, simple woman you were pretending to be."

Chapter 24

Alec drew his watch from the pocket of his waistcoat and glanced at the time: half past eleven. He'd been sitting here for more than an hour, keeping watch over Betsy Milbourne as she danced and flirted and fluttered around the drawing room— a greedy gypsy moth painted up like a butterfly.

Although Miss Milbourne claimed his eye, his ear now belonged to Arthur Stewart, who had regrettably indulged himself in one too many brandies this evening. He'd pulled up a chair only a few minutes before, having made the decision to unburden himself and seek advice from his hapless friend, Alec Dalton.

"I've done all that she asked of me," he complained to Alec, his words slurred with drink, "yet still she puts me off."

Alec let go an exasperated sigh. "These ladies are like high-strung thoroughbreds," he told him. "You need to show them a firm hand."

Alec had to suppress a smile as he considered what

Kate would make of such a philosophy. Kate. He'd tried not to let his thoughts stray to her and the errand she'd undertaken, but now that they had, he could no longer deny the apprehension that gnawed at him. She had been gone a long time. What if something had happened to her, out there on an unfamiliar road in the dark? On its own, Alec's mind conjured up the still-vivid memory of Kate lying in a tangled froth of petticoats in the red dust of a Mississippi road, and a shudder coursed through him. Or what if she had reached her destination and could not convince Ellis to help them? But, no, Alec had too much confidence in Kate's abilities to believe that.

As for Arthur Stewart, he was determined upon making a nuisance of himself. "What if you spoke to Betsy for me, Dalton?" he proposed now, turning a bleary but nevertheless hopeful eye on Alec. "You're a likeable fellow. She'll listen to you. Tell her my feelings are sincere, even if I can't find the words to tell her so myself. I was sure my letter would serve, but I don't even know if she's read it."

"I'm afraid you'll have to face the lady on your own," Alec concluded, pulling himself out of his chair. He was fast losing patience with this spineless, sorry excuse for a man. He could waste no more time on him, at any rate, for Betsy Milbourne—in company with two young lady friends—had just stepped out on the terrace, and he could not afford to lose sight of her.

Excusing himself, Alec followed them out into the garden and noticed the three young ladies at once. They were sheltering near the base of a spreading oak.

328

tree, and in their fine silk dresses, they resembled a clutch of soft-hued wildflowers. Alec kept to the shadows, advancing as near as he could without giving himself away, and when he looked again, he saw Betsy draw from her waistband the slip of paper that Stewart had given her. At once, his interest was piqued.

With her companions crowded around, Miss Milbourne glanced at the words, stifled a childish giggle behind her gloved hand, and with a melodramatic air, began to read: *"My dearest Betsy . . . I hope that you will look more favorably upon your poor servant now that I have proven my worth. There is nothing I would not do for you, my precious angel. I am bewitched. . . ."*

The recitation was punctuated with unladylike snickering, and Alec was struck by how deceptive appearances could be. Beneath the veneer of charm and sweetness, these women's hearts were as cold as ice.

It was not disillusionment, however, that caused Alec's own heart to slam against his ribs with such force that it jarred him to the core. It was the realization that the paper that Stewart had passed to Betsy Milbourne was a love note, nothing more. And now Alec recalled that Arthur Stewart had, indeed, mentioned a note he'd written to Betsy. Still, he knew that Stewart had been carrying the information he'd stolen; he'd told him as much, and in his role as conspirator, Alec had urged him on. But Stewart had not wholly confided in him; he'd not told him to whom he'd been instructed to deliver it. Alec had only assumed that person would be Miss Milbourne.

His mind racing, Alec considered who—among all those assembled here tonight—might have received the stolen plans from Stewart. It was ludicrous to speculate. Most all of these guests bore sympathies for the South. So Alec took another tack. He'd spent most of the night in Arthur Stewart's company. All he needed to do was to concentrate his thoughts, to try and remember if he'd seen Stewart pass a folded paper to anyone else.

The first realization came to him slowly, as a mere prickling of uneasiness deep in the base of his spine, but as his thoughts took shape, an icy wave of dread swept through him. Only one other time tonight had Arthur Stewart reached into his pocket and drawn out a folded paper, and that was when he'd written out the note to cover his gambling debts. And the man he'd handed that paper to was a Federal Army officer, Mrs. Greenhow's godson—Robert Ellis.

Kate twisted her hands sharply back and forth, hoping the movement might loosen the rough hemp ropes with which Ellis had tied her hands behind the uncomfortable, wooden chair. Despite a concentrated effort, she only succeeded in chafing her wrists.

Captain Ellis finished shoving the remainder of his belongings into his saddlebag and, as if aware of her actions, crossed the room to speak to her. "I do hope you'll forgive me for binding you hand and foot, Kate," he said, sarcasm running deep in the words, "but I'm sure you understand that I can't afford to have you setting the dogs on my trail before I've crossed the Union lines."

Kate did not like this feeling of helplessness. She glared at him, wishing the action might somehow do him ill.

"I can't leave until my men have settled in for the night," he explained, "so lets you and I have a little chat, shall we?"

Once he'd reached to remove the cloth with which he'd kept her tightly gagged, Kate ran her tongue across her parched lips and worked the stiffened muscles in her jaw. "I have nothing to say to you," she snarled.

Ellis was undaunted. He ambled carelessly over to the mantelpiece, selecting the ripest apple from the willow basket which rested there, then settled in behind his desk. "Let's begin by discussing who it is you're working for, and how much they know about our activities."

Kate ignored his questions, posing one of her own instead. "What's to prevent me from screaming for help right now?"

Captain Ellis only smiled, and from beneath the papers scattered over his desk, he produced a knife. Its slender blade glittered in the lamplight. Against her will, Kate's eyes were drawn to his. They were two cold, black beads of jet, his intentions unfathomable, and she felt a sliver of fear pierce through her shield of outward calm as she realized how completely she'd been taken in by this man.

"Oh, I think if you were going to try that, you'd have done it the moment I turned on you. As it is now, we're quite alone up here, you and I, and the sound doesn't carry that far down into the valley."

Ellis eased back in his chair, resting his booted feet

on the desktop, and began to deftly peel the skin from the apple with his knife. "You've only yourself to blame, you know. 'Tis you who rode up here at an hour when no decent lady would come calling. My men have no doubt already made up their minds about you, Kate, and even if they should hear any peculiar sounds coming from this house tonight, they'll ignore them. Officers are gentlemen, and gentlemen must have their amusements."

Kate swallowed hard, struggling to maintain the cool composure she prided herself on, and sought a new approach. "But that's just it, Robert," she said, her words soft and soothing. "You are a gentleman, a man of your word, and you've already chosen sides. You're a Federal Army officer. Why betray your men? Why take such a risk?"

Ellis flicked the last of the apple peel onto the floor and then pared himself a thin wedge of fruit. "I might ask you the same question, Mrs. Katherine Potter from Mississippi—or whoever you may be."

The sound of creaking wood carried in the open windows and brought Ellis quickly to his feet. Kate felt a flutter of hope in her breast. Was there someone on the porch? After casting a warning glance at her, Ellis strode across the room, roughly pulled open the door and peered outside. He seemed to stare out into the darkness for a long time, but finally, when he was satisfied that there was no one lurking in the shadows, he shut the door and rejoined her.

Kate's hope dissipated. As he regarded her now, she saw signs that his nerves had begun to fray. His face was taut and pale, and a muscle in his jaw had begun to twitch. "Do you enjoy this little spy game you're playing?" he asked, sounding far more sinister than she could have imagined. "I expect a woman of your talents is much in demand in Washington. What are your duties exactly? Do they have you seduce your suspects, take them to your bed to steal their secrets? Was that what you intended for me?"

Despite the danger in her situation, Kate felt an irrepressible anger rising in her. "No," she retorted. "Such methods are better left to the amateurs at this game, such as your precious aunt, Rose Greenhow, and her like."

There was only a glint of warning in Ellis's dark eyes before his arm flashed out and he struck her face with the back of his hand. "Abolitionist whore!"

Kate's head reeled as a profusion of stars lit up before her eyes. Her jaw was throbbing, and she was aware of the salty taste of blood in her mouth; but still she held her chin high. "Be assured, Captain Ellis," she told him in a carefully controlled voice, "if there were anything I wanted from you, I'd have had it—without you being the wiser and without having to compromise myself."

His dark eyes narrowed as he bent down on one knee and drew nearer to her. Carelessly, he tossed away the remainder of his apple. It struck the floor and rolled unevenly into a corner. "Ah," he sighed, and Kate sensed new danger as his mouth curved into a cunning smile, "but what if there's something I want from you?"

Ellis's face was only inches away now. He was running the tip of the knife's blade lightly under her chin as his free hand reached to pull the pins from her coiled hair. Next he threaded his fingers through the silken mass to send it tumbling down her back. "All the time we spent together in Washington, Kate, while I was enjoying your company . . . you were only waiting for me to betray myself, weren't you?"

Kate's heart beat a frantic tattoo. She would not deny it, but pride would not let her admit that in the end, it was she who had been deceived. It was humiliation enough that she had come to trust him, that she had come here tonight seeking his aid.

Using the knife's point, Ellis traced an invisible line, following the arch of her throat to the lace-edged collar of the borrowed riding jacket she wore. With a twist of the blade, he severed the threads that fastened the top button. It sailed off into the darkness and skittered across the floor. The next three followed in quick succession, and Kate's jacket gaped open, revealing her filmy, muslin chemise.

"I've some time left yet," he advised her. "Perhaps I'll show you the error of your ways."

Snatching her chin between his thumb and forefinger, he forced her to look into his eyes. "You've not half the grace or breeding of our Southern ladies, but you'll do for tonight."

Kate was utterly helpless, and as frustration welled in her, the hated tears were gathering. They clogged her throat and stung her eyes. Unwilling to face the triumph in her captor's face a moment longer, Kate wrenched free, turning her head away. And as she did, she glimpsed a flash of white outside the window at the far corner of the room. Had Ellis seen it, too? But, no, his attentions were centered elsewhere, his knife now toying with the ribbons on her chemise.

Kate strained her eyes to see. Yes, there was

334

someone in the shadows just outside the open window—a tall man in evening dress, his white shirt and waistcoat reflecting the scant moonlight. Alec!

Standing before the window, made to watch the evil unfolding before his eyes, Alec felt no less helpless than Kate. He dare not make his move now, for Ellis's knife was poised perilously near to Kate's throat, and he would not risk her safety. Calling upon all his strength, he kept his head and bided his time.

It had been easy enough until now. With no time for explanations, he had "appropriated" a horse from Mrs. Bonham's stables and ridden across the countryside in pursuit of Kate as if the devil were at his heels. Unlike Kate, though, Alec came armed with the identity of their true enemy, and so when he'd caught sight of the Union camp, he'd hidden his horse in the woods and kept to the trees to avoid the sentries. It was the sight of Kate's tethered mount that led him to the farmhouse.

Alec stood motionless before the window now, fists clenched with barely bridled rage. He tried, but could not drag his eyes away from the scene playing out before him: The sight of Kate's pale profile, her face bruised and bleeding, tore at his heart. But Ellis was not content to merely strike her. He went still further, unfastening Kate's bodice with the point of his knife, cruelly snatching her face in his fingers. As he drew her toward him, Kate's bodice draped open, and a silver chain slipped free, dangling in the air between them. Alec's eyes fixed on the silver snowflake pendant as it glinted in the lamplight. He recognized it only too well. It was the one he'd given her three years ago, before their differences had torn them apart, yet she wore it still. Even at this critical moment, Alec did not miss the significance of that.

When it seemed she could stand no more, Kate turned her head away from her tormentor to the window where Alec stood, and their eyes met briefly. He knew, in that instant, that she'd drawn strength from the realization that he was near. But how was he to save her?

As it was, he needn't have worried, for as Ellis sliced through the ribbons that tied Kate's chemise, Kate made her own move. Before the fabric had slipped from her shoulders, she pulled back in the chair, drew up her still-bound legs, and aimed one great kick at the nearby table leg. Her own chair overturned in the process, but she achieved her intent. The table tipped awkwardly, spilling papers everywhere, then toppled sideways. The lamp that was set upon it crashed to the floor, and as the wick ignited the spilled oil, tongues of fire chased over the floorboards.

It was the distraction that Alec was waiting for. Momentarily dumbstruck, Ellis dropped his knife. When he noticed the flames, he hurriedly gathered up his discarded tunic and flailed it, feebly striving to beat them out. Meanwhile, Alec bounded in the window, crossed the room in two long strides, and catching Ellis roughly by the arm, turned him around.

"I ought to kill you for touching her, you traitorous bastard," he said, and with a grim satisfaction drove his fist into Ellis's face.

It did not end so easily, though. Ellis rebounded

with a vengeance, swiping a hand across his bloodied mouth. Alec was by far the heavier man, but by thrusting a shoulder into his midsection, Ellis knocked him off his feet. Soon, they were rolling on the floor trading blows, oblivious to the acrid smoke rising in a thick, black cloud around them and the ravenous blaze that sought to consume strewn papers, curtains, floorboards—all that stood in its path.

Lying in a helpless tangle, Kate watched as Alec struggled to regain his footing, only to have Ellis once more slam the full weight of his body against him. The impact sent them both sprawling still nearer the searing yellow wall of flame. Too late, Kate saw Ellis's purpose. He had urged their battle nearer to the place on the floor where his knife lay, and now, with surprising swiftness, he reached out to retrieve the weapon. With a demonic grin, he curled his fingers tightly around its hilt, turned on Alec and slashed a wide arc through the air. Kate screamed.

But years of barroom fights and chasing down criminals in dark alleyways had served Alec well. His body was accustomed to abuse, his reflexes as quick as a cat's. Ellis made only a few wild swipes before Alec's hand shot out and caught his wrist in a merciless grip. When at last the knife clattered to the floor, Alec kicked it far out of reach and landed a blow that dropped his opponent.

With Ellis pinned beneath him, he pummeled him again and again, needing to exact revenge for every moment of pain that Kate had suffered. Driven by a blind rage, he continued the attack even after Ellis had given up the struggle. Only the sound of Kate's screams finally stilled his hand.

"Alec!" she cried out shrilly, and her voice broke into a choking cough as she breathed the roiling smoke. "Alec, for God's sake, let him be! I can't move!"

By now, Kate had managed to extricate herself from the chair, but with limbs still bound, she could only tuck herself into a corner on the floor as flames lapped close at the hem of her skirt.

Alec swept through the rising flames with no thought of the danger to himself and was beside her in an instant. Before Kate could so much as draw a breath in relief, he had tossed her over his shoulder and carried her out the front door and across the porch to set her down gently in the grass. With shaking hands, he removed the knotted ropes from her wrists and ankles and gathered her tightly in his arms, scattering kisses across her brow. "Are you all right, Kate?" he whispered urgently. "Are you all right?"

Kate's limbs felt as heavy as lead, her eyes were tear-filled and smarting from the smoke, but as they settled on Alec's bloodied, soot-smudged face, a swell of emotion filled her heart. Choking back a sob, she summoned a smile for him, then stilled his fevered questions by swiftly covering his mouth with her own.

It seemed so simple now, so right, that Kate did not know why she'd been fighting against it for so long. But she'd seen things clearly as she'd watched Alec struggle with Ellis, when she'd thought he might be killed. She'd felt his pain then as surely as he had felt hers. There was no denying it. If he should die, then she would die as well. That's what they had become, each a part of the other. How could they live apart?

Alec drew back grudgingly. "I have to go in and fetch Ellis," he told her.

First, though, he stripped off his jacket and draped it over Kate's shoulders to hide her deshabille. Kate caught his hand in hers. "I love you, Alec. I've always loved you, no matter what I might have said. You do believe me, don't you?"

Alec traced her jaw lovingly with the back of his hand, then fingered the silver chain and snowflake pendant where it lay against her skin. "Yes, Kate. I believe you," he said, "and this time nothing will come between us. This time it's forever."

The soldiers in the valley had seen the smoke by now and were making their way up the hill. While they might well have ignored an errant noise, fire was something that required immediate response. One sergeant who'd perceived the danger barked orders to his men, and in short order, buckets of water were being passed man-to-man from the well to douse the blaze.

Alec had gotten to his feet and was heading for the house when the sergeant called out. "Here, you two. Who are you, and what's going on here?"

"There's a man still inside," Alec explained, but before he could take another step, Ellis stumbled out onto the threshold on his own. He appeared barely coherent. His face was misshappen and bloodied, but he'd thrown his saddlebag over one shoulder and was now pointing an accusing finger. "Arrest these two at once," he ordered. "They're Confederate spies."

After all that had happened, Alec was in surprisingly good humor. "Now there's the pot calling the kettle black," he remarked, winking at Kate with his badly bruised eye.

Kate pulled Alec's jacket close around her and rose with as dignified an air as she could muster. "Excuse me, Sergeant, but my partner and I are federal agents, reporting to Major E. J. Allen and acting under direct order of the assistant secretary of war. Your Captain Ellis is not all he appears to be, and if you'll check his saddlebag or perhaps his waistcoat pocket, I believe you'll find the evidence that will bear out my claim."

Chapter 25

The summons came late in the afternoon on the following day, but Kate still had to drag herself out of her bed to answer the knock upon her door. Her head was throbbing, and she could feel the pull of each strained muscle as she stretched out her arms to slip them into her dressing gown. It was no comfort to her that the face that greeted her when she peered into the bureau glass sported a swollen left cheek, decorated with a mottled greenish purple bruise, nor that the messenger who met her when she opened the door regarded her mangled visage with widening eyes, as if she were something not of this world.

The note informed her that she was to report to Major Allen as soon as she was able, and so dutifully, Kate dressed, concealing her injuries beneath a heavily veiled bonnet, and went down to ask the desk clerk to arrange a carriage. It was half an hour later when she finally presented herself at Pinkerton's door and was ushered into the parlor, which served as his office.

"Well, good afternoon to you, Mrs. Warne," he said, rising to greet her. "I understand my two best operatives got themselves in quite a scrape last night. Come here and let me have a look at you."

Kate threw back her veil, removed her bonnet and obediently went to stand before him. Drawing a steady breath, she tilted her chin upward, ready to accept the chastisement she deserved. The evidence of her rash actions was, quite literally, there upon her face. Pinkerton placed a finger gently under her chin, turning her head so that he might examine her bruises.

"You and Dalton both look as if you'd gone a few too many rounds with a bare-knuckled boxer. Are you sure this wasn't some personal scrap between the two of you?"

The mention of Alec brought a pensive smile to her, but she stifled as soon as she felt the tug of skin that threatened to reopen the cut on her lip. "We've had our differences, I'll admit, but we've never come to blows."

As he regarded her more closely, Pinkerton's own amusement evaporated. "I am sorry, Kate. This wasn't meant to be a dangerous assignment."

"What happened was entirely my fault," she confessed. "Events got out of hand, and I made an unforgivable mistake. I put my trust in the wrong man. I'd seen Ellis coming out of your office and assumed you'd had dealings with him, that maybe he was working for you."

"Aye, I'd called him in, but only to ask him a few questions. A man of his background, with connections to Rose Greenhow . . . you can understand why

342

I'd want to interview him myself. But I could find no proof, not till you stepped in."

Kate cast her eyes downward, features set in deep frown as she appeared to study the hem of her dress. "Till I stepped in and nearly botched the whole affair," she finished for him. Then after a long pause, her chin lifted once more, and she met him eye-to-eye. "I want you to know, Allan, that Alec bears none of the blame for this. He tried to caution me, but I wouldn't listen."

"It's all worked out well enough," Pinkerton observed. "Captain Ellis and young Mr. Stewart have been arrested, and Mrs. Greenhow is being confined to her home under the watchful eye of two of our men. I don't doubt that we'll soon have enough evidence to jail her as well."

Kate expelled a barely audible sigh. "That's good news, at least."

"Let it go, Kate," Pinkerton ordered. "I haven't called you here to scold you, if that's what you're thinking. I've other things on my mind. I need your help."

At once, Kate was aware of the effervescent surge of blood through her body, the familiar stirring of curiosity and excitement that overtook her each time he proposed a new challenge. Not even the dangers she'd encountered last night could change that, it seemed.

But there had been a change in her nonetheless, for her thoughts went at once to Alec. She would speak to him before she took on this new case, she decided. Her heart leapt at the realization that they had a whole future to decide upon. Now that she had put her foolish fears aside, what was there to stand between them?

Alec had said he wanted "forever," and with all her doubts fled, Kate was determined to give it to him, starting tonight. They'd have a late supper in her hotel room, maybe even order a bottle of champagne, and together they'd make love and make plans.

"You're tired after your adventure, I realize that," Pinkerton said, interrupting her thoughts, "but 'tis only a simple task, which requires a woman's touch, and we can trust no one else. I'm sending a courier south who'll carry a new set of codes for my operatives already in place in Virginia. We've hidden these codes in the lining of his waistcoat, but, well, none of us here can make a row of stitches neat enough to finish the job. We need you to sew up the seams we've ripped out."

Kate laughed. She could not help herself. He'd sounded so serious, so solemn. "You want me to sew up a seam?" she echoed. "That's all? Now, there's a task I can handle with ease."

Ignoring her amusement, Pinkerton strode toward a heavy, panelled door that closed off another room, pulled it open and impassively motioned her inside. But no sooner had Kate crossed over the threshold than he himself withdrew and discreetly shut the door behind him.

Kate was perplexed. She looked up to find herself in a small sitting room with the afternoon light streaming in the windows, throwing into stark silhouette an all-too-familiar figure standing there in his shirtsleeves, the sun picking up the golden highlights in his hair. Tossed over his arm was the waistcoat of which Pinkerton had made mention, and suddenly, everything became terribly clear. When Kate spoke, the voice that emerged was thin and confused. "Alec?"

"I'm going to Richmond, Kate," he said, putting on a warm smile as he came forward and placed the raw-seamed waistcoat in her hands.

"You're the courier?" Kate's mind was racing as her hand clutched convulsively at the fabric, still warm from contact with his body and full of his masculine scent. "But Pinkerton can't ask that of you. You need time to rest, after what happened last night, and we need to . . . to. . . . Why didn't you tell me about this?"

"It's only just been decided," he explained. "I'm to leave tonight."

After all the foolish, romantic plans she'd been making in her head, Kate was stricken by the news, but determined to ignore the hurt by focusing her attentions on the sewing basket that lay upon a nearby table. With a trembling hand, she reached out for a spool of dark thread.

"You'll be back in just a few weeks," she said, hoping the confident words would reassure her. "And then after you've finished with business, you and I can . . ." Somehow she couldn't finish the thought.

Alec tried to smile. Failing in that, he went back to the windows and gazed out over the street, as if something there had caught his attention. Kate sensed the hesitancy, so strong within him; she was afraid to learn what lay behind it. "I'll not be coming back, Kate," he revealed at last. "Leastways, not for a while. Pinkerton has decided I'll be more useful scouting the rebels in Richmond.''

Alec watched, his eyes mirroring concern, as Kate's face paled and the spool slipped from her fingers, struck the carpet and rolled lazily to a halt. The waistcoat dropped as well, pooling at her feet. Only a soft, quivering breath escaped her as she turned from him. With shoulders sagging, she carried herself to the sofa, sank down into the cushions and silently buried her face in her hands.

Somehow Alec hadn't expected this. He'd expected her to lash out at him, the way she always did when she was hurting. Anger he could deal with, but this was something else again.

"I have to go," he tried to explain. "You, more than anyone, ought to understand. You've watched me leave before."

When Kate looked up at last, Alec was surprised to see that there were no tears at all in those wide sapphire eyes of hers, only the lost and lonely look of an abandoned child. "This time it's different. This time it's war. The world doesn't need another hero, Alec," she said simply, calmly, "not as much as I need you."

The admission was a hard one for her to make. Kate had always prided herself on her independence; Alec knew that only too well. He watched from across the room as she clenched her two hands tightly together, whitened knuckles the only visible sign of her distress. Alec longed to go to her, to take her in his arms and tell her that he'd changed his mind and that he'd stay. But he could not, and no matter what her heart might have her ask of him now, he knew that in the end, Kate would understand his devotion to his duty.

And then, as if what had transpired between them was of no consequence, Kate got to her feet to retrieve the items she'd dropped, took up a needle from the sewing basket, and settled on the sofa once more, where she began to stitch the torn seam.

"What would you have me do while you're gone?" She asked coolly enough, but Alec did not miss the bitterness caught up in her words.

He considered the question. "Go back to Chicago, if you like," he told her, "or stay and do what needs to be done here in Washington. Just don't meddle in anything dangerous, Kate. Swear to me that you won't. And don't go south. Don't cross the lines, not even if Pinkerton should ask it of you."

Kate seemed to accept his suggestions impassively enough. With head bent over her work, she concentrated upon each tiny stitch she made. But her hands were not so steady as she would have him believe, and without warning, the needle flashed out and pricked her finger. Her whole body tensed as she rose up, cast aside the work and turned on him, her eyes accusing. "If you can't deny him, what makes you think that I can?"

As Alec's frustration increased, he began to pace. "Damn it, Kate, you'll have to! How can you expect me to go off and leave you this way? How can I do the work that needs to be done, if all my thoughts keep coming back here to you?"

"Then, don't go," she said simply. But the wall she'd built so carefully was crumbling, and her composure gave way at last. A breathless sob caught in her throat, and she put out her hands. "Oh, God . . . Alec, please don't go! Not now!"

With that, Alec rushed to her, dragging her into his arms. When their lips met, he drank in her sweetness, filled himself with it, and cursed the world for coming between them. He crushed her so hard against him that he feared he must have broken her bones. Each frantic beat of her heart vibrating against his own reminded him that time was running out, and he would soon have to leave her. Yet for all this while, Kate was surprisingly still. Only when he felt the warm, slick wetness of her tears against his cheek did he realize that she was crying. It did not help to strengthen his resolve.

In his arms, Kate found all the strength she needed. In his arms, she could believe that this delay was nothing, that they'd be together soon enough. They'd waited so long for happiness, what did a few months matter?

But there was something more that she needed to hear before she could let him leave her. "When you come back to me," she questioned, "what then?"

Alec cupped her face in his hands and met her with love reflecting like brilliant stars in those eyes of his, those eyes as green as bottle glass. "Don't you know, Kate, after all this time? All I want, all I've ever wanted is you. I want you for my wife, nothing less."

"And my work?" she murmured, afraid to hope.

He bent to breath a kiss against her lips. "I know how much it means to you. For now, I'll be content to share you with the work, if that's what you want. But when the children come, we'll need to talk again."

"You won't care what the rest of the world says, what the newspapers might accuse me of?"

Alec caught up her hands, squeezing them tightly. "Damn the newspapers!" he exclaimed at the top of his voice. "Damn what everyone will say, and yes, damn Allan Pinkerton, too, if he tries to stand in our way!

"Promise me, Kate," he entreated, his voice dropping to an urgent whisper, "promise me that as soon as this war is over, we'll make a life, some kind of life for ourselves—together."

Kate smiled, and the warmth of that smile left no room for doubt. "I promise, Alec. You and I . . . forever."

Author's Note

In October of 1871, a great fire destroyed much of the city of Chicago, Illinois, and along with it, the offices of the Pinkerton National Detective Agency. Nearly twenty years of the agency's history perished in those flames: files containing operatives' reports, case histories, and all written record of the contributions made by a number of dedicated detectives whose names and faces are, unfortunately, lost to us now.

All that remains to tell us of those early days are Allan Pinkerton's own reminiscences, set down from memory. This series of adventure stories was immensely popular when first published in the 1870s and 1880s and helped make Pinkerton's name well-known the world over.

It was through these stories that I first became acquainted with one of the founding members of Pinkerton's organization, a remarkable woman by the name of Kate Warne. In a time when so many women's lives were controlled for them, she openly flouted convention and decided her own destiny.

In preparation for the writing of this book, I sought to find out more about this woman. Alas, the evidence available is scant, and she remains as much a mystery today as ever. But those incidents of her life that did come to light were so intriguing, so worthy of note that I could not wholly abandon her story.

My only alternative was to weave a tale around the available facts, to create a work of historical fiction that blends "what was" with "what might have been." It was a task I have undertaken with a great deal of trepidation. To bring to life the historical character of Kate Warne, it was necessary to fill in the many gaps in her story, and to endow her with certain motivations, thoughts and emotions. These are, of course, of my own design. But, by far, the most remarkable events related in this story are based on truth.

I only hope that this book serves to illuminate, for the reader, the life of this fascinating woman, who would otherwise have languished as a footnote in the pages of history.

Catherine Wyatt
P.O. Box 88082
Carol Stream, IL 60188-0082